# A LOVE OF CONVENIENCE

Adesuwa O'man Nwokedi

# PRAISE FOR ADESUWA

Never stop writing, Adesuwa. Your hands are blessed.
**—Glory Abah, Bestselling Author**

Adesuwa writes beautiful, authentic African characters.
**—Amaka Azie, Bestselling Author**

Adesuwa's characters get me talking to, laughing at, and crying with them.

**—Feyi Aina, Bestselling Author**

Adesuwa blows my mind every time I read her books.

**—Mosunmola Rose, Bestselling Author**

Adesuwa's pieces have never fallen short of exceptional.

**—Mara Abutu, Bestselling Author**

Adesuwa's writing is seamless and beautiful.

**—Aminat Sanni-Kamal, Bestselling Author**

A LOVE OF
CONVENIENCE

# A Love of Convenience

By Adesuwa O'man Nwokedi

# DEDICATION

To Yvonne, who beat the damned thing!

And to Uju Egonu and Emeka Obinna.
Thank you for New York.

6

# CHAPTER ONE

## Handbags & Gladrags

MY EYES OPEN AT 7AM as Bill Withers' ***Lovely Day*** blares from my alarm clock radio, and a wide smile forms on my face.

What better song to wake up to on my wedding day!

I sit up and stretch in the most exaggerated manner I can, before I hop off the bed and do a small dance to the catchy song. Oh yes, it sure as heck is going to be a lovely day.

When the song stops playing on the radio, I put it on repeat on my phone in the most permissibly loud volume my neighbours won't call the cops for. I sing along with all gusto, my heart, body, and soul reverberating with the words. How else would one feel on the day they marry the person they have loved for pretty much all their lives?

Yep, today is the day I marry the man I have loved since I was five years old; Okwudili, or as he's more popularly called, Dili.

Sitting with a cup of coffee at my study table overlooking my busy Manhattan neighborhood, I smile as I travel down memory lane. While it was love at first sight for me, it wasn't quite the same for him. Our parents, our fathers specifically, were childhood friends, and even though life took them down different paths, what with my dad opting for the more modest civil service and Dili's hitting the jackpot with his manufacturing business, the two men remained friends. Despite the distance that separated our humble abode in Yaba from their luxurious one in Ikoyi, both families saw each other at least twice a month.

I remember the day I knew I was in love with Dili. It was at his fifth birthday party, four months and twenty-four days after mine. While my own 'party' had been little more than a few friends gathered round our small living room stool, on which was perched a teeny-tiny cake flanked by bottles of soda and beer, Dili's party was a full-on carnival. But all the fancy food and games had paled into insignificance the moment I saw him emerge from their grand mansion in a jet-black corduroy trouser and waistcoat set with a sparkling white shirt beneath, his lustrous black hair combed into a shiny afro. I lost my heart to him then and there. Even at that age, I'd noticed the cleft in his chin, the light brownness of his eyes, the aquiline structure of his nose, and I knew I wanted nothing more than to be his wife one day.

Hoping to be Dili's wife was one thing, being noticed by him was another. For some reason, I remained totally invisible to him, not only at the age of five but even when we were teenagers. The truth is I was invisible to pretty much everyone. While my siblings inherited our father's caramel-coloured skin and dainty, almost feminine, features, I'd inherited our mother's more severe facial structure; my eyes too large, my nose too broad, and my lips too thick. Add to that the fact that years of sucking my thumb gifted me dentition straight from hell, it was no surprise that I was often overlooked, despite being the oldest.

As we grew, the distinction between my sisters and me became even more apparent, with their Amazonian height and blossoming bodies. I lost count of how many times Ebere and Uchechi were mistaken for models or approached by agents trying to get them to be. For me, no such luck. My body didn't blossom like theirs and I remained rake thin for the longest time; no boobs and no ass. And as my height decided to freeze at five feet and four inches, a model I was never mistaken for.

So I guess it was no surprise that Dili never noticed me, either. Instead, he noticed my sister, Ebere. I was fifteen when I realised the boy who had my heart had his eye on my thirteen-year-old sister. I watched, heartbroken, every time his family visited ours, or vice versa, as Dili and Ebere would giggle in a corner, knowing I had lost him to her. I was too ashamed to confront her about it and, instead, suffered in silence for the next two years, until Dili's family abruptly moved to Enugu. While I was sad to see them go, I was glad not to be subjected to watching him cavort with my sister any longer. But the most annoying part of the whole thing was that Ebere didn't even care. Of the multitude of the boys pursuing her, Dili was just one, not the beginning and end like he was for me.

Thankfully, for everything I lacked in looks, God gave me in brains. I excelled in my studies, and when I got an almost perfect score in my SATs and was offered a scholarship by the University of Pennsylvania in the United States of America, I finally got the chance to shine. For the first time in my life, I was the center of all attention, my parents the proudest I had ever seen them. Even my siblings were excited, bragging about my feat to all their friends. Their sister was going to school in America. It wasn't something that happened often to people in our social and financial circle.

The ringing of my phone jolts me out of my reverie and I smile as I see the name of my colleague, Mia, on the caller-ID. She squeals as I answer the phone, and I know she is just as excited as I am.

"It's your wedding dayyyyyyyy!" she screams over the phone. "I hope you're getting yourself all sexy as we speak."

"I haven't even had a shower," I laugh. "It's not 8 o'clock yet, and our ceremony isn't till 11. There's still a lot of time."

"Just make sure you look amazing."

I smile as my vanity rears its head. "I look amazing everyday, Mia."

She laughs in return. "That you do, Ezi. That you do." She pauses briefly and I already know what she wants to ask. "Are you sure you don't want me to go with you? Won't it be lonely getting married without your family there?"

"Thanks babe, but that's how Dili and I want it. His family won't be there, either. It'll be just both of us at City Hall. No thrills or frills."

Mia sighed. "That's so romantic, though. Almost like you're eloping."

I smile and nod. Yep. Almost like.

"Take lots of pictures, okay?" she says, as I shoo her off the phone. "I can't wait to meet him!"

"You will," I say before I disconnect the line, eager to finally hop in the shower and get myself prettied up for the man who will be my husband in a matter of hours.

It's so wonderful to say that word. Husband!

After a long soak in a strawberry, vanilla, and coconut infused bath, I embark on getting myself beautiful for my wedding day. Thankfully, good dental work has taken care of my teeth, and an expensive skin care regimen has added a nice glow to my dark skin, but I still have to spend considerable time on makeup to give me a less severe look. It took years to perfect, but I can proudly say I am now able to transform into a very nice-looking woman indeed. It just takes something of an hour or two to achieve.

This morning, I spare no effort and put all my expensive beauty products to work. Satisfied with the outcome, I slip into the lace Dolce and Gabbana slip dress I have splurged on. I'm glad I didn't go with my first instinct to buy a no-name suit for the occasion. It's my wedding day after all. What better excuse do I need to look amazeballs?

I finish off the look with a large red rose attached to my long and wavy weave. I wish I had enough hair to pull into a nice, sleek bun, but after struggling with my limp, lifeless, and uncooperative hair for decades, I finally gave up on it, chopped it all off, and have been hiding under weaves and wigs ever since.

Flagging down a taxi, I'm glad I live in Manhattan, where a woman can be dressed like this and not even raise an eyebrow. In my white figure-hugging designer dress, red hair accessory almost the size of my face, and sky-high red stilettos, I'm overdressed for a Thursday morning. But hey, so is half of New York.

It is a short ride to Lower Manhattan where City Hall is, and as I disembark from the taxi, I see a few other women dressed in the same understated bridal manner as me. I smile at all of them, my fellow City-Hall brides, my heart still dancing from the excitement of the day. I make my way upstairs, and just as I walk into the room, I see him…the love of my life!

Dili walks up to me and embraces me. "You look spectacular, Ezi!"

I blush, happy to be getting the desired response from him. "So do you," I say to him, even though he hasn't bothered to wear a suit, but is instead in a striped shirt and dress pants.

We take our seats, wait our turn, and by 11:30am, Dili and I have been married by a Justice of the Peace. We exchange a broad grin as we are pronounced husband and wife and walk out of the room hand in hand.

"That was quicker than I thought it would be," Dili says.

"I know, right," I answer. "We did it!"

He pulls me into a hug. "Thank you so much for doing this, Ezi. You're a life saver."

I look around nervously. "Not so loud. You want us to get arrested?"

He makes a *yikes* face, and I have to stop myself from laughing.

"I need to call Onyeka to tell her how it went. She's been texting all day," he says as he walks away. "I'll see you later, Ezi. I'll bring my things over to the apartment later today, like we agreed."

The smile on my face fades as he walks away, and I can tell when Onyeka is on the phone as his face lights up like Christmas lights at Rockefeller Plaza.

Onyeka is his fiancée back home in Nigeria.

And our marriage is a sham marriage so he can get his Green Card.

I stand alone on the sidewalk, now feeling overdressed in my expensive white dress and unreasonably high red shoes. I know I have no right to be sad or disappointed. I was the one who made the offer to him anyway. I was the one who stretched out a hand to help when I saw that he was drowning. But I think somewhere deep inside, the five-year-old Ezioma wished he would take one look at her in that City Hall room and fall head over heels in love.

But, alas, by leaving me standing alone on a Lower Manhattan Street, dressed like something out of a Calypso music video, it is a painful reminder that this is just a marriage of convenience for him, and that his heart belongs to a beautiful, light-skinned, six foot tall, twenty-seven-year-old woman back in Nigeria.

Later that day, sitting before my laptop preparing to write my daily column, ***Soundtrack of My Life***, for the *Manhattan Buzz*, as is my ritual before I write, I prepare to play the song that has been the soundtrack of my day. When I woke up this morning, I'd thought it would be ***Lovely Day*** for sure. But as I sit with my heart on the floor, it doesn't quite feel like such a lovely day after all.

So instead, I select Stereophonics' ***Handbags and Gladrags***.

# A LOVE OF CONVENIENCE

## *Handbags & Gladrags – May 15, 2014*

*Deception is a bad thing. Self-deception, the worst.*

*Sometimes, we paint a picture of a fairy tale, when we know that our reality is more like a scene out of* A Nightmare on Elm Street.

*So, here's to all of us who have once, or maybe even right now, lived in a fool's paradise. If we can't get out of it, we can at least make it a fun place to be…no?*

I am startled by the sound of my buzzer. Stealing a look at my clock, I see that it is 5:32pm and just about the time Dili would be arriving. Taking a deep breath, I pray for grace, not just to face him today, but for the rest of the time we must keep up this charade.

God help me.

# CHAPTER TWO

## There She Goes

I DECIDE AGAINST simply buzzing him in and go downstairs to receive him instead. Riding the twenty-eight floors from my apartment down to the ground floor, my heart is in my mouth as I wonder if I'm doing the right thing. Am I truly able to share an apartment with Dili, my new fake husband, to keep up the charade of our marriage? Especially as it appears my childhood crush on him was not just a childhood one after all. As the elevator makes its way down, I find myself humming the song I've been intermittently humming since the first day I saw him in New York; Six Pence None the Richer's ***There She Goes***.

I sight him the moment I step out of the elevator, and butterflies flutter in my stomach. In his Abercrombie & Fitch t-shirt and track-downs, he is the very definition of sexy. His face lights up when he sees me, and he walks over to give me a friendly embrace.

"Your tenant has arrived," he laughs. "I hope I didn't come with too much luggage. I thought I'd be able to leave a few things at Folarin's place, but it appears he and his wife were more than ready to see me go!"

I smile, looking at his meagre two suitcases and a travel bag. If I were to move all my things out, we'd be talking in the dozens of boxes and bags. "As long as you have everything you need, it's not too much."

Taking him by the hand, I walk up to the doorman on duty. "Hi, Tomas. I'd like to introduce you to my husband, Dili. He's moving in."

Tomas face breaks into a broad smile and he shakes Dili's hand vigorously. "Oh wow! Congratulations! This is fantastic news!"

"I've already arranged for him to have his own card and key," I continue. "But I wanted to introduce you. I'll do the same with Stuart when he's here." Stuart is the other doorman.

Dili looks on in awe as Tomas and I talk, and, as we make our way into the elevator, says, "I can't get over the fact you live here. It must cost you a fortune."

I smile at the look of unabashed admiration on Dili's face. We had this same conversation the first time I brought him here a week ago. He'd been even more shocked to hear that I'm not renting and that the flat belongs to me. I bought it a few years ago with my ex-fiancé, Seth. Seth was an Investment Banker like me, and, back in those days when our bonuses where out of this world, we'd easily been able to afford the apartment in Manhattan's Upper East Side. When Seth decided to give up his career on Wall Street in favour of one in the academia, leading to our breakup, I bought him out and took full ownership of the place.

How did I get here? How did the girl with such humble beginnings who came to America with only six hundred dollars, money her parents had barely been able to raise, end up owning her own luxury Manhattan apartment? Through a lot of sweat and hard work, that's how. And a decent dash of good luck, I'll have to admit.

I arrived America in August of 1995, a bright and eager eighteen-year-old, ready to take on the world. Luckily, my father had found me a chaperone in Philadelphia, an older sister of one of his colleagues at work. Aunty Amaka took me in like her own daughter and ensured I was not only comfortable, but that I had all I needed to start life at UPenn. She took me to school herself, settled me in my dormitory as best as she could, scrutinized my room mates to be sure she was comfortable enough to leave me there, and made it a point of duty to check on me almost every week. She was as good as a mother to me and, even then, I knew how lucky I was. Quite a few of the international students I soon befriended did not have it quite as good; some were completely alone there in Philly and others had family or chaperones literally from the pit of hell. Very few had caring guardians like mine, who not only checked on me frequently, but often visited with coolers of delicious Nigerian delicacies. So, yeah, I knew I was very lucky.

Towards the end of my freshman year, I started dating a Nigerian boy, Eze. His major was Electrical Engineering and mine was Mechanical Engineering & Applied Mechanics, but that didn't stop us from becoming Siamese twins. For the first time in almost nineteen years of my life, a guy was paying me attention. I had long resigned myself to the fact that my brain was all I had to offer and didn't take it to heart when I was overlooked by sororities or didn't get the kind of male attention my friends did. It was okay. I'd accepted I just wasn't that girl, and instead chose to focus on shining the one way I knew how; academically. Eze was also something of a nerd, so I guess it was no surprise he was drawn to me. By our sophomore year, everyone knew us as a couple. Eze & Ezi. Even our names had a rhyme to it. We were always together, and I was soon helplessly in love with him, so much so that I gave him my virginity in the fall of 1996. He was my everything, all that I lived and breathed.

By the time we got to our junior year, Eze and I moved into an apartment off campus together. Aunty Amaka wasn't too happy about this, but her love for Eze made her overlook the fact her twenty-year-old ward was cohabiting with a boy. Thankfully, she didn't tell my parents about this, as they most surely would not have been as understanding. The good part of living with Eze was that he made sure we studied round the clock, because, left to me, I was happy to just lie in his arms all day long. My passion had shifted from my books to my boyfriend, and it's a wonder my grades didn't crash too hard.

Then came our senior year, and everything fell apart. Eze became cranky and irritable, and started spending more and more time away from the apartment. After weeks of agonizing over the change in his behavior and crying myself to sleep almost every night, in January of 1999, at the start of the Spring Semester, he broke up with me. He told me I wasn't the same fiery and passionate girl he'd fallen in love with, and that he'd met someone else. This 'someone else' was a young Nigerian freshman called Bodunrin. She was also in UPenn on a scholarship and was apparently something of a whizz kid. She was everything I'd been in my own freshman year, the only difference being she had the looks to go with her brains. She had the face of an angel and the body of a porn star, and there was no way I could compete with that. Luckily, my friend, Melissa, let me move into her apartment, and I'd spent the next few weeks refusing to leave the couch, crying myself awake and to sleep every day. I probably might have done that for the rest of the academic year if my friends hadn't staged a mini intervention, reminding me why I was in America in the first place, and that it wasn't because of a boy called Eze.

That was he kick up the ass I needed, and I shook off my funk and immersed myself into my studies once again. Not only was this enough to help me forget about Eze and Bodunrin, I was able to graduate Summa Cum Laude, the equivalent of First Class. My parents gathered all their coins and flew to America for the ceremony. Seeing the look of immense pride on their faces more than made up for the months of sacrifice that had led me there. Eze, on the other hand, only managed to graduate Cum Laude. His intoxication with his new girlfriend had seen his grades topple, and I'm not ashamed to admit it gave me immense satisfaction. Hearing Bodunrin dumped him for an all-American frat boy made it even sweeter, but the highest satisfaction came when he tried to get back with me, bombarding my inbox with non-stop e-mails. Thankfully, life after UPenn took us in opposite directions, with him returning to Nigeria and me getting to choose between several job offers and a Graduate Assistant position I'd been offered at UPenn's business school, Wharton.

My friends, and even Aunty Amaka, thought it was a no-brainer. They all wanted me to accept a very enticing job from a Silicon Valley company offering a very tempting salary. But I'd surprised them all and opted to heed my father's advice to take up the Graduate Assistant position at Wharton, as it was an opportunity to go to an Ivy-League business school without having to pay a dime.

So I started my MBA, with a focus on Statistics…and never looked back. People thought I would struggle, especially as I didn't have a business or finance background, but I made them eat their words as I was soon top of my class. By the end of the internship after my first year, I'd received job offers from Goldman Sachs and several other companies on Wall Street. When I was done with my MBA, I accepted the role with Goldman, and that was when I moved to New York.

It was a totally different Ezi who moved to New York. Towards the end of my MBA, after an exercise of self-assessment, I decided it was time to start focusing on *me* for a change. I was only twenty-four years old and determined to finally start acting my age, instead of decades older. So what, if I wasn't born with supermodel looks? I now had enough money in the bank to do something about it.

I learnt how to dress for my petite stature and found out what kind of beauty products worked for my features. With my first salary, I began the three-year long process of remedying my dentition, and with all of this came a new-found confidence in myself I'd never had before; not when I was with Eze or even when I graduated top of my class. Looking good made me *feel* good, and I finally came into my own. For the first time, I was not known as just the smart girl, but as Ezi, a killer dresser and arguably one of the most fashionable women in Goldman Sachs' West Street office. Yes, I was still known for my smarts and my ability to murder just about any brief that came my way, but I was no longer overlooked as a wallflower. Yes, I still wasn't the prettiest girl in the room, but if I walked into that room, people noticed. And that was good enough for me.

I was now more attractive to members of the opposite sex. It didn't matter that almost all this attention came from Caucasian guys. Frankly, after what Eze did to me, I was ready to try something different. My first boyfriend after Eze was Matt, a nice guy from a tight-knit Bostonian family. We dated for about a year until things fizzled out naturally. Then came several others, most of the relationships lasting anything between six to eighteen months.

And then came Seth.

Seth was a good-looking Jewish guy who had been on my case for years, but I was adamant about not dating anyone who worked in Goldman like I did. Office romance, I'd decided, wasn't for me. So, I'd blown him off and went on to date several other guys instead. But after my breakup with my last boyfriend, I decided to take a break from men and instead focus on passing the Chartered Financial Analyst – CFA - exams I was writing. Seth had been writing the same exam level and we'd gravitated towards each other during group discussions at work. By 2005, not only were we both certified CFA professionals, we were by then very much in love. By the time he proposed to me on my thirtieth birthday in 2007, I was convinced I had found THE ONE.

In 2008, we both made Vice President at Goldman and decided to buy a house together. Our initial plan was to buy a proper house in the suburbs, especially as we were hoping to soon get married and start a family. But with most of our friends buying homes in the decidedly swankier Manhattan, we followed suit and put down twice what we had budget for a nice town house in Connecticut on a 2-bedroom condo with a fancy Manhattan address instead.

However, 2009 came with the global economic crunch and, even though neither of us lost our jobs, the strain on our sector led to more pressure at work. There always seemed to be a looming cloud of uncertainty hanging, as nobody knew if they would be a victim of the next round of job cuts. Bonuses vanished into thin air and there was less incentive to put in the tedious hours required to stay afloat in the world of investment banking.

It was around that time I got the part-time gig to write for the *Manhattan Buzz*, an online newspaper for the young Manhattan professional. I'd met the then-editor at a friend's party, and what had started off as a joke had led to a daily column. We'd been talking about music, I'd mentioned something about having a soundtrack for everyday of my life, he'd offered me a column to write about it, and that's how ***Soundtrack of My Life*** was born. It started out a sleeper column, but soon gained a cult followership. At the time, I didn't know I had it in me to write, but not only did I find it a great outlet to release all the stress I was struggling with, the money that came from it was a much needed supplement to my salary, a salary I didn't know how much longer I'd have it for.

Seth couldn't understand why I was 'distracting' myself with such an unnecessary 'hobby', but while I had an outlet to express myself, he didn't, and it didn't take long before the strain of work was too much for him to handle. By 2012, not only was our five-year long engagement looking unlikely to lead to the altar, Seth made the wild decision to quit his job and take up a teaching position with Duke University. Leaving my job and moving to North Carolina was not an option for me, so we'd made the amicable decision to break up. Not wanting the mess that came with co-ownership, I bought him out of the apartment and moved on with my life as a single thirty-five-year-old woman. Even though I was sad about the end of the relationship, it hadn't broken me, and, somewhere deep in my heart, I was relieved.

Thankfully, by now there was less pressure at work and my day job was no longer a chore that had to be endured. My passion for it returned, I got back into the dating scene and fell in love with life again. My parents had both passed away – my dad from a heart attack in 2002 and my mom from breast cancer in 2005 – so I had no pressure from home to get married, as my siblings were themselves also busy with their own lives.

And that was how I remained footloose and fancy-free. Until about a month ago.

I'd been nursing a cup of coffee and a muffin at a Starbucks near my office when I saw him standing across the street. I stopped chewing as I strained to look, to make sure the man I was looking at was, indeed, my childhood crush, Dili, whom I hadn't seen in over twenty years. Even though so much time had passed, there was no mistaking those eyes and that chin. And I knew, without a shadow of doubt in my mind, that it was him.

Jumping to my feet, I ran out of the store and yelled his name. "Dili! Okwudili!"

He looked across the street, surprised, and waved at me, still confused. I could tell he didn't recognize me, a fact that both pleased and saddened me. When the pedestrian light flashed green, I dashed across the street to meet him.

"Dili, don't you remember me?" I exclaimed, excited about seeing him again after so long.

Recognition lit up his eyes and a smile broke on his face. "Ezioma!"

And then we hugged like the long-lost friends we were.

"What are you doing here?" I asked. "When did you come to America?"

Something in his eyes shifted, and I could tell he didn't have a happy story. "Almost two years. But I've only been in New York a few weeks."

That was when I noticed he didn't look so good. His eyes looked weary and tired, and there was a fray to his shirt that betrayed the fact it had been worn a few times too many.

"Are you busy? I was having coffee across the road. Would you like to join me, so we can catch up?" I asked.

He smiled. "I'd love that."

With hands interlinked, we crossed the road and returned to my table in the café where my half-drunk and half-eaten coffee and muffin still sat.

"You look amazing, Ezi. I'd heard you were doing well, but you look absolutely amazing!" he remarked. "Do you still work on Wall Street?"

I nod. "Goldman Sachs, thirteen years now."

"Thirteen years! Wow! You must be a big madam there now."

I smiled. I'd just been promoted to Executive Director but didn't think saying that was appropriate, not with what I could sense.

"So how are you, Dili? What have you been up to here in NYC?" I asked, trying to change the subject.

His smile waned again, and he sighed deeply. "*Mehn*, Ezi, I can't lie to you, it's been tough, really tough. I was hoping to have better luck here in New York than I had in California, but it's been really tough."

I stared at him, surprised. Tough? How could life be tough for Chief Dike's son? Yes, the old man died around the same time as my father, but surely, he'd left enough of a legacy for his children, especially his first-born son.

Dili saw the surprised look on my face and laughed. "I can understand why you're shocked. The truth is, so were we. When my father died, we realized he was neck deep in debt. I spent the next decade trying to clear up the mess he made. It also didn't help that the man left behind about a dozen illegitimate children to feed."

"What?!" I exclaimed.

"You didn't know?" Dili asked, surprised by my uninformed state. "Why do you think we moved to Enugu in such a hurry?"

He went on to tell me how his mother found out his father had another wife in the Enugu home he frequented. With one of his major factories in the town, he'd had seemingly authentic reason to spend more and more time there, until he'd finally stopped returning to Lagos altogether. Dili's mother went on to hear the man was not only living with another woman in Enugu but was expecting a third child with her. That had been all she'd needed to pack up everything - and everyone - and move to Enugu finally. Dili, having just finished his SSCE exams, had no choice but to move along with his mother and younger siblings. While they'd succeeded in uprooting the new 'wife', her spawn had stayed back. They'd thought the worst was over, but what they hadn't bargained for was the emergence of several other women…with several other children. Dili's mother, who'd always had a heart of gold, opened her door to every one of those children. By the time Dili's father passed away in 2002, there were thirteen children living in the house, in addition to the four Dili's mother had borne. But more was to come, as the old man's death revealed he was steeped in debt in the hundreds of millions. They'd gone on to sell off all the man's factories, houses, and assets to pay off most of it off, and Dili had become saddled with the responsibility of caring for his large family. He'd asked his mother to send away the illegitimate children, but she'd refused each time, insisting it was her duty and obligation to take care of them.

"Can you imagine that? Duty and obligation to a man who cheated on her? A man who played her for a fool?" Dili retorted, and I could feel his pain was still raw, so many years later.

"I worked like an animal just to take care of them. I moved back to Lagos and got a job with one of the New Generation banks, but I could barely make enough to take care myself, let alone all the man's kids. I had to rent a small place for my mom after we lost the house in Enugu, and all the kids moved there with her like little rats. As if that wasn't enough, some of their mothers returned, and my mom welcomed them in!"

"Your mom has always been a very kind person, Dili. I'm not surprised she wasn't able to turn anyone away," I answered. "Is that why you came here? To make a better living?"

"I lost my job with the bank and couldn't get another one. For months, I was pounding the streets of Lagos, searching for any job at all. It was my fiancée who suggested trying America. We figured I'd get better chances here."

My stomach dropped at the word 'fiancée'. "You're engaged?"

He smiled and nodded. "Yeah. Her name is Onyeka. I really don't know what she sees in me, really. She could have chosen any guy without the same family troubles I have, someone better able to take care of her the way she deserves. But she chose me. I'm an incredibly lucky man."

I'd forced a smile, surprised I was affected hearing he was taken, a man I hadn't even seen or thought about for years. "How long have you been together?"

"A year after she finished university, so about six years now. She turned twenty-seven yesterday," he said, showing me his phone. "This is the picture she sent me this morning."

An image of a light-skinned goddess with flawless skin and features stared back at me. "I think this picture was meant for your eyes only!" I teased Dili, as the top she was wearing revealed a hell of a lot of cleavage. "She's very pretty."

"She is. That's why I had to propose to her before leaving Nigeria. I had to lock her down, you know," he said. "I also had to give her the assurance I wouldn't forget her upon getting here. I had to prove to her I'm not anything like my father."

"So what happened when you got to the States?" I asked, eager to change the topic from Onyeka.

"I found out the hard way that my visiting visa was not going to get me legitimate work. I also found out the hard way that friends have a very limited amount of time before they start to get irritated by your presence, especially if you're not bringing anything to the table. I did a few odd jobs here and there, but nothing really clicked. I had to leave when someone I was hoping would hire me threatened to report me to immigration instead. That was when someone suggested I come here to New York."

I sighed inwardly. If he was having a hard time in California, he was bound to have an even harder time in New York. "And how has that been?"

"Worse," he said. "Much worse. My visa has expired now. I can't even get menial work to do. I'm out of money. My friend who's been housing me is already hinting to leave. It's been really difficult."

My heart went out to him. "That's horrible, Dili. Why don't you just go back to Nigeria?"

"I haven't sent money home since I got here. The consolation has always been that I'll get a good job that will make up for all this time. If I go back worse off than I left, wouldn't that be tragic?" he answered, before shrugging. "Anyways, I'm off to see a guy about the possibility of driving his cab for him. If that works, that will be something, at least."

"I really hope it works out," I said, reaching into my wallet and handing him my card and a hundred dollar note. "I wish I had more on me, but just hang on to this for now. The card has my phone numbers, so call me anytime you need anything, okay?"

Dili reached across the table and hugged me tightly. "You don't know how much of a difference this will make for me, Ezi. It means I'll actually get to have a proper meal today."

We hugged again and parted with the promise to keep in touch.

But he remained on my mind for the rest of the day. Even when I got home and sat before my laptop to write my article, he was still there.

I could think of nothing else.

And then, I was hit with the most radical of ideas. I tried to laugh off an idea so ludicrous, but the more I thought about it, the more evident it was to me that it was the only way to help him.

Reaching for my laptop, I typed the song title that perfectly described how I was feeling now.

***There She Goes (Six Pence None the Richer) – April 18, 2014***

*Love is an immortal beast. It never dies, no matter how hard you try to kill it, or how long you try to stifle it.*

*True love is immortal.*

*True love can bring out the little girl you have inside you, the one who has given out her heart to someone unable to reciprocate.*

*Just when you think you've been able squash her to silence, to get her to kill off all her realistic dreams….*

*There she goes again!*

I paused as I wrote, before smiling and shaking my head.

*There she goes again…about to do something really and truly stupid!*

# CHAPTER THREE

## Once in a Blue Moon

I'D TOSSED AND TURNED in bed, unable to get Dili off my mind, or, more truthfully, unable to shake off the wild idea that was taking root.

But I simply couldn't.

I'd been an American citizen since 2008 and knew I was probably the best option he had to remain in the United States legally. I also had a large two-bedroom apartment, which could help solve his accommodation problem. The more I thought about it, the better an idea it seemed to me.

But there was just one catch. I didn't have his phone number.

In our haste and excitement, I'd given him my details but forgotten to take his. As the days went by, I was filled with panic over the thought of him never getting in touch. I worried about him losing my card or, worse, deciding not to call at all.

"What exactly is your deal, Ezioma?" I muttered to myself, when the fifth day after our chance encounter was about to roll to an end. "Why do you even care? If he doesn't call and he ends up getting deported, that's his problem, not yours!"

But as much as I tried to convince myself of my indifference, it still weighed heavily on my mind.

And then a little over a week after the day we met, as I sat on my sofa watching *Frasier* re-runs, he finally called.

"Hi, Ezioma," came his voice, sounding tentative. "I didn't want to disturb you during the week. I know how late you investment bankers work."

I could feel my heart pound furiously in my chest, and I was amazed his voice still had the same effect on me twenty years later. "I was beginning to wonder if you'd lost my card."

"Are you kidding? I've been guarding it like the prized item it is," he laughed in return.

"How did it go with the guy you went to see? The cab guy."

He sighed. "Not great. It turns out I don't have the right kind of license I need to drive here. Ezi, at this point I've run out of ideas. I'm beginning to think it might be best for me to go back to Nigeria after all, instead of waiting to be deported."

I sat up, knowing the time had come for me to do what I had to do. "Can you make it over to Manhattan tonight? For dinner? My treat."

"That's the best thing I've heard all week. Maybe it'll be the last time we see before my ass is hauled back to Naija."

I smiled. "How about we meet at Gallagher's Steak House at 7pm? It's on 52nd Street. You think you can find it?"

"7pm sounds perfect, and I most surely can," was his gleeful answer.

Quickly getting off the phone, with barely two hours, it was just enough time for me to get ready. As I primped and prepped myself, a tiny voice in my head wondered why I was going through all that effort. From the doe-eyed, love struck look on his face when he spoke about his fiancée, Onyeka, it was clear Dili only had eyes for her. But another naughty voice in my head urged me on. He was engaged to her, not married.

And if all went well, I'd soon be the one who'd have that honour.

By the time I left my apartment at 6:53pm, I knew I looked the business. Yes, I was not as pretty as Onyeka, but I knew there was absolutely no way she could compete with me in a host of other ways.

Gliding into the informal steakhouse, I smiled when I saw Dili already seated. His face lit up when he saw me, and he rose to his feet, waving. I'd chosen this location because it was informal enough for him not to feel uncomfortable. Celebrities and the New York elite favoured most of the restaurants I frequented, and the last thing I wanted was for him to feel out of place.

How ironic, though! That I was worrying about Dili, Chief Dike's son, feeling out of place. It saddened me how greatly the tables had turned.

"Ezioma, you look wonderful!" Dili gushed. "You've really blossomed with age."

"Is that code for I was ugly as a kid?" I teased.

"Of course not. You were also…cute then."

"God hates liars, Okwudili!" I laughed, hitting him playfully on his arm. This relaxed him, and we were soon laughing and bantering about old times.

We were midway through our meal when I decided to ask him the million-dollar question. "Have you ever considered getting married to a citizen? You know that would help you, right? Or is Onyeka opposed to the idea?"

"I tried that in California," he answered, his eyes clouding over. "My friends introduced me to this girl who was supposed to help me. We agreed I'd pay her five thousand dollars. I didn't have the money, so I had to give her a down payment of a thousand, while I hustled for the rest. Will you believe when I was finally able to put the money together, she denied it was five thousand we'd agreed on and instead asked for eight? I didn't have it, and that was the end of everything. She even refused to refund my one thousand."

"So why didn't you get someone else to do it?" I asked.

He shrugged. "Before I knew it, I'd already blown the four grand I'd saved and had no money to start that kind of discussion again."

We ate our meal in silence for some minutes before I decided to go for it. "I could do it for you."

He looked at me. "You could do what?"

I shrugged, trying my best to look casual. "I'm an American citizen. We could get married so you can get your Green Card."

His eyes widened in amazement. "Are you serious?"

"And I won't charge you, don't worry." I laughed, trying not to let him sense my own nerves. "I've been speaking with a friend of mine who's an Immigration Attorney, and she told me that, with proof of a valid marriage, all we have to do is sign some paperwork, send in the required applications, and you might be able to get your Green Card in less than a year."

"Ezioma, you would do that for me?" he asked, his eyes glistening.

"Oh, come on, Dili. Why are you getting emotional?" I teased, trying not to cry myself. "We're as good as family. And I know you'd do it for me if I was the one who needed help."

He suddenly reached over the table and pulled me into a tight embrace. "Thank you so much, Ezioma! Thank you!"

As we held each other, I shut my eyes as I inhaled his scent, savouring the mix of his natural smell and a mild cologne. It took everything in me to detach from the hug and give him the most casual smile I could manage.

We spent the rest of the evening talking about the logistics, he got emotional again by my offer for him to move into my apartment, and I grilled him about how he intended to break the news to Onyeka.

"That won't be a problem at all," he said confidently. "She knows that's the quickest way for me to get my papers here. She was aware of the whole saga in California, and I know she'll be glad to hear someone as good as my sister has offered to step in. Heck, even some of her married friends have had to 'divorce' so they could marry American citizens here."

"To remarry their original spouses after they get their papers?" I asked, shocked.

"I kid you not. I know several couples who have had to do that," he answered. "So Onyeka will definitely understand."

We finally left the restaurant at about 10pm and agreed to meet at the Immigration Lawyer's office the following Monday. Michelle had been a good friend of mine since UPenn, and I knew she would be discreet.

On Monday, taking advantage of my lunch break, I left for her office a few blocks from mine. Dili was already there, and we were soon seated before Michelle, who confirmed most of what I'd already told him. Once we could prove we were legally married, we could commence the process of filling the necessary paperwork.

"However," she stressed, "There might be need to show proof of your union. This could be by way of joint financial bank statements, joint ownership of property, a lease showing joint tenancy, things like that."

Dili and I exchanged a look. Even though we had neither of these, I was confident we could come up with at least one.

"And pictures. Lots of pictures. Pictures that can give some credence to your claim of a relationship," Michelle continued. "And if your online or social media footprint is also reflective of the relationship, all the better."

By the time we left the office, we were both mentally exhausted.

"It's a lot of paperwork!" Dili remarked.

"That won't be a problem," I answered. "What could be the problem is the social media stuff." I'd hoped this was something we could do quietly, but by going social media public, that would mean everyone we knew finding out about it.

"I know, right! I'm not sure Onyeka is going to like that part of it. We have a lot of mutual friends on Facebook," he remarked.

This statement irritated me, and I shrugged. "If you don't think she'll be cool with it…"

"No, she'll be cool. She has no choice but to be cool with it," Dili cut in, a desperate lilt to his voice. "Or is it something that could hurt you? Maybe your…your boyfriend might not like it?"

I raised a brow at him, wondering if he was genuinely unsure or just trying to fish for information. "I'm not answerable to anyone, Dili. I just don't want us to get your girlfriend all frantic and frustrated back in Nigeria."

"If this is what it takes, then it is what it takes," he answered, looking me square in the eye. "You're doing a wonderful thing for me, Ezi. God knows you don't have to, but here you are doing it anyway. I will never be able to repay you, not even if I tried."

I couldn't help but smile at the sincerity in his face. While it might have been an offer I'd made lightly, this had become a lifeline for him.

"We're family. I know you'd do the same for me," I said, punching him playfully.

I opted not to return to the office and, instead, took him to my apartment to show him where he'd soon call home. He gaped at the place like it was a palace, and I couldn't blame him. I knew he stayed with his friend in Queens, and I also knew there was a huge difference between apartments on that side of town and mine.

We parted, agreeing to, first, share the news with our families, before going social media public with it. We also agreed to spend the weekend together, taking as many 'loved-up' pictures as we could.

Sitting in front of my laptop that evening, I thought about events of the last seventy-two hours, and it hit me for the first time how much our lives were about to change. Yes, this would just be a sham marriage and a means to an end, but it would forever be on record that we were once married.

And I found myself wishing it were all under different circumstances.

***Once In a Blue Moon (Lighthouse Family) – April 28, 2014***

*Wouldn't it be easier if we could write, by ourselves, the script for our lives? We are in control of the basic things like where we go, what we do, what we eat, what we wear.*

*But wouldn't it be perfect if we could plot our wider destinies?*

*For the most part, we can control whom we fall in love with…but wouldn't it be so much better if we could also control who falls in love with us?*

*But maybe we can.*

*Maybe we can control who will love us. Maybe we can work it all out in such a way that the day will come when that happens.*

*Maybe.*

I stared blankly out of my window, my heart on the other side of town. I thought about Dili, probably talking to his precious Onyeka at that very moment despite the time difference, and I wondered.

I wondered if that day would ever come.

# CHAPTER FOUR

## Russian Farmer's Song

IN THE THREE WEEKS that followed, Dili and I shared our 'news' with our friends and family. As my family consisted only of my sister, Ebere, and brother, Enyinna, they were the only two I bothered to call. Enyinna, being the pragmatic person he is, seemed satisfied when I explained it was only a temporary measure to help our old family friend, and didn't even dwell on it beyond the few questions he asked. Ebere was another case entirely.

"Okwudili!" she exclaimed when I told her. "What kind of blast from the past is that? The last I heard, he was pretending to be a big boy in FUTO. When did he go to America? How did you two even meet? And you want to marry him? *Hei hei! This one na serious sometin!*"

"It's just temporary," I answered, my irritation rising. "It's just to help him with his papers, that's all."

"*I bụ onye nzuzu*! You're so foolish! Is it a fake marriage or a real marriage? Won't you two have to divorce at the end of it all?" she retorted. "So you want to have a failed marriage under your belt? Don't you remember how tough it was for Chinedu's people to accept me as a divorcee. Yet, you *wan* open your two eyes and enter fire! *Ichọrọ ịbanye n'ime ọkụ*! And he is not even paying you! *Chai*! Ezioma, when did you become so foolish?"

I chose not to take offence by her outburst as I realized she felt strongly about it because of her own bad experience. Having married her university sweetheart immediately after graduating, they relocated to Germany where her husband went on to turn her into a punching bag. By the time we found out about it, she'd already suffered years of domestic violence. Despite our entreaties for her to leave him, she'd chosen to remain with her violent husband, but the marriage finally came to a dramatic end when he beat her up to the extent their neighbours had to call the police. That had marked the end of the marriage, and, after floating from one women's shelter to the other, she had made the painful decision to return to Nigeria.

Luckily, their five years together had produced no children, so Ebere only had herself to worry about. As fate would have it, shortly after her return home, she started receiving attention from a young London-based doctor, Chinedu, who was in Nigeria for his father's funeral. He'd taken one look at her as she walked down the road and decided she was the one for him. Ebere, on the other hand, was still smarting from the disappointment of her failed marriage and rebuffed him for months. It took almost a year of serious wooing before she finally gave in to his advances. But that was only the first hurdle, as Chinedu's family vehemently opposed the idea of their beloved son marrying not only a divorcee, but one who hadn't even been able to give her first husband any children. The battle with Chinedu's family lasted another year, until he'd given them an ultimatum; accept Ebere as his wife or cease to be a part of his life, because he was going to marry her whether they liked it or not. With that, his family had no choice but to agree, and he and

Ebere married a few months after her thirtieth birthday, following which she went on to have three children in quick succession, her youngest son just having turned a year old.

"Ebere, relax. Nothing is going to happen to me. It's the least I could do for Dili. Remember, he's like family to us."

"*Okay o!*" she reluctantly conceded. "As long as you're sure."

Dili, lucky for him, didn't have it quite as hard. His mother and siblings were happy he'd found a solution to his problem, and they were happier still when they realized it wasn't a random stranger he was marrying, but one they knew well.

"And Onyeka?" I asked him, as we sat across from each other at a small diner a few blocks from my apartment. "Have you told her?"

He nodded. "She was the first person I told, even before my mom. At first, she was glad I've found someone to help. But when she heard it's a Nigerian, I could tell she was worried about that. It wasn't until I told her how far back we go, how you're like a sister to me, and even showed her some of your pictures, that she finally relaxed."

I couldn't help but chuckle. "Oh, she relaxed when she saw I'm not your usual spec of tall and light skinned, *abi*?"

"Don't be silly, Ezi." Dili laughed, but we both knew I'd hit the nail on the head.

"Don't forget how long I've known you, Okwudili. I remember how you wanted to kill yourself because of Ebere when we were younger," I teased him.

He smiled nostalgically. "Ebere! I was in love with your sister, but she didn't even give me the time of day. How is she? Is she still in Germany? I heard she and her husband moved there."

My hiss was long and intense. "You knew Ejiofor?"

"Not really. The guy was a notorious cult member in UNN, and he was known across all higher institutions in the east. I remember being surprised that a girl as gentle and sweet as Ebere was dating someone like that. I was even more surprised when I heard she went on to marry him."

I hissed again and filled him in on the violence and abuse Ebere had endured in the hands of the beast called Ejiofor. "But before you get too excited and start nursing any ideas, she's remarried now and has three beautiful sons."

"Me nursing ideas? After all these years? You're a clown, Ezi!" Dili chuckled, shaking his head. "What about Uchechi? How is she doing?"

The smile on my face faded. "We lost Uchechi seven years ago. Breast cancer."

The sadness on Dili's face was so sincere, I had to look away to prevent myself from sinking into the depression remembering my youngest sister's death always triggered.

"I'm so sorry, Ezi. I didn't know," Dili said, regretful.

I shrugged and smiled. "It's just me, Ebere, and Enyinna now."

Dili's eyes widened. "Don't tell me your mom…"

"Okwudili, come on! My mom died three years after dad. It will be ten years next year."

"I heard about your dad's death, but I didn't know your mom had passed as well. I don't even think my mom knows because she would have mentioned it if she did."

"Breast cancer, just like Uchechi," I shrugged again. "It sucks, yes. But that's life for you, isn't it? Ebere and I know we're high risk, so we make sure we get regular mammograms and checks." I hit him playfully on the arm, desperate to change the topic. "So you only like tall, yellow babes, *okwiya*?"

Dilly threw his head back in a throaty laughter, this time not bothering to deny it. He told me about the girl he'd dated all through his university days, Uloma, who had been so beautiful, she'd been a Runner Up in the Most Beautiful Girl in Nigeria competition in 1997. As he talked about how broken he was after she left him, I realized I was fooling myself thinking Dili would ever be attracted to me, not when every woman he had ever been involved with was drop dead gorgeous.

As we talked, it was soon my turn to tell him about my dating history, and I told him about Eze, Seth, and the several casual relationships in between.

"I just knew you were the kind of girl who only dates white guys!" he exclaimed. "You mean you were actually engaged to one?"

"We were together for seven years and engaged for five," I answered. "We bought the apartment together."

"So, what happened?"

I shrugged. "We grew apart, I guess. He got tired of New York and decided to take up a teaching job at Duke."

Dili nudged my shoulder with his. "Are you sure that's what happened? Or is it true what they say about white guys in the bedroom?"

I shrieked, and we were soon both laughing hysterically, drawing angry looks from the other diners.

"Of course not!" I exclaimed. "I'll have you know that is just a big myth. Most of the white guys I've been with haven't had any issues down there, I can promise you that."

"If you say so," Dili said, his eyes twinkling. "But I don't know how you guys do it, though, you people that date other races. The cultural differences would be too much for me. Tell me you and your ex never had any instances where your differences made things difficult."

I smiled. "If I'm to be honest, food was a big issue. That was where our differences were the most apparent. He thought my food was too spicy and, good Lord, I couldn't stand the amount of cheese he consumed."

This set us off again, and we were soon laughing with reckless abandon.

"Jokes apart, Seth was a great guy," I said after the laughter subsided. "He loved me deeper than anyone ever has. By the time I found a way not to cook with too much spice, and learned to tolerate his insane love for cheese, we were able to live a good and happy life. Maybe if investment banking hadn't taken such a hit during the global recession, he'd still be here. But hey, life happens, and we are where we are, I guess."

Dili looked at me long and hard. "You're a special girl, Ezi. I'm going to make it my duty and objective to find you a great guy by the time this is all over."

I forced a smile, even though his statement killed me inside. By the time we left the diner and I got back to my apartment, I realized I was fooling myself thinking Dili would ever fall in love with me that way.

In the weeks that followed, I shared the news with my friends; a few close friends consisting of some work colleagues and a handful of friends from UPenn. The only difference being I didn't tell them it was a sham marriage. No. Instead I concocted a story of running into my childhood sweetheart on the streets of Manhattan, and how, after a whirlwind romance, he'd proposed. I told myself I'd lied to them to protect our ruse, but the truth was I wanted to live that fantasy, even if only through their eyes.

Dili and I changed our respective Facebook profiles to *Engaged* and uploaded the perfunctory pictures together, as we had been advised to by our Immigration Lawyer. I had never been very active on the social media platform, so I only had to respond to the odd congratulatory message or two. Dili, on the other hand, had to deal with the uproar that arose from his own revelation, and had to pacify a very distraught Onyeka, who herself had to deal with curious and confused questions from their mutual friends. But hey, we had to do what we had to do, right?

Now, three weeks later, as I lead him into the apartment with his luggage, I know I must be realistic. Dili and I will never be an item. He will never be attracted to a girl like me, talk less of love me like he does his darling Onyeka. All I have gained for myself is someone to keep me company for the year it will take his Green Card to be processed.

"Wow!" he exclaims as I lead him to the second bedroom of my apartment, one that I have had specially redecorated for him with top of the range beddings and furnishing from Pottery Barn and William Sonoma. "I've been rotating between sleeping on sofa beds and the floor for almost two years, Ezi. I can't believe you're offering me all this."

I smile at him. "How can I have such a big apartment and not help a friend in need? You're free to call this home for as long as you like."

"How will I ever repay you, Ezi?" he asks, his eyes glistening with tears.

"You are too emotional for my liking *oh,* Okwudili!" I tease him. "*Every small thing na cry! Na wa for you oh!*"

"If you knew all I've suffered in the last year, heck in the last decade, you'll understand why this means so much."

"Whatever, son!" I tease. "Just unpack quickly, so we can go out and grab dinner. It's our wedding day, remember?"

He nods and smiles, just as I shut the door. Once the door is closed, I exhale deeply. Yep, it's going to take everything for me to keep my feelings all nice and casual. But I know I have no choice.

That weekend, we go to Long Beach for our fake honeymoon. Our Immigration Lawyer has insisted honeymoon pictures will help make our case more believable, so off we go, first thing Saturday morning. As soon as we get there, we hit the beach and take several pictures we hope will be convincing enough. We also have a 'romantic' candlelit dinner afterwards, taking several pictures as well.

By the time we retire to our suite, I am not just mentally drained from a day of forced picture-taking, but emotionally as well. I wonder how long I'll be able to keep up this charade.

The suite has two bedrooms with a connecting lounge. When Dili retires to his room, I sit on the couch in the lounge, prop open my laptop and cue on the one song I know that captures just how I am feeling now, Keane's ***Russian Farmer's Song***.

I close my eyes and drink in the lyrics of the song, never more apt than they sound now.

***Russian Farmer's Song (Keane) – May 17, 2014***

*What do you do when the love you want is simply out of your way…blowing out of the rain?*

"What are you doing?" comes Dili's voice, startling me. "And what are you listening to?"

"*Oga,* you frightened me!" I say, trying to compose myself as I slam my laptop shut. "I'm writing my article. I told you I write for the *Manhattan Buzz,* didn't I?"

Dili sits on one of the chairs in the lounge, his interest piqued. "You didn't. That's amazing! So you're an investment banker by day and a writer by night. Impressive."

I shrug. "It's an additional source of income, no big deal."

"What do you write about?"

"I write about the soundtrack of my day," I answer, smiling. "I basically write about how my day is captured by a song, any song at all."

"Really? I'd never have thought you the musical type."

"That just shows how little you know me, Okwudili Dike," I say, with a sly smile. "I've always been musical, and this article is the perfect outlet for me after every day; be it a good or bad one, a happy or sad one."

He nods. "Interesting. You're full of surprises, young lady," he cocks his head to the side and listens to the song playing. "And this is the soundtrack for today? What song is this *sef*?"

I look at him incredulously. "You don't know Keane? This is one of their more popular songs, and one of my favourites of all time!"

He laughs and shakes his head. "Underneath this dark skin, you're a white girl at heart, Ezi. I've never heard it in my life." He rises to his feet. "Don't let me interrupt you. Carry on with your writing, my lovely wife!"

I watch him as he returns to his room, his words enveloping me like a much-needed embrace.

My lovely wife.

If only he knew how true I wish those words were.

*Definitely out of my way.*

*Definitely blowing out of the rain.*

# CHAPTER FIVE

## Moonlighting

BY THE TIME WE RETURN to Manhattan after our stay in Long Beach, I have resigned myself to fate, to the fact that Dili will never love me, and that the woman he does love is his Onyeka. What did I expect anyway? For him to just take one look at me and forget the woman he has pledged forever to back home in Nigeria? Besides, before I ran into him, he was the last thing on my mind. So I decide to return my focus to what it was prior to that April morning of our meeting; work, my writing, fashion, and searching for love online. In that order.

Immediately we are back home, we fill the required paperwork, consisting of the standard Form I-130 and the Form I-485 to adjust his status. We have agreed with Michelle that there is no need to send any joint financial or property ownership information, considering our story is that we were lovers back in Nigeria and he only just moved to the States, and, as such, won't be expected to have that kind of financial or property ownership footprint. So we only include our marriage certificate, pictures, and my financial information as supporting documents.

And so begins the waiting period.

As the days turn into weeks, and the weeks turn into months, Dili and I are soon more comfortable in each other's company. Having talked myself out of my crush on him, I can now act normal around him and no longer parade around the apartment with a full face of make-up from dawn to dusk. Instead, I am comfortable enough to ditch my weaves and sport my natural cornrows when I'm in the apartment. And the more comfortable I get, the more I enjoy his company.

Despite his limited options for employment, I pull in a few favours from some friends to get him a short-term IT support contract with a small financial services company downtown. Due to his immigration status, he can only work for them remotely, which is just as well, as it gives him the time he needs to study for a Project Management Professional certification exam, which he has registered for.

Both of us fall into a comfortable routine, one we are both happy and content with. He has a comfortable roof over his head, a decently paying job, the time and opportunity to work towards a certification that will help advance his career and, most importantly, the dream of getting his Green Card soon. I, on the other hand, now have company at home, someone to chat with about old times, gossip with about happenings at work, and just be silly with.

I am no longer bothered when I overhear him talking to Onyeka at odd hours. I have accepted her as a part of his life and have even spoken with her on a few occasions. I was quite surprised the first time we spoke, as I had expected her to be one of those arrogant, yet empty-headed, Lagos girls. But she turned out quite the opposite.

"Ah, sis! *Kedụ ka ọ dị? Nne, daalụ!!* Thank you so much for what you are doing for us! *Chukwu gozie gị*! God bless you!" had been her emphatic words.

We went on to speak for about a minute more, with her rattling in Igbo half the time. So, nope, she certainly wasn't what I'd expected.

"She's awesome, right?" Dili beamed as soon as I got off the phone.

"Mmhmm," I said, forcing a smile. "Did she grow up in the east?"

Dili laughed. "She did. She only came to Lagos for her Youth Service."

"And how old did you tell her I am? The way she was talking, one would think I was her mother's age."

"She's just very respectful. You'll like her when you meet her."

Ah yes. When I meet her. I have come to realize that Dili's Green Card will signal his ability to bring his fiancée over, so my meeting her in the near future is almost a certainty.

But rather than be depressed about that, I choose to continue enjoying his company and soon start seeing him like the sibling he also sees me as.

One Saturday afternoon, as we are sitting in a nearby patisserie having breakfast, I see him admire a beautiful, tall, light-skinned African American woman and I chuckle. "Okwudili! Don't let your eyes pop out of your skull oh!"

He chuckles back. "Just admiring God's creation, that's all."

After a few moments, I ask what I have always been curious about. "Have you cheated on Onyeka? Since you've been here?"

He shakes his head. "Never. Not once. Yes, I've admired beautiful women, but that's where it always ends."

"Not even once?" I exclaim. "So that means you haven't had sex in almost two years? *Mehn, your agro no go be here oh!*"

Dili smiles. "You're silly." Then with a shrug, adds. "Yes, it hasn't been easy, but I've made up my mind never to be that guy."

By 'that guy', we both know he is referencing his father. After the mess the old man left his family in by procreating all over the place, I suppose it's no surprise Dili wants very little to do with that kind of life.

"Onyeka is a very lucky girl. I hope she knows that."

"The truth is, I'm the lucky one!" he says, a dreamy smile on his face. "She can have any guy she wants, but she has chosen to wait for me. If anyone of us should count themselves lucky, it's me."

I nod as I take another sip of my cappuccino, angry that I feel a sudden stab of envy. My consolation is that I, too, once had this kind of love. With Seth, I once had a man who was incredibly faithful and devoted to me. And hopefully, one day soon, I will again.

"So," Dili says, a wide smile on his face as he scans the room. "Let me guess who your type would be. That one?"

He points at an olive-skinned guy reading a newspaper as he sips his coffee, and I shake my head. "Nah. Too pretty. I've never liked guys who are too obviously handsome."

Dili raises his brows in piqued interest, before turning to scan the room again. "That guy?" he asks, pointing at a guy who looks like he just awoke from the 1990's Grunge era, with his dirty blonde hair, faded tee-shirt and painfully distressed jeans.

I frown at Dili. "Preferably one who's had a bath in the last month."

Before Dili can respond, I smile as a familiar song starts playing on the sound system; *You Get What You Give* by New Radicals. "I love this song."

Dili shakes his head. "Why doesn't that surprise me?"

But I ignore him, choosing to instead sing along to a song that has a very special place in my heart. *"But when the night is falling. You cannot find the light. You feel your dreams are dying. Hold tight. You've got the music in you!"*

Dili watches me in amazement as I sing along, and then nods in the direction of the Grunge guy. "Your boyfriend is also jamming the song."

I look across to see the guy, and a few other people in the café, also singing. By the time it gets to the ending bridge, we are all singing along like people in a flash mob. We break into mild applause when the song is over, and each return to what we were doing beforehand.

"Must have been a popular song," Dilly remarks.

"It takes me all the way back to 1999. My flat mate and I loved it so much, we played it every day. Such a feel-good song!" I say, nostalgically. "I was in Wharton then, doing my MBA."

Dili nods in understanding. "I know what you mean. Some songs just teleport one all the way back."

"Exactly. For me, songs are even stronger than photographs when I want to remember a certain period of my life," I say, getting excited the way I do when I talk about music.

"So if I name a year, you can tell me the song that best captures that year for you?" Dili asks, leaning closer in interest.

"Try me," I say, leaning in as well.

"1985!" he challenges.

"That's easy. The *Moonlighting Theme Song*," I answer proudly. "That was the year I fell head over heels in love with Bruce Willis, aka David Addison."

"Interesting. 1988?" he asks.

I laugh. "You and I know what song that would be. Can't you remember the song our dads jammed to that year?"

"*Silent Morning*," we exclaim in unison, before bursting out laughing.

"Oh, my goodness, I can vividly see the old folks dancing the Cabbage Patch to this song! What were we then? Eleven?"

I nod, happy to see he has gotten into the vibe of things. And we go on to play the game for the next hour.

"1992?" I throw at him.

"*Rumpshaker*!" he answers. "You?"

"Boyz II Men's *End of the Road*." I answer but omit to tell him this is my song because it was what I would cry myself to sleep with every time I encountered him and Ebere in their stage of poppy love.

"1995? First year of university," he throws at me.

"*Don't Speak* by No Doubt," I answer. It had not only been the anthem almost everywhere on my campus that year, it had also been Eze's favourite song.

We continue that way, working our way through the years.

"2001?" Dili asks me.

A wide grin breaks on my face. "That's easy! Outkast's *So Fresh, So Clean*! That's the year I moved to Manhattan and experienced something of a rebirth."

"You mean your deliverance from white music?" Dili chuckles. "Funnily enough, it was one of my favourites that year as well."

And we find ourselves encountering several common songs as we work through the years.

"*Lean Back*," we both answer for 2004, and "*Gold Digger*," for 2005, and we go on to laugh over Dili's story of the 'gold digger' he dated that year, a girl who erroneously thought he was wealthy and had inherited his late father's riches, and who disappeared the moment she found out it he actually hadn't.

But after 2006, Dili draws a blank.

"Music was the last thing on my mind when I was dealing with my father's mess. That was the peak of when we were trying to negotiate with the banks, so I didn't have time for music at all," Dili answers, bringing some somberness to our conversation.

I nod, sad he had to grow up so fast. But I continue with the game, hoping it will cheer him up. "For me, 2008 was all about D-Banj's *The Entertainer* album! That was the best of the year for me."

Dili laughs in surprise. "So you also listen to Naija music?"

"Are you kidding? I'm probably more up to date with Naija jams than you are," I beam, not adding that I have two of my friends from UPenn, Adaeze and Joko, to thank for this.

"It wasn't until I met Onyeka that joy, real joy, returned to my life," he says. "Bruno Mars' *Nothin' on You* is our song. It's the song I sang to her when we first got serious, when I realized I was in love with her. And every time I hear it, I think of her."

Again, that stab of jealousy. "Yeah, it's a lovely song. Really nice."

We finish our meal and are soon strolling home. With summer having given way to fall, it is getting colder. Without warning, Dili grabs my phone from my hand and opens my *Tinder* app.

"*Eeeehn*! So you're on Tinder, Ezioma!" he laughs. "I caught a glimpse of the app when we were at the café. I would never have pegged you for online dating."

I shrug casually. "Not all of us are lucky to find love walking the streets. These days, you're more likely to find it online."

"But why Tinder, though? Why not any of the others like eHarmony and Match? Those seem like they'd have more serious guys. Isn't Tinder all about the booty call?"

"I tried those before and only got hit up by creepy guys," I answer. "Mia was the one who suggested Tinder."

"And how has that been so far?"

I shrug again, reluctant to admit how much of a disappointment it has been.

"Ah, no wonder you don't seem enthusiastic. Your profile is very dull, Ezi. For God's sake, why did you use this picture?"

I grab the phone from him. "What's wrong with my picture?" I ask, closely examining the image of me sitting on a park bench, a broad smile on my face.

"You look too serious. You should change it to something more flirty…more fun," he suggests. "Trust me, you'll get more hits that way."

"I've deliberately not been active since we got 'married'. We don't want the authorities seeing me actively dating online, do we?" I mutter, shoving my phone in my pocket.

"Ah, true!" Dili answers, before looking at me wide-eyed. "I have the perfect guy for you, Ezi! Why didn't I think of this before?"

I look at him quizzically. What perfect guy?

"My friend from university, Madufuro. He is a Medical Doctor, and he lives in New Jersey. He's perfect for you!" Dili exclaims, his excitement bubbling over. "You two will be perfect for each other. As soon as we get home, I'll call him."

I have mixed emotions about this, and we walk to the apartment in silence. While I might have resigned myself to us never being together, the thought of him setting me up with another guy is not a pleasant one, either.

Once in the apartment, Dili calls his Madufuro friend and makes small talk with the guy as I busy myself with other things.

"He's not in town at the moment," Dili says regretfully, once he is off the phone. "He's away in Europe for some training program and will be back in about a month or two." He smiles eagerly. "But he was very interested when I hinted him about you, and he's asked me to send him your phone number. Will that be okay?"

Realizing I have nothing to lose, I shrug in agreement. Meeting this Madufuro person shouldn't hurt. It's not as if I have a better option right now.

Later that night, sitting before my laptop, I stare out the window into the Manhattan night sky. I listen to the typical sounds of nighttime;, the intermittent blast of a siren, laughter from twenty-somethings bar hopping, and the low-frequency hum of the city. But my mind is on none of these. Instead, I find myself gravitating to the *Moonlighting Theme Song*. I play the song on my phone, and the lyrics could not be more apt than they are today.

***Moonlighting Theme* *(Al Jarreau) – September 13, 2014***

*You can share your life with someone, but if your hearts are not aligned, if your hearts don't walk together, you are nothing but Moonlighting Strangers*

*Walking by night, flying by day…who just met on the way.*

"I'm off, Ezi!" Dili says, walking into the living room, on his way out for drinks with his friends. "Are you sure you don't want to come? I've met your friends, so don't you think you should meet mine?"

"I'm really tired," I answer. "Maybe next time?"

"I'll hold you to that," he answers, before smiling coyly. "Madufuro sent me a reminder for your number, so I've given it to him. I'm sure he'll call you any minute."

"I can't wait!" I say with feigned excitement.

As he disappears behind the shut door, I shut my eyes.

Yep, we're moonlighting strangers alright!

# CHAPTER SIX

## Knocks Me Off My Feet

DILI'S MADUFURO FRIEND doesn't call me for another week, but it is long enough for me to lose any interest I've managed to muster. All I can imagine is some Igbotic guy with an accent just as bad as his dress sense. Especially after speaking with Onyeka, I find my perception of Dili's crowd somewhat altered. Maybe if I weren't seeing him through the eyes of childhood infatuation, he would also appear razz and local to me.

Every day, Dili asks me if Madufuro has called, and every day, I answer in the negative. The truth is, I really don't need his pity and can very well find a guy of my own if I'm serious about it. But having lied to all my friends that I have married, not to help a friend, but out of love, I find myself handicapped and unable to socialize as I ordinarily would. I accept that I am probably going to be hopelessly single until this arrangement with Dili is over.

Alas, the dreaded call comes by weekend. Having forgotten all about it, I erroneously assume the call from the European number is from my sister, Ebere. With the way she and her husband holiday from one exotic location to the other, I can't be blamed for the assumption. Alas, it isn't Ebere, but finally Doctor Madufuro.

"Hi. Am I speaking with Ezioma?" comes a soft-spoken voice, which is nothing like I'd imagined.

"Yes, this is Ezioma."

"Hi. My name is Madu. Dili gave me your number," he says, and I am pleasantly surprised to realize he is nervous, and not arrogant like I thought he'd be.

We have a pleasant conversation, with him telling me all the nice things Dili has said about me. He also admits to looking me up online and being extremely impressed by what he's seen. Knowing nothing about him beyond his first name or that he is a doctor who lives in New Jersey, I ask him questions about himself and find out that, even though he started out at FUTO, he left for the States in his second year, where he went on to qualify as a doctor. At thirty-nine, he is two years older than I am, and I hate to admit that he is ticking all my boxes.

"Ezioma, you're a very fascinating woman and I hate the fact we're connecting when I'm at the start of a six-month program here in Berlin," he says, after we've spoken for almost an hour.

"Six months? That's a long time," I remark.

"Look, I know this is the first time we're speaking, but I think there's something here. But I don't want to keep you hanging for the time I'll be here in Europe. So I'm not going to call again until March next year, when I'm about to leave for home. If I'm lucky and some guy hasn't swooped you up yet, I'd be glad for us to continue this conversation from where we've left off."

It sounds like a great idea to me. At this age of mine, I'm too old for any telephone love across the seas. If, when he gets back to town, if I'm still available, we can always see where this leads.

But Dili is less than impressed when I tell him. "I don't understand. You guys have agreed not to talk until next year?"

"What's the use? He's not in town for over five months. Why waste each other's time and incur high phone bills?"

Dili raises his hands in surrender, and I can tell he thinks neither Madu nor I is serious about taking things further. But I respect Madu for it. Just because Dili and Onyeka are happy to carry on an indefinite long distant relationship doesn't mean the rest of us are.

The months roll by, and it is soon Christmas. No matter how sad or depressed I am, in December I am always cheered by the typical New York festivities. The lights, the carols on every corner, the chill in the air, the snow if we're lucky. It is unarguably my favourite time of the year. Dili has just passed his PMP certification exam, so there is a lot to celebrate.

On December 23rd, he asks me to accompany him for his friend's annual Christmas party here in Manhattan. Apparently, both the friend and the wife have their birthdays this Christmas week, so they have a combined party every year to celebrate. Having dodged Dili's invitations to meet his friends all year long, I feel obliged to accept this one.

"How come this friend of yours didn't help you out when you were having a hard time?" I ask as we leave our apartment. With an address like that, his friend is not a pauper.

"Nnamdi did help me out with about a thousand dollars when I first got to New York," Dili says in his friend's defense. "The truth is he's not making as much as he used to. He lost a lot of money in the global financial crisis, and he and his wife are just making the most of whatever they can get from his real estate business and her book publishing."

I nod in understanding. The story of pretty much half of Manhattan.

We get into the taxi, and I am excited anew by the sights and sounds of Christmas everywhere.

"Don't you just love Christmas?" I exclaim, feeling like a little girl experiencing the holiday for the first time.

Dili shrugs and smiles. "Obviously not as much as you do. Before I left Nigeria, it was no big deal. And last Christmas, I was having such a difficult time in LA, it was hard to find anything about the holiday to smile about."

"Well, you're going to enjoy this one. I'll make sure of it!"

He smiles at me, and we ride in silence for a few minutes, before he says, "One thing I love about going to visit Nnamdi is his piano. He has a grand piano in his living room, and just being able to play it makes me forget every and anything."

"You play the piano?"

"You're the reason we all learnt to play. Don't tell me you don't play any instrument!"

I shrug. "I did for a short while, but I dropped it when it was proving to too much of a distraction for me in school." I look at him, his words suddenly dawning on me. "What do you mean I was the reason you all learned to play?"

Dili laughs. "My father used you as the benchmark for everything. He would always come home and yell at me, especially, about what fantastic feat Ezioma had achieved. It was always how Ezioma had done this, passed that, excelled at this, accomplished that. To be honest, I hated you."

I squeal with laughter. "And there I was thinking you didn't even notice me."

"Notice you? You were a thorn in my flesh!" Dili laughs. "The worst was when you got good enough grades to get you into Queens

College on Merit, whereas I couldn't even manage to get a place in Kings College on quota. My Dad made me feel I was a failure by only managing to get accepted into Saint Greg's. Or how about when you smashed your SATs and got a scholarship to America, while I went ahead to fail my JAMB exam that year? The old man didn't let me hear the last of it."

I giggle, very tickled by this information. It feels good to know I was held in such high esteem in their home.

We soon arrive at the impressive apartment building on 59th Street and Madison Avenue. It is clear that, once upon a time, Dili's friend indeed had a lot of money. Getting to their condo on the 37th floor, I am impressed by the opulence of the place. Just like Dili said, grandstanding in the middle of their expansive and expensively furnished living room is a magnificent white piano, the kind one would see in Hollywood movies. But a Naija party will always be a Naija party, as the blare of The Mavins' *Dorobucci* overshadows the condo's uptown luxury.

As we make our way across the crowded room, Dili introduces me to his friends, and from the warm way they greet me, it is obvious they know who I am and what I am doing for him.

"Ezioma!" Nnamdi exclaims, hugging me like we are old pals. "It's so good to finally meet you. Thanks so much for what you are doing for my brother."

I am introduced to Nnamdi's wife, Azuka, and I am pleasantly surprised to see she is a familiar face from my early party-hopping days in Manhattan. As the party progresses, I gravitate to Azuka and a few other wives and girlfriends, almost all of whom are Nigerian and thankfully not the nose-in-the-air, stuck-up kind you'd typically run into in Manhattan. These women are extremely down-to-earth and so funny, I am soon in stitches listening to their stories.

Ever so often, I steal glances across the room to where Dili and the other men are playing snooker. He is also enjoying their company and I am glad to see him having a good time. He has come such a long way from when I ran into him months ago and looks so much better; fresher and more relaxed. It is amazing what difference a few months can make.

I look up to see Azuka studying me intently. I force a smile and look away, suddenly feeling flushed. She probably knows of Onyeka and must think me foolish gaping at Dili like that that.

"Ezi, do you want to give me a hand in the kitchen? I need to dish dessert," she asks, rising to her feet.

Knowing she absolutely doesn't need my help, I trudge along anyway. Just as I expected, her kitchen is full of all sorts of hands doing one thing or the other, but she takes a tray of chocolate truffles and macarons from one of the caterers and starts idly arranging the treats by size and colour.

"It's a wonderful thing you're doing for Dili," she says, smiling at me. "When Nnamdi told me about it, I couldn't believe Dili's luck. Finding someone he doesn't have to pay to help him with his Green Card *and* give him free accommodation here in Manhattan? The guy won the jackpot!"

I shrug. "We go way back. He's like family to me."

She smiles at me. "You're sure? I saw the way you were looking at him just now, and you weren't looking at him like a brother."

I force myself to laugh. "Dili is exactly like a brother to me, nothing more. Besides, he has a fiancée back in Nigeria."

Her smile doesn't waver. "Just be careful, Ezi. We're not as hard as guys can be. Try not to get carried away, okay? I like you, and I don't want to see you get hurt."

Her words are still ringing in my head as we make our way back to the living room. I am so deep in thought that I don't hear Dili walk up to me. "Where have you been? I've been looking all over for you."

"I had to help Azuka with a few things," I mutter as he takes me by the hand and leads me to the piano.

"I told you this is my favourite part of coming here." he says, taking a seat. "And you haven't heard me play before."

I sit beside him. "So you want to play the piano above P-Square singing in the background."

He smiles coyly as his fingers start to glide across the white keys, playing what I can clearly make out to be Stevie Wonder's *Knocks Me Off My Feet.*

I stare at him as he sings the song while playing its melody on the piano, completely mesmerized. For me, the whole world stops, and I realize that I am just as in love with him as the first day I saw him at his fifth birthday party. Maybe even more. The party continues around us, and the DJ continues spinning his Naija tracks, but for me…for me, it might as well just be us two, Dili and me, in the room.

"Wow!" I say, when he is done playing. "That was amazing. You play so well. And that's one of my favourite songs ever."

"Yeah? It's Onyeka's favourite as well. She loves it when I sing it to her," he answers, beaming.

And that brings me crashing right back to earth.

I look up in time to catch Azuka's eye, and she shakes her head at me. It appears we are the only two people in the room who know I have lost my heart to Okwudili Dike.

I excuse myself to go to the toilet, and, while there, I look at my reflection in the mirror for a long time. "What is wrong with you, Ezioma?!" I demand from my reflection. "You better get a grip of yourself!"

After finally composing myself, I walk out and return to the party. Dili and his friends have their backs turned to me and I stop walking as I overhear them talk.

"I don't know why you are wasting your time with that girl in Nigeria!" Nnamdi says to him. "You've gotten yourself a sweet catch here. The babe owns her own apartment here in Manhattan, is a Director with Goldman, isn't bad looking…what do you want again?"

"Exactly what I was thinking. *You nor dey see her type everyday*!" says Udeme, another friend of theirs.

"Guys, it's not like that with Ezi and I," Dili says. "She's like a sister to me. And she knows my heart is back home in Nigeria."

I decide to make my presence known and emerge as if I haven't been standing behind them, eavesdropping on their conversation. We make some more small talk before Dili and I leave for home a little before midnight.

I am quiet all through the taxi ride home, citing a headache for the change in my mood. Settled in my room, I lie awake for hours, thinking of Dili singing the Stevie Wonder song, a song he apparently also sings to the woman who has his heart.

Unable to sleep and uninterested in writing my article, I go to the living room at about 2am and proceed to watch old episodes of my favourite show, *Sex and the City*.

"What are you doing up at this time of night?" Dili asks, emerging from his bedroom.

"I'm sorry, did the noise wake you?" I ask in concern.

"Nah. I was on the phone with Onyeka," he answers, taking a seat next to me. "She and her family are headed to Umuahia this morning, so she called when they were about to leave the house."

I shrug, trying not show that knowing he's been on the phone with Onyeka for hours isn't boring a hole in my heart.

"*Sex and the City*! Why do women love this show so much? Onyeka can watch it all day without any toilet breaks," he chuckles.

I shrug again, wishing this time he'd just return to his bedroom instead of bombarding me with this endless talk about Onyeka.

"But I see why you'd like it though. I see the Carrie Bradshaw link; the designer shoes, the fancy clothes, the column writing…" he says, a rueful smile on his face. "You two are very much alike."

This time, I can't help the smile that forms on my face. "Yeah? Carrie Bradshaw is my ultimate inspiration. When I first moved to Manhattan, I modelled my life after hers. And as for being as glamorous as her, I wish!"

"Oh, but you are! There's no difference between you both. She's also not that pretty but dresses just as stylishly," he says, before realizing his goof. "I didn't mean…What I meant was…"

The funny thing is I don't even take offence.

"No need to stammer, Dili!" I laugh. "You are indeed correct. Neither Carrie nor I are that pretty. Maybe that's why I can relate with her so well!"

"I'm really sorry, Ezi. I didn't mean it the way it came out. You are a very pretty girl…"

"In my own way. I know." I answer sarcastically, smiling at him.

"I better go back to bed before I allow my sleepy brain put my mouth into more trouble," he mumbles. "Try not to stay up too late. It's Christmas Eve."

When his door is shut, the smile fades from my face, and I have lost interest in even the *Sex and the City* reruns I'd used to console myself. Rising to my feet, I walk to my study table and pull open my laptop. I try to think up a song, any song, I can use as my song of the day, but all that keeps looping in my head is the song Dili played at the party.

# A LOVE OF CONVENIENCE

*Knocks Me Off My Feet (Stevie Wonder) – December 24, 2014*

I am about to write the narrative for the article when I see a notification for a comment on a previous post.

***You've been referencing a lot of soppy songs lately. Very unlike your usual. Sounds like you're in love.***

I pause as I stare at the comment. My first inclination is to ignore it, but apart from never ignoring interaction or feedback on my columns, something about the comment tugs at me. I guess because I know the writer is correct, and that I *am* in love. Despite the fact the object of my affection is head over heels in love with another. Despite the fact he has just told me to my face that he doesn't even find me attractive.

***You're correct,*** I write in response. ***I'm in love. As a matter of fact, I just got married.***

Heck, I might not have him in real life, but nobody can take him away from me in the land of make believe, can they?

# CHAPTER SEVEN

## Simple Kind of Life

MY COMMENT IN THE ARTICLE sets off an avalanche of messages from my readers. I wake up the next morning to a staggering two hundred and seventy-nine comments, all expressing their joy over my new 'marital' status. I am amazed because, even though my anonymously written column is widely read, I have never exceeded thirty comments per column. But sitting in front of the laptop reading all their comments as I drink my morning coffee, I can't help but be tickled by it all. So I thank every one of the commenters, and even tell the few that ask the same story I concocted for my friends about how Dili and I met and fell in love. Nobody can stop me from fantasizing, can they?

The charade is enough to see me through the holidays and gives me the stamina to listen to Dili's ongoing commentary about Onyeka's older sister's traditional marriage going on in Umuahia. Why he thinks I'd care about his lover's sister getting married is beyond me.

But my online fairy tale world gives me the strength to feign interest and even console him when he laments about Onyeka's parents' growing impatience with him.

"It will soon be three years since we got engaged," he says sadly. "And I can't even give them an idea when we'll be moving on to the next stage."

"Don't worry. You should get your Green Card before we hit the one-year mark in May, and you can make your plans then," I say, trying my best to sound reassuring.

By the time we enter the New Year, and the Christmas Magic has packed its bags not to return for another year, the novelty of my online lie starts to wear thin. I have less people commenting to ask about my marriage, and I am no longer as enthused about living in the land of make-believe. But more so, with my thirty-eighth birthday looming, I realize I can not continue pining for another woman's man…not at this age. I am not a star struck teenager who, even though knows the truth, chooses to lie to herself instead. At this age, continuing to do that would be the ultimate tragedy. I know the truth, the truth being that this man will never love me, and I might as well get with the program.

The months roll by with us continuing with our comfortable pattern; me working sometimes fifteen-hour days at work, and him continuing his job from home. Even with him now PMP certified, without his Green Card, he is still not eligible for legal work. But our friendship deepens in the few hours we do get to spend together, and as we confide in each other our deepest secrets. I tell him about what really went down with Seth, and how badly our relationship silently deteriorated before he made the decision to leave, and he tells me about his lowest point of helping his mom sell off all her jewellery, including her wedding and engagement rings, when things got really bad for his family. Thankfully, he is now better able to support his mother with the little he makes from his remote job. A few times, I have offered lending him money, but he rejects the offers each time, saying what I am doing for him is more than enough.

As for Madufuro, even though he is not a permanent fixture in my mind, I think of him fleetingly. As we approach the month of March, I find myself looking forward to his call to let me know he's back in town, and that we can pick up from where we left off. In the months since we've spoken, I have checked him out online and, apart from him being better looking than I'd imagined, I am impressed by all he has achieved at such a young age, garnering numerous awards and recognition for his exploits in Thoracic Surgery.

But as the days in the month go by one by one, the chance of Madufuro calling dwindles. Yes, our initial conversation might have been interesting, but so much could have happened in the five months since then. He could have met someone else and decided I'm no longer worth his time. By the time March is officially over, and I change my calendar to April, I accept that Madufuro and I will never have that reconnection, so I condemn him to my box of DOA relationships.

Whilst I can't say I really grieve the end of the daydream of whatever could have been between Madufuro and I, I do find myself slipping into a depression I don't understand. I find myself worrying I will never find that special person, that I will never get married, that I will be alone for the rest of my life. Not even after breaking up with Seth did I feel this kind of emptiness. It is worsened when Mia's longtime boyfriend finally proposes to her. As she gushes in excitement about how romantic the proposal was, even though I am squealing and excited on the outside, on the inside I am dying with envy. How wonderful it would be to have the love of the man I love! Whilst my friend is happily about to begin life with the man of her dreams, I am living a charade with mine. Alas, as she is one of those who thinks Dili and I are the real deal, I keep up the pretense, act all happy for her, and even accept to be her Maid of Honour for her summer wedding.

The final nail in the coffin comes when I get the call from Uju, the person I have been friends with the longest since I got to America. We bonded as fellow Nigerian undergrads in UPenn, and we have bonded even more over the years with her also not toeing the typical line of getting married to the first Nigerian boy that came her way after school. Instead, she has also been climbing the career ladder in Atlanta where she now lives, and whenever she's in my town, or I'm in hers, we catch up over drinks, laughing at our friends who no longer have the luxury of freedom like we do.

"Can you imagine she actually came to the club with her baby's diaper bag?!" she once giggled about a mutual friend who had insisted on carrying her child's supplies when they went on a night out, so that she wouldn't have to stop over at home before heading to the babysitter's house to pick up her daughter. "If that's what having kids does to you, *biko* count me out!"

So even though most of our friends have been getting married and procreating, and even though Uju, like all my other friends, thinks I married for love, I have always held on to the comfort of knowing I'm not the only one content and happy with the kind of life I live.

Until that day in April when she calls to tell me she is not only pregnant but that, her boyfriend - an Igbo guy for that matter - has just proposed, and that the wedding will be in Nigeria in December.

"By then, I would have had the baby," she says, her voice high pitched in excitement. "You and your hubby better buy your tickets now. *I no go hear story*!"

I go through the motions of giving her my heartfelt congratulations and talking about the pros and cons of getting married in Nigeria, but as soon as I get off the phone, it feels like I have just been hit with a sledgehammer. Uju is not just getting married, she is having a baby!

And I am here, still single to stupor.

I continue to live my life as normal, putting on a happy face to mask the growing depression I feel every day. From the minute I open my eyes in the morning to when I close them at night, I can feel despondence so heavy, it is like it is lying in bed right next to me.

Thankfully, at the end of April, we get the call we have been waiting for from Michelle. Dili's Green Card has been approved.

"It's a CR1 Green Card, though," she says, when we meet with her the next day. "Meaning it's a conditional one because you have been married less than two years. You should qualify for an IR1, a permanent Green Card, when you hit your two-year anniversary, or, worst case, two years after the issue of the CR1, which would be two years from today."

I steal a look at Dili, wondering how he is taking the news of us having to continue our arrangement for anything between another year to even two, but he is as excited as ever.

"Can I work with the CR1? Can I travel?" he asks, his excitement palpable.

Michelle smiles in understanding. "You most surely can. Congratulations!"

Dili is a ball of energy as we return to our apartment, talking non-stop, oscillating between raving about hitting the job market immediately, travelling to Nigeria to see his beloved Onyeka, and thanking me profusely for my help.

"God bless the day I came to Manhattan to see that guy!" he continues to ramble on. "God bless the day I found you, Ezioma! You're an angel specially sent to me by God! God bless you!"

"You're my brother, Dili, no need to thank me," is my perfunctory answer.

That night, I listen to the endless phone calls he makes to Onyeka, his mother, his siblings, his friends, announcing his Green Card, albeit a conditional one. I smile through him celebrating with every phone call, but I am saddened by the finiteness of it all. This is the official beginning of the end for us. The minute he gets a good job, he just might decide to move out. If he gets a good job out of town, it won't be a hard sell to convince Immigration that we are only living apart because of work. It hits me that the bigger tragedy isn't that Dili will soon be leaving me…but that I will once again be well and truly alone.

At the grand old age of thirty-eight! Only two years separating me from the age of forty.

But I put on my happy face, which is what I do for the next few weeks, smiling through his excited chatter and as his job search starts to yield early results, with him getting invited for multiple interviews. By the middle of May, he has accepted an offer from a major software company in Manhattan, with a very mouth-watering salary. Three years after arriving in America, he has finally made it.

On May 15th, I do not even remember it is our one-year anniversary. As I typically would, I leave home before he rises, and soon am totally immersed in work as soon as I get to the office. My work has once again become my crutch, my means of escape, and I am burying myself in it more and more, all in a bid to forget about the emptiness that is eating me alive.

I am surprised to get a bouquet of flowers from Dili delivered to my office late morning and can't help but smile when I see the *Happy* Anniversary inscription on the accompanying card. Anniversary indeed! Of course, my colleagues 'oooh' and 'aaah' over it, and, once again, I have to plaster on smile through it all.

"I got the flowers. Thanks," I say, when I sneak a phone call to him during my lunch break.

"You didn't think I'd forget, did you?" is his cheerful answer. "This was the day you changed my life, and I am going to celebrate you today for it. Try to get away from work early if you can, okay?"

I smile, wondering what he has up his sleeve. "Sure."

I am not able to leave work before 8pm, but as soon as I walk into the apartment, I almost have to look at the number on my door to be sure I'm in the right place. Dili has rearranged the living room, bringing my small dining table to the middle of the room, a tall candle burning on a holder right in the middle of it. There are rose petals everywhere, and *Tony Toni Tone's* ***Anniversary*** plays on the sound system. I didn't expect this kind of romantic ambush at all.

"Ah! Finally, you're home!" comes his voice from the kitchen as he walks up to me, takes me by the hand, and leads me to the table. "Have a seat, Mademoiselle. I am spoiling you tonight."

I snigger. "So you couldn't even take me to an expensive restaurant! It has to be home service?" I tease. "Cheap much!"

"Home service with a difference," he smiles, before disappearing into the kitchen and returning with two bowls of fresh fish pepper soup, and bread from my favourite bakery all the way in Soho.

"You made this?" I exclaim even though I'm not really surprised, as Dili has cooked for us several times before. But never like this.

"All for you, my dear Ezioma. You deserve it all," he says, serving me the appetizer, which is soon followed by fried rice, made Naija style, accompanied by stewed lamb, and even fried plantain. Okwudili has really pulled all the stops tonight.

"This is one of the most delicious meals I've ever had in my whole life!" I remark as I wolf down the food. "I'm still amazed you can cook this well. Your mother really did a great job with you."

"I want to thank you for everything, Ezioma," he says sincerely. "What you did for me, very few would have. Without even worrying that I was some sort of scam, you welcomed me into your life…into your home. You married me without even insisting on a Pre-nuptial Agreement, without even worrying if I was one of those scammers who would clean you out financially. You've had me living like a king here in Manhattan. You got me a job even when I couldn't legally work, you supported me while I wrote my exams, and gave me the enabling environment to seek new opportunities.

I am forever indebted to you. After my first few months in America, when I was still in L.A, I honestly thought I'd made a mistake coming and that I would never be able to achieve the American dream. But one encounter with you and everything changed. Ezioma, you changed my life, and I just want to say a big thank you!"

I smile sadly, wondering if this is the big speech before he tells me he is moving out.

"All I want to do is show you my gratitude…somehow, someway," he continues. "I could only think of this dinner because you have everything. I don't know what I could buy for you, what I could get you, that would even make any sense. I just want to show you my gratitude any way I can."

I look at him, and the words are out of my mouth before my brain even has a chance to process, screen, and approve them. "I want a baby."

"A what?"

Suddenly emboldened, I sit up and look him straight in the eye. "I want a child. I'll be thirty-eight in July and there is no hope in the horizon of me meeting anyone any time soon. If I can't have a man, let me at least have a child."

By now, he is proper confused. "I don't understand, Ezi. Are you asking me to…"

"It would just be between the two of us. Nobody would need to know you're the child's father. After all this, you could walk away from us without having to look back. I'll take full responsibility for the child," I say, reaching for his hand. "I've been miserable the last few months. Miserable. I even considered going to a sperm bank, but I don't want a stranger to father my child."

Dili pulls his hand away. "Ezioma, I can't do that. How can you even ask that of me? You of all people know that was the one thing my father did that I abhor the most. How on earth would I explain this to Onyeka?"

"She doesn't have to know!" I plead. "I swear to you, Dili, you'll be able to walk away without even having to look back. We will never, ever bother you. The child won't even have your last name."

He shakes his head. "I'm sorry, Ezioma. I could never do that. It would be too messy. Way too messy."

I place my hands on my laps and nod in understanding. "I understand, Dili. Forgive me, I don't know what came over me. I guess I'm panicking about getting older. Please, forget we ever had this conversation."

He nods but the mood is destroyed, and we sit in silence for a few minutes.

"I got your favourite Pineapple Upside Down cake. Should I get you a slice? With some apricot ice-cream?" he asks, breaking the uneasy quiet.

I smile and shake my head as I rise to my feet. "I'm completely stuffed already. Thanks, Dili. And please, forgive me and my loose mouth this evening. I had a few cocktails after work, so it was probably the alcohol talking. Thanks for the awesome meal…and happy anniversary."

I don't wait for an answer as I make my way to my bedroom, where I throw myself on the bed, my eyes fastened to the ceiling.

Ezioma, what exactly have you just done?

What on earth was I thinking, asking Dili to give me a child? I cringe as I remember my words, my words pleading with him to father a secret child for me.

I must have a screw loose for sure.

Later that night, after finally regrouping and having a shower, I sit before my laptop and play No Doubt's ***Simple Kind of Life***.

***Simple Kind of Life* (No Doubt) – May 15, 2015**

*How does a person go from being happy and carefree…to wanting a child with every piece of her soul?*

*How does one go from laughing at parents struggling with babies…to wanting one of her own?*

*How does one go from reveling in her perfect, stress-free, commitment-free, responsibility-free life…to wanting all of it; the stress, the commitment, the responsibility that comes with having a baby?*

*And not just any baby.*

*A baby with the only man who makes her heart beat?*

I stop writing and peer out of the window, realizing the sooner I stop fantasizing over the impossible, the better it will be for me. I worry that my inability to control my mouth might have cost me the only thing Dili is able to give me.

His friendship.

And that realization breaks my heart.

# CHAPTER EIGHT

## I Can't Help It

THE TAP ON MY DOOR is so light, it's a miracle it awakens me. I open my eyes, and another timid knock sounds, making me sit up abruptly. A cursory glance at my wall clock indicates it is 5am in the morning, a clear hour earlier than when I would normally awake on a weekday, lest of all a Saturday morning.

"Come in," I call out, wondering why Dili would be knocking on my door so early in the morning.

The door opens and a subdued Dili walks in. I am all too aware of my flimsy nightgown and raise my duvet higher to cover myself. He also looks unsure of himself.

"I'm so sorry to bother you this early," he says, unable to look me in the eye. "I haven't been able to sleep all night."

"Are you okay? Is everything alright?" I ask in concern.

He shrugs. "I've been thinking about the conversation we had at dinner. About what you asked me for."

It is now my own turn to look away. Before I managed to fall asleep, I made myself believe I hadn't made an absolute fool of myself with my crazy request and was determined to pretend none of it ever happened. But here I am now, reminded of it.

"Ezioma, you've never asked me for anything. All you've done is give and give. It was ungracious and ungrateful of me to have declined the way I did," he continues. "What you have given me, I will never be able to repay you for. Giving you this thing you want is the least I can do."

I look at him, stunned. "You'll do it?"

He nods. "I'll do anything I can to express my appreciation."

I find myself awash with happiness, excitement, and agitation. "Don't worry, nobody will know the child is yours. I promise."

He nods. "Thank you, Ezioma, but Onyeka is much smarter than that. She'll figure everything when the child is born. When the time is right, I'll have to tell her. I'm sure she'll understand that it's the least we can do to express our gratitude for what you're doing for us."

*Us*. The word doesn't miss me at all. This is a favour Dili *and* Onyeka will be doing for me. Not quite the way I envisioned, but I guess a beggar has no choice.

"So…how do you want to go about it?" he asks. "Would you want me to donate my sperm? Or would you prefer we do it organically? I'm fine either way."

I find myself suddenly on the spot. "A donation might be the more straightforward way, but that only gives me one or two chances in a cycle."

"It would also be more expensive," Dili agrees.

We look at each other awkwardly for a while. "I guess organic might be better. If it's okay with you."

Dili shrugs. "Ezioma, I would do anything for you. Just tell me when, and I'll be here."

With my period just ending, I have a few more days before I enter my fertile window. "Tuesday is day eight of my cycle. From what I read, I'm supposed to start having sex every other day from then, until about day eighteen or so."

Dili nods. "Tuesday it is then. Let me leave you to get some more sleep. I know how much you cherish your Saturday morning shut eye."

I am still in an upright sitting position long after he has left the room, unable to believe what we have just discussed, and that he has agreed to father my child…the old-fashioned way. Meaning, come Tuesday, he and I are going to have sex.

The thought pleases and frightens me at the same time.

Somehow, I manage to get some more sleep, and by the time I awake at 10am, the silence in the apartment lets me know Dili has already left for the gym. He doesn't return until later in the day, during which time we make stilted conversation before he retires to his room. Normally, the weekends are when we spend the most time together, chatting, or surfing Netflix. I can already feel the strain on our relationship, even before we do the deed. The same thing happens on Sunday, with him out of the house for most of the day and retiring to his room immediately he returns. On Monday, by the time I am back from work, he is already in his bedroom.

Journeying to work on Tuesday morning, a part of me is tempted to call the whole thing off. What is the point getting him to father my child if I lose him as a friend in the process? But my selfishness spurs me on. Having a part of him with me for the rest of my life is much more important than whatever friendship I think we have. What is the use of the friendship if it will involve a lifetime of having to watch him all loved up with another woman anyway? No, that has less value to me than him giving me a child of my own.

I leave work at about lunchtime and go shopping for sexy lingerie. He will probably not be turned on by me in my natural state, so wearing sexy lingerie should help speed things along. Getting to La Senza, I select a black organza slip that covers absolutely nothing. It is transparent as glass and will have all my goods on display for him…which is exactly what I want.

From the shop, I head to my hair salon. I have decided to present myself in my most natural state, meaning without my wig. Yes, Dili has seen me in the untidy cornrows I usually sport underneath them, but today I decide to condition my natural afro to give myself a different look.

I get home at about 4pm. Dili isn't back from work yet, so I take the opportunity to luxuriate in the bath, more to relax my nerves than to feel sexy. I tense when I hear him return at about 6:00pm and have to shut my eyes to remind myself why we are doing this in the first place. Getting out of the bath, I pamper my body with an array of scented creams, primp my shiny afro into place, before slipping on my new nightgown. I decide against using makeup and instead pour myself a glass of wine, before setting the Lauryn Hill and D'Angelo duet ***Nothing Even Matters*** on repeat.

And then I sit on my bed…and wait.

At exactly 8pm, there is a knock on my door, and I know the hour has come. I rise to my feet and open the door. Our eyes meet, and I can see my nerves reflected in his. His widen as he takes in my semi-nakedness and, feeling brazen, I stand back to let him into the bedroom, giving him a better look. He walks into the room, and once he's inside I release the hooks fastening my slip and it drops to my feet, revealing me in my full nakedness. Whilst I am not endowed with the same full breasts and rounded hips I have seen him admire on other women, I know I have a beautiful body which, even though slender, is hourglass shaped thanks to my small waist.

Without saying a word, I lie on my bed. I watch as he nervously takes off his t-shirt and joggers, and I am glad to see that his body is already ready for what lies ahead. He gets into bed with me and without any preamble, no kissing nor foreplay, he slips into me. But even without all that, I'm ready for him. I've been ready for him all my life.

Maybe it's because I haven't been with a man in a long time, or maybe it's because my body is finally connecting with the first man it ever wanted to, I let out a soft moan as he silently thrusts. I grasp him by the shoulders as my own moaning intensifies and as I reach an earth-shattering release. He moans as he reaches his, and we both lay still for a few minutes, neither of us quite knowing what to do. He eventually rolls off me and we exchange a nervous look.

"I better go," he says, as he sits up. "So…till when?"

"Thursday." I answer, suddenly unable to look him in the eye. "The suggestion is every other day."

He nods. "Okay then," he smiles stiffly. "Good night, Ezioma."

When he is gone, I close my eyes and bask in the memory of the feel of his skin against mine. I relive the magical moments over and over again, and despite how awkward it was afterwards, I would not trade what has just happened for anything in the world. That night I sleep more soundly than I have in a long, long time.

The next morning, I am tempted not to leave for work early, so I can see him. However, I think better of it, realizing he might need more time before having to face me. But when I get home that evening and realize he has continued his new pattern of retiring to his bedroom early, I know I must do something about it.

So I walk to his door and knock.

"Can I come in?" I ask, peering my head into the room.

He looks up from his study table and smiles. "Hi, Ezi. I didn't know you'd come back from work."

"Dili, is this how things are going to be from now on?" I ask. "You doing everything you can to avoid me?"

His eyes drop for a moment, and he shrugs. "I didn't know if you'd need your space, considering…considering what we've decided to do." He laughs awkwardly. "I'm also ashamed of the way I rushed you last night. It was my first time in three years, so I guess I got a little too excited."

"Dili, I totally understand. Didn't you hear the way I was groaning like a porn star?" I laugh. "We're only human beings, and neither of us has had sex in a while. So, it's only normal."

He laughs and is finally able to look me in the eye. "I suppose so."

"It's just sex, Okwudili. And not just casual sex, it's sex for a purpose," I say, trying to sound cavalier. "So let's not let it spoil our friendship."

"I'm sorry," he apologizes sincerely. "I promise not to act weird anymore."

"You can start by coming to the kitchen with me and telling me about your day!" I say, taking him by the hand and leading him out of his room, so we can continue our typical after-work tradition.

Luckily, this works and by the time we both retire for bed that night, things are back to normal for us.

Well…sort of.

Lying in bed, I can't deny the fact that my body is so much more aware of his now. As we ate and laughed in the kitchen, I found myself aware of his every movement. I found myself stealing several glances at his toned and taut arms, remembering how they felt as I held him in the throes of passion. But each time my mind drifts, I immediately recompose myself, determined not to scare him off. Because, if he realizes this is not quite as casual for me, it might destroy everything.

Luckily, on Thursday night, when he knocks on my door, things are not quite as awkward. Also like before, we do not waste any time on preamble and go straight to it. But it is just as enjoyable this time as the first, and even as we continue until I hit day twenty of my cycle the following Friday.

"Do you want me to come back on Sunday?" he asks, lying next to me after his release, that Friday night.

Everything in me wants to scream YES, but with my twenty-eight-day cycle, having sex on day twenty-two would not be for baby making. In fact, going all the way to day twenty has been unnecessary.

"Nah, I think we're good. I believe we've covered all the bases." I answer.

He nods. "So fingers crossed from now until…?"

"Till I miss my period," I smile at him. "I have a good feeling about this cycle. From everything I've read, I think we've done enough."

And so we both return to life as normal, without having to have sex every other day. But even as I hope and pray that I have conceived, I cannot help but crave his body yet another time.

On the morning of June 6th, right on the dot of the twenty-eighth day of my cycle, I get my period. I am saddened as I sit on the toilet bowl just before I insert a tampon, the full impact of the failure of the cycle hitting me hard.

I do not realize I am brooding all day until Dili takes his seat beside me as I absentmindedly pop grapes into my mouth. "You got your period?"

I look at him, shocked. "How do you know?"

"I saw an open box of tampons in the bathroom," he answers.

I cover my face with my hands and start to quietly sob. "I'm so sorry, Dili. This isn't what I was expecting would happen."

He puts his hand around my shoulder. "Ezi, even for couples who do this every day of their lives, these things take time. Don't beat yourself up about it. It's just one cycle. We have others to keep trying."

I look up at him. "You wouldn't mind trying again?"

He shakes his head. "I made a promise to you, Ezi, and it doesn't matter how long it will take."

I hold him and it feels like a heavy weight has been lifted from chest. I go through the rest of my period uneventfully, and on the evening of June 13th, exactly day eight of my cycle, I hear a knock on my door, and I am so relieved, I could cry. I hadn't bothered reminding him about it and didn't expect him to remember, let alone show up. But as I open the door, there he is, Dili, ready to try again.

And as I yield my body to him, as I cling to him, I am more excited about this sexual reunion of ours than any desire to have a baby.

After he has returned to his room, I pull out my laptop. For the last month, I have only written about generic topics, keeping my true feelings off my keyboard. But tonight, with my heart, soul, and body all singing a symphony, love is all I can think of…all I can write of.

***I Can't Help It (Michael Jackson) – June 13, 2015***

*Is there really anything like casual sex? A friend with benefits? Isn't there a time when lines become hazy, borders become crossed, and feelings reassessed? Isn't there a time when you realize your feelings transcend the bedroom? A time when you discover you just can't keep away? A time when you realize that no matter what you do, you just can't help it…not even if you wanted to.*

*But the truth is, you really don't.*

I sit back in my chair, shake my head, and laugh. "Ezioma! You better get it together."

While I know I have no choice but to, in fact, get it together, a part of me knows that with each trip Dili makes to my bed, he takes away a little piece of my heart each time.

# CHAPTER NINE

## Edge of Desire

AS ANOTHER CYCLE comes to an unsuccessful close and yet another one starts, Dili and I find ourselves more and more comfortable with our arrangement. There is less awkwardness with each visit to my bedroom, and by our fifth cycle of trying, we are comfortable enough with each other to lie in bed afterwards to chat. Even though we have managed to avoid the kissing level of intimacy, there is a whole lot more touching and caressing than there was at the beginning of our journey. I attribute it to the fact that we are both so at ease with each other, the fact we're also having sex is now inconsequential. On the one hand, that could be true, as the strain has totally disappeared from our relationship and our friendship is even stronger than ever. Gone are the self-consciousness and tension that characterized those earlier days. Now, we have returned to life as it used to be, and I'm glad about that. On the other hand, though, I can't deny that my physical attraction to him is increasing by the day. But I'm sure it's something I can continue to contain.

Or at least that's what I tell myself.

I convince myself I am not bothered anytime I hear Dili and Onyeka on the phone, which is pretty much everyday. Especially on nights when he and I have been together, I try to make myself ignore the pangs in my heart when I hear them talking when he returns to his room. But the truth is it still hurts. It really does.

Luckily, despite his unwavering commitment to his fiancée, he is still willing to go along with our agreement, month after month. We have reached the conclusion that, as I am older, conception could take a little longer. And, as we still have a few more months until he gets his permanent Green Card, we have enough time to keep trying.

In early October, Mia invites us for dinner to celebrate her new husband's birthday. I am pleased when Dili agrees to accompany me, and as we make our way uptown, I can't help but think wistfully about what a lovely couple we make. In his Brooks Brothers blazer worn over a crisp, white Ralph Lauren shirt and dark blue jeans, he looks like he just stepped out of a *GQ* magazine, a far cry from when I ran into him almost eighteen months ago. In a nude-coloured bodycon dress that clings to my slight curves like a second skin, I know I also look great. And when we get to the upscale restaurant of Le Bernadin, which is in such high demand it is usually booked months in advance, our friends compliment us on what a beautiful couple we make.

If only they knew!

We go on to enjoy our very expensive dinner. One of the things that drew Mia and I together was our love for the finer things of life, which, in my case, has always been mainly fashion. We would notice each other's shoes and vintage clothing in the elevator at work, and soon realised we were kindred spirits. However, expensive shoes and clothing are where my extravagance end. Having grown up in Hoboken, New Jersey, and raised by immigrant, working-class parents from Venezuela, the minute Mia started making good money at Goldman, she acquired the lifestyle to go with it. While the rest of us were still renting small squats in Harlem and Brooklyn, Mia had long since moved to Manhattan, renting an uber chic apartment. Ironically, her husband, Todd, is the exact opposite and is a down-to-earth graphic designer originally from Oklahoma, happy to live in comic character t-shirts and faded jeans all day everyday, and whose annual salary might be less than what Mia makes in a month. But as different as they are, their love has waxed stronger and stronger for almost a decade.

"I can't get over how adorable you look together," Mia gushes when we are in the Ladies Room, touching up our makeup before we head out dancing.

I smile politely. "Thanks. I see you got Todd all nice and cleaned up today."

She rolls her eyes. "I spent almost a half hour trying to convince him a Batman polo shirt would not be the best choice for tonight, not even if it does have a collar!"

We giggle like schoolgirls, even though the truth is that no matter how disheveled Todd looks, he is still better looking than a lot of men out there.

"You look amazing, Ezi!" Mia says, looking at my mirror reflection as I powder my face. "And that dress is smoking hot. No wonder Dili has been looking at you all evening like a piece of raw meat."

I look at her, shocked. Looking at me? "You think so?" I ask, trying not to sound too surprised because, to her, he is my husband after all.

"Don't tell me you haven't noticed," Mia teases, shoving my shoulder playfully with hers. "It's obvious he can't wait to get you right back to the bedroom!"

I manage a strained laugh and, as we walk back to meet our men, I watch Dili's face closely...and I see that Mia is correct. Dili's eyes are fixed on me as I approach the table. Whilst a part of me attributes it to the fact he has never seen me in a dress this revealing, a bigger part of me is enjoying every minute of this newfound attention.

The four of us head to a Latin nightclub a few blocks away. Whilst not as well known as others, it has remained a favourite for us over the years, not only because of its mostly South American music, but its amazing food and cocktails. We settle in and are soon nursing some of the best *Mojitos* in the whole of Manhattan, when one of my favourite songs, *Mas Que Nada,* starts playing. Emboldened by the alcohol, I grab Dili by the hand and lead him to the dance floor. We maintain eye contact as we dance to the sultry, high-tempo Brazilian song, and the lethal combination of a little bit of alcohol and a hell of a lot of confidence from my dress, gives me the bravado to gyrate all over him. But rather than step away, his hands remain on my hips as I twirl them sultry and sensual, grazing his only slightly…but enough to feel his desire.

We remain in the nightclub for about an hour afterwards, after which we take a taxi back home. The minute we are back in the apartment, Dili pulls me to himself, raw desire in his eyes.

"I'm not yet in my fertile window." I manage to say.

"Who cares?" is his response, as we both fall into my bedroom.

That night, our sex is wild and passionate. That night, our sex is unguarded and unrestrained. That night, we officially cross a line. That night marks the last time we can use procreation as an excuse to have sex.

We do not leave my bedroom all that weekend, unable to get enough of each other. But as many times as we have sex that weekend, he still refrains from kissing me on the mouth. And when he dashes out of the room to answer a call from Onyeka, I am reminded that I should not lose my head over this. I am reminded that as wild and passionate as it may be, what we have is simply just sex. Onyeka clearly has his heart.

But the sex is so good, I decide nothing else matters.

When I am back at work on Monday, it is all I can think of, and apparently all he can as well, as a quick phone leads us to meet up the apartment for a lunchtime quickie. And when we are back home that evening, we pick up from where we left off. And so it continues for the rest of the week, and even the weeks after; us having fiery, intense, steamy sex.

Which is why when the phone call from Madufuro comes in early November, I am completely thrown.

"Hi, Ezioma. It's been a long time," he says, when I answer my phone that Friday evening. "I'm back in town and here I am calling, just like we agreed."

It takes everything in me not to hiss. "It's been a year since we spoke. If I remember correctly, you were supposed to have called in March. This is November," I retort instead.

"Didn't Dili tell you? I lost my father in March. I had to go to Nigeria to bury him," is his own perplexed answer. "I thought Dili told you. We spoke a few times around that time."

"No, he didn't," I say, feeling ashamed of myself. "I'm so sorry for your loss. You've been in Nigeria all this time?"

"While we were trying to sort out my dad's will and estate, my mother decided she'd rather follow her husband to the land of the dead than stay with us. She died in June, a day before I was set to return to the States."

I gasp, my hands flying to my mouth. "That is awful! I am so sorry."

"Yeah, it was very tough, especially for my younger siblings. I had to stay back a few more months, just to be sure they'd be okay," he answers. "I only got back to Jersey last night."

As saddened for him as I am, I am relieved there is a good reason for his prolonged silence, and that he hadn't ghosted me like I'd feared. We spend a few minutes on small talk about his stay in Nigeria, before he finally asks if we can meet over the weekend.

"Sure," I answer. "My weekend is free. Maybe we can do drinks tomorrow?"

"That sounds perfect," he says in response, a smile in his voice. "I'll pick you up for 6pm. Text me your address."

I am smiling from ear to ear after I get off the call. Maybe I am destined to have a man that belongs to me after all. Maybe I am meant to get married and have a proper family of my own. Maybe it has been a blessing from God for me not to have conceived after all these months of trying with Dili.

When Dili returns from the gym, I am eager to fill him in. "Guess who just called me. Madufuro!" I exclaim. "Why didn't you tell me his parents died?"

Dili's brows are crossed in what appears to be irritation. "I didn't think you two were serious. In fact, I felt I'd wasted my time and energy hooking you up."

"Anyway, it's all fixed now," I grin. "He's back and we're having drinks tomorrow."

Dili's brows remain furrowed. "You're having drinks with Madufuro? Why?"

"What kind of question is 'why'?!" I retort. "*Na only you wan marry?* Let me explore this to see if anything will come out of it."

Dili shrugs. "Cool. I'm sure you'll have fun."

I am puzzled by his lack of enthusiasm, especially as he is the one who introduced me to the Madufuro in the first place. Does he expect me to be a wallflower forever? Surely, after he leaves my apartment next year, I am expected to have a life!

For the first time in weeks, Dili doesn't come to my room that night. As I lie stewing in my bed, I am torn between sexual frustration and anger, especially as I am unable to decipher why he is acting the way he is. I know it cannot be him being possessive. Not after how crystal clear he has demonstrated that Onyeka is his beginning and end.

With the dawn of Saturday comes even more tension. We hardly speak to each other the whole day, but I choose to ignore him. Instead, once it is 4pm, I set about readying myself for my date with Madufuro. By the time the buzzer goes off at 5.50pm, I am more than ready to finally meet the mysterious doctor.

I decide not to buzz him in and instead grab my purse before heading out of the apartment. Dili is watching TV and pretends not to notice me leave. But I truly can't be bothered with him. I am too excited about what lies ahead.

Getting to the lobby, I smile at the sight of the pleasant-faced guy standing there. From his crisp Oxford shirt and immaculately ironed trousers, I can see that, even though he might not be too stylish, he takes excellent care of himself, as evidenced by his impeccable head-to-toe grooming. I notice the stark whiteness of his teeth, his neatly cut fingernails, and closely cropped hair. Though not drop dead gorgeous, he is a good-looking man.

"Wow, Ezioma!" he exclaims, hugging me like a long-lost pal. "You look even better in person."

"You don't look bad yourself, Doctor!" I say in my most flirtatious voice.

From the corner of my eye, I notice the doorman, Tomas, give us a quizzical look. He is probably wondering why I am brazenly flirting with another man when my 'husband' is upstairs in our apartment. But I could care less. All that is on my mind is finding a way to move forward and get a safety net for life after Dili, which could very well be sooner rather than later.

As we head to the bar of Madufuro's choice, it feels good for a man to take the lead for a change. Even though he lives in Jersey, he knows Manhattan well, and I relish being the one getting the treat and not giving it.

As we chat about our lives, neither of us notices the hours go by. The more we talk, the more we realize we have so much in common. His late father was a civil servant like mine, and both our mothers were the dominant parent. We laugh over our 'new-in-America' stories, with me regaling him about my life in Philly, and him telling me about the difficult experience he had in DC attending Howard University.

"So how come you're still single?" I finally ask the million-dollar question.

"I was all about trying to accomplish everything I could in my career," he answers truthfully. "I honestly didn't have time for anything that didn't have to do with getting my specialty, so dating was out of the question. Women were the last thing on my mind for a long time. But when I was ready, it became close to impossible to find the right person. I was either meeting American girls I had nothing in common with or Nigerian girls who were more interested in my bank account than me as a person." He cocks his head to the side to look at me. "And how come a beautiful woman like you is still single?"

I consider telling him about my long engagement to Seth but decide against it. "Same." I shrug casually. "I was also doing the career thing."

Even though that is less than the truth, the answer seems to satisfy him, and we move on to talking about other things. By the time we are ready to leave, it is almost midnight. We ride back to my apartment in a cab, and he is chivalrous enough to walk me to the door.

"I had a wonderful time, Ezioma," he says. "I know this might sound eager, but I'd really love to spend time with you tomorrow. Is your Sunday free?"

I smile in response. "It is. Maybe you could invite me over to your place for lunch?"

"You'd come to Jersey?" he grins. "That would be fantastic. I could come get you."

"No need for that. I'll get a rental car," I answer, hugging him goodbye. "Thanks for a wonderful evening. I had a great time!"

I have a huge smile on my face as I let myself into the apartment, and I am startled to see Dili still in the living room, watching TV.

"That was a long one," he remarks. "It's well past midnight."

"And we could have stayed there for much longer, if the bar didn't have to close!" I say, smiling. "We talked for hours. He's such an amazing guy."

"Are you seeing him again?" he asks.

"As a matter of fact, I am. Tomorrow. He's having me over for lunch," I answer smugly.

Dili's face clouds over. "You're going there? To his house?"

I shrug in response. "Yeah. He came over to Manhattan this time, so it's only fair that I return the favour for the next date."

"By going to his house, you know you're indirectly agreeing to sleep with him, right?"

I shrug again. "Not necessarily, but if it happens, what's the big deal? I like him, and I'm hoping this is the beginning of something."

And then for the very first time, I see Dili lose his cool. "What's the big deal? You mean you're actually considering sleeping with him? Even when…me and you…"

"When me and you what, Dili?" I retort back. "Because you're sleeping with me, you think I should close my eyes to other options?"

"I thought we were exclusive, Ezioma!" he shouts back. "God knows I'm not dating or sleeping with anyone else!"

"What about Onyeka?" I throw at him. "She doesn't count, *abi*?"

His nostrils flare. "Onyeka isn't here. It's not the same thing."

"Oh, it's okay for you to be whispering sweet nothings to your babe every night, but not okay for me to try to find a stable relationship of my own?" I explode. "What is this? You don't want me, but you don't want others to want me?"

"What I'm saying is how can you possibly want to sleep with two men at the same time?" he shouts back. "Is that the kind of woman you are?"

I flinch at his words. "Is that the kind of woman I am? I don't blame you, Okwudili. I'll tell you the kind of woman I am. A very foolish one, it appears."

And with that, I storm off to my bedroom. I am so livid I can hardly breathe. The nerve of Dili to judge me! I am mad at him for insulting me, but even madder at myself for getting in this messy situation to begin with.

The next day, I leave the house as early as 10am, so I can rent a car and run a few errands before heading off to Madufuro's house in Chatham, New Jersey. Thankfully, I do not see Dili before I leave the house, which is just as well. I don't leave Manhattan until 1pm, but still make it to Madufuro's place before 2pm. Driving down the long driveway leading to his imposing mansion, I find myself wondering why a bachelor would need to live in such opulence. Well, I guess to each his own.

I park my car, walk up to the house and the door is opened even before I get a chance to knock. A beaming Madufuro embraces me happily.

"Welcome to my home, gorgeous!" he exclaims. "I'm so glad you made it."

I walk into the house, and it takes my breath away. I might as well be standing in the home of a *Love & Hip Hop* star. With its glistening chandeliers, domed ceiling, French doors, arched hallways, and glossy white and gold furnishing, the house is magnificent.

"You have a lovely place," I remark, feeling a bit intimidated.

"Thanks!" he smiles proudly. "It used to belong to a player with the New York Knicks. Let me show you around."

And so begins an elaborate tour of the almost five thousand square foot mansion, with six bedrooms, a home theatre, an elaborate gym, tennis court and Olympic-sized swimming pool. But the more he shows me, the more vulgar and unnecessary I find it all.

"Why did you spend so much on property like this?" I just have to ask. "Or do you live here with any family? Siblings or cousins?"

He laughs and shakes his head. "No, it's just me. I guess it's always been a dream of mine to have a big house. So as soon as I could afford it, I bought one."

I manage a smile in response, and, taking me by the hand, he leads me to his exquisite dining room, with its wall covering, table and chairs all from Ralph Lauren Home. Rather than impress me, it sickens me the more. I am even more irritated by the emergence of a Japanese chef, who proceeds to serve us an exotic five-course meal. The more we talk, the more I can't help but be amazed that a single man is happy and comfortable to live in such an elaborate house and be waited on hand and foot by servants. In addition to the Japanese chef, I sight a few other uniformed staff walking around, and it only serves to astonish me the more.

After lunch, we go to his private living room, where I see he has tried to set the mood with an artificial fireplace and *Kenny G* playing from hidden speakers.

"I'm so glad I met you, Ezioma." he says, sitting closer to me than I'm comfortable with. "You're everything I've been praying to God for."

I force a smile, my discomfort rising.

He takes my hand and raises it to his lips. "I'm not looking to play around. I want to marry you."

"You only just met me," I mutter.

"But it's enough for me to know you are the one," he answers, leaning in to kiss my neck. "I need someone to share my life with. Come and spend forever with me, Ezi."

I pull away from his hold, literally feeling my skin crawl. He stares at me, perplexed by my reaction, and I realize that the problem really isn't him. It's me. Unnecessarily elaborate house aside, he seems a nice enough guy. The only problem is I didn't come along with my heart.

I left it back in my apartment in Manhattan.

"I have to go," I say, rising to my feet. "Thank you for a wonderful afternoon."

He nods in understanding and stands. "I'm sorry if I rushed you, Ezi. I'm ready to slow things down if you want. Maybe we could do lunch during the week or something?"

"Sure," I say, even though I know that won't be happening. I know there is no point wasting any more time, when it is clear he isn't the one I want.

The drive back to Manhattan seems much longer than the earlier one to Chatham, and I know it is because of the things weighing heavily on my mind. I am saddened that I feel absolutely nothing for Madufuro, and also because it is clear Dili has completely consumed all of me; body, mind, heart, and soul. And the latter angers me more than the former.

Returning the car, I decide to walk the eight blocks to my apartment - heels and all - hoping the crisp November air can clear my head and maybe even administer some sense. Because I can't understand how, after everything, all I want is Dili.

Getting to the apartment, I find it empty. I wonder where Dili could have gone on a Sunday evening, and I kick myself for even caring. Desperate to think of something, anything, else, I decide to take advantage of the peace and quiet and write my article early. But even when I am seated before my laptop willing myself to think of words to write, maybe even about the disastrous date with Madufuro, all I can think about is Okwudili Dike.

I select *John Mayer*'s ***Edge of Desire*** and shut my eyes as I meditate on its lyrics.

*Edge of Desire* *(John Mayer) – November 08, 2015*

***I want you so bad I'll go back on the things I believe***
***There I just said it, I'm scared you'll forget about me.***

Listening to the song's lyrics, I stare at my keyboard, not even knowing what to type, overwhelmed by the realization that my heart prefers the crumbs Dili offers to a ten-course meal from another person.

Just then, the door opens, and he lets himself into the apartment. He is surprised to see me.

"I didn't think you'd be back so soon."

I shrug. "It's almost 6pm. What time did you think I'd come home? I have work tomorrow."

"To be honest, I didn't think you'd come back today," he says. "I thought you'd spend the night there."

I don't dignify him with an answer and instead return to stare at my laptop, the song still playing in the background.

"It's all that's been on my mind since yesterday," Dili says, still standing behind me. "I don't think I got a wink of sleep last night. I was haunted by images of you and Madufuro in his bed. It's the reason I had to take a walk now, to see if I could get them out of my head."

I look at him. "Why are you so obsessed with this idea of me sleeping with Madufuro? What's it to you anyway?"

He says nothing, and I decide I'd rather be alone in my room than sit there and get more hurt by his words. As I make to walk away, he holds my hand.

"I can't stand the thought of you with another man, Ezi."

I stare at him, shocked, unable to process his words. "But we're just casual. You said so yourself…" I manage to say in response.

"There is nothing casual about this," he answers. "I don't know how or when, but this is no longer just about sex, Ezi. It's a lot more than that."

Our eyes make contact and I find myself unable to breathe. And then in what seems to be a split second…and eternity at the same time…he lowers his head and claims my mouth in a kiss.

Our very first kiss.

I wrap my arms around him as our kiss deepens to John Mayer's lyrics, in a union that transcends our lips.

But which, this time, also involves our hearts.

# CHAPTER TEN

## The Fear

I THOUGHT I KNEW what it was to be happy. I thought with Seth I'd experienced true love, true contentment. But it turns out I hadn't even scratched the surface.

Not until Dili and I gave in to our hearts.

Till this very day, I can't adequately articulate the wonderful feeling, the feeling of having Dili desire me for more than my body. That night, for the very first time, it is not just sex. That night, we make love. All through it, our eyes hold. We make love not just with our bodies…but with our eyes…and with our hearts. And lying in his arms afterwards, it feels like I have died and gone to heaven. It feels like I am floating in the clouds. Falling asleep in his arms for the very first time…words will never explain how wonderful it feels.

The next morning, awoken by his kiss and making love all over again, it feels like I am living a fantasy. We are oblivious of time. For us, it stands still. And so it should. After all the bumps in our road, we have finally found our way to each other.

We share a cab, and it is difficult to part for work. We spend a good minute kissing in the taxi and would probably have stayed longer if it not for the driver's impatient coughing, the running meter not enough of a deterrent.

Once at my desk, I am unable to concentrate on anything at all. I break into smiles every time I remember our magical night and as I relive every moment. But as the day progresses, I worry that it was all a big fluke. I'm scared I imagined it all. I panic about returning to the apartment only to find that nothing has changed, and we are still as casual as we could ever be. I am increasingly desperate to return home, but I get roped into a long conference call that sees me unable to leave the office before 8pm.

The moment I walk into the apartment, a wide smile breaks on my face. Right from the door, the floor is littered with rose petals and John Legend's *Tonight (Best You Ever Had)* is playing. I set my bags on the dining table, looking out for Dili, and he soon emerges from his bedroom.

"Hey, beautiful," he says.

"What's all this?" I ask, my cheeks hurting from smiling.

He walks to me and takes me by the hand. "This is me seducing you."

He leads me into his bedroom. Even though I have been in his room many times before, we have never been intimate there.

Inside, the floor is littered with even more rose petals, the only illumination coming from several dozen candles scattered all over the room, perfectly setting the scene for a night of romance.

Wordlessly, I give in to him and we have an even more magical night than the previous one, dispelling all my worries about what we had being a fluke. He shows me this is no fluke, proves to me what we have is real…and beautiful…and all we could have ever hoped for.

That night leads to several other magical days and even more magical nights, and, with each passing day, I fall deeper in love with him. With each passing day, our relationship solidifies. I no longer overhear him talking to Onyeka. I am overjoyed she has finally been discarded the way she should have a long time ago. I begin to dream of when we will be able to renew our vows I dream of a proper wedding ceremony, a beautiful and romantic one at sunset, maybe on a Caribbean beach or on a rooftop beholding the Manhattan skyline. I dream of spending the rest of my life with him. And these dreams are finally becoming my reality.

I am living my dream.

We are just as intimate when we are simply lying on the living room couch, legs entwined, me writing my article and him reviewing documents from work. We are just as intimate when we take turns in the kitchen, talking and fooling around like kids. We are just as intimate when we watch TV together, each of us discovering the other's favourite shows and movies. I rope him into *Sex & the City* reruns, and he gets me hooked on *House of Cards*. And when we watch the *Sex & the City* movie, we both agree that the scene where Miranda and Steve reconcile on the Brooklyn Bridge is the best part of the movie.

Putting it simply, I am the happiest woman in the world.

The first week of December, Dili convinces me to attend the birthday party of another friend of his, this time all the way in Queens. Distance aside, I get myself all beautified and we make our way there. As expected, it is your typical Naija party and we spend the first few minutes exchanging pleasantries with Dili's friends, most of whom I have already met. The party gets into full swing, and Dili and I are soon on the dance floor, gyrating to Naija jams.

When Burna Boy's comparatively low tempo ***Like to Party*** comes on, we slow things down and he pulls me close as we dance. With my hands around his neck and his on my hips, we are sensual enough for any onlooker to know we are a couple, a proper couple. I'm laughing over something he has said, our foreheads touching, when I feel a pair of eyes on me. I look up to see Azuka, Dili's friend's wife, watching us closely. This makes me uncomfortable, and I pull away from him. This coincides with the end of the song, so he doesn't read any meaning into my sudden withdrawal. He walks away to get us drinks, and Azuka takes advantage and walks up to me.

"Ezioma!" she exclaims, hugging me. "*So na only Christmas time we dey see your face!* You didn't even keep in touch after our party last year."

"So sorry, babe. Work has been crazy," is my lame excuse. "But I always ask after you and Nnamdi from Dili."

"Speaking of Dili," she says, leaning closer. "You two looked very cozy when you were dancing. I take it you don't see him as a 'brother' anymore."

I smile coyly. "Well…I guess not."

"What about the Naija babe?" she asks.

"Past tense." I answer with a wink.

Before Azuka can say anything more, Dili and Nnamdi walk up to us, each bearing drinks, and we are soon chatting away like the happy foursome we are. Just as we are debating the pros and cons of living in Manhattan and raising a family there, a woman, who obviously just arrived from Nigeria, walks up to us. It is easy to spot the people who are fresh off the plane from Lagos as they are always overdressed, and often inappropriately. Looking at the woman's open-toe stilettos in this chilly late fall weather, it is clear to any onlooker that she is not from these parts.

"Dili!" she squeals, hugging him. "I'm so happy to see you! Tagbo told me you were coming, and I've been waiting anxiously. How now?"

"*I dey o!* When did you get into town?" he exclaims, equally happy to see her. "Onyeka mentioned you'd be arriving soon."

The name Onyeka is a kick to my gut, and I can feel Azuka's curious eyes on me. But I choose to keep my cool instead. He must be referring to speaking to her weeks ago, not anytime in the weeks we have been *really* together.

"I got in a few days ago," the girl answers. "She said you'll be in Nigeria for Christmas. When do you leave?"

This time, it is my turn to look at Dili quizzically. Nigeria for Christmas? Why is this news to me? With my friend Uju's wedding postponed to Easter, my earlier plans to travel to Nigeria had to be cancelled, and Dili never mentioned any trip of his own even when I was lamenting my foiled one.

"I can't go for Christmas anymore, I'm afraid. Work," he answers the woman. "But I hope to travel to surprise her for Valentine's Day."

This time, it feels like I have been slapped across the face. I look at Azuka and I see sympathy in her eyes. No, this can't be happening.

"Awww, she'll really love that!" the woman exclaims. "It's been too long. Long overdue."

I walk away, unable to listen to any more. Dili and Onyeka are still in touch? This can't be happening!

I don't even know when I'm outside the house. All I want to be is far, far away from there.

"Ezi! Ezi!" comes his voice behind me. "Where are you going?"

"You're still talking to Onyeka?" I explode. "You're planning to go to Nigeria to surprise her for Valentine's Day?"

He looks at me, confused. "Of course, I'm still talking to Onyeka. She's my fiancée!"

I stop walking, feeling like a truckload of snow has just been tipped over me. "Your fiancée? So what have we been doing these last few weeks?"

"Ezioma, I never told you anything otherwise!" he exclaims. "You've always known her to be my fiancée. Why are you acting like you're hearing something new?"

I stare at him, speechless, wondering how he can stand there and so cavalierly wonder why I am surprised, not after how deeply our relationship has evolved in the last few weeks.

"I thought you said it wasn't just about sex, Dili," I say, when I eventually find my voice. "I thought you said what we have means something."

"And it does, Ezi!" he answers, proper frustrated now. "I have deep feelings for you…and you will always be special to me. But I made a promise to Onyeka, and I can't walk away from her after she's waited over three years for me…"

I throw my hands in the air, not wanting to hear anymore. Deep feelings for me, special to him. Is that all the last few weeks have meant to him? I turn around and continue walking, wanting to be as far away from him as possible.

"Ezi! Ezioma!" he calls out.

But I don't turn back this time. I keep on walking until I get to the subway station, where I get on the Queens Boulevard Line back to Manhattan. Though a longer commute than returning by taxi, I am grateful for the time I am accorded, to think about what has just happened.

Dili is still with Onyeka.

My fantasy has turned into a nightmare.

I walk from the subway station back to my apartment. Once inside, I change into warm flannel pajamas and head to my room for the first time in weeks. I am still awake when I hear Dili let himself into the apartment about ninety minutes later. But as I sit on my bed, waiting for him to come and tell me it's all a joke and that I'm the only one he wants, I soon realize that won't be happening. I realize that, for the first time in a long while, we will be sleeping apart.

But rather than feel heartbroken, I am simply numb.

The truth is that deep down inside, I have always had this fear, the fear that he will return to her one day.

I walk to my writing table and open my laptop, selecting Travis' *The Fear* as my soundtrack for the day, because I know that writing is the only thing that can help me tonight.

***<u>The Fear</u> <u>(Travis) – December 12, 2015</u>***

*You spend all your life running away from something. You try to convince yourself that maybe, just maybe, it doesn't exist, and you made it all up in the first place.*

*You get comfortable, convinced what you were afraid of never existed at all. You get used to living your life as if it were never even there.*

*Until the day it shows up, making you realize it never left. Making you realize it has always been here.*

*The fear.*

A lone tear rolls down my nose and drops on the character 'B' on my keyboard.

Yep…the fear is still truly here.

# CHAPTER ELEVEN

## Ordinary People

SLEEP ELUDES ME all night, the only thing on my mind that my dream, my perfect dream, has been shattered.

I am still lying in bed, wide awake, at 5am when there is a knock on my door. Before waiting for a response, it opens and Dili walks in.

"Ezi, we have to talk."

I remain still in bed, not acknowledging his presence, not wanting him to verbalize my darkest fear…that what we've had these last few weeks has been nothing but a mirage, a mere fantasy.

"Ezi, please look at me," he says, sitting on my bed.

My back remains turned to him, more so for him not to see the tears that are pooling in my eyes.

"What we have is special. I've never felt this way about anyone before. It's funny, because I never would have imagined ever feeling like this when we first started this. Somehow, you've taken over my whole heart and soul, Ezioma," he says, before inhaling deeply. "But I made a promise to Onyeka. She has given me nine years of her life, three of which have been with me here in America. I started dating her when she was just twenty-one years old and next year, she'll be thirty. For crying out loud, I was the one who took her virginity. I can't hurt her this way."

I bite my upper lip to keep from crying aloud, tears fast rushing down my face. With everything in me, I want to lash out at him, hit him, claw his eyes out, demand why he has led me on for weeks if he knew we never stood a chance. But I know all that will be futile. It will not change the fact that he is Onyeka's. Always has been…and always will be.

"There's no way I could disappoint her that way, no matter how I feel," he continues. "Not after I made promises to her and her family. I could never do that. That was the way my father acted, and I don't want to ever be like him. Not ever."

I remain motionless and so does he, and we are that way for what seems like forever. In the end, with a resigned sigh, he gets up from my bed and lets himself out of the room. I remain lying for a few more minutes before I also rise from the bed and head to the bathroom for an early shower. I lock the adjoining door that leads to his bedroom to keep him from ambushing me there, and I stand under the shower for the better part of the hour, allowing the water cascade from my nappy hair all the way down to my feet. But it gives me little relief or escape from my current reality. Instead, it only serves to paint the picture in its more explicit and crystal-clear reality.

Dili and I will never be.

By the time I am out of the shower and back in my room, as I prepare for work, I put my game face on. Dili is not going to see me broken. He has eaten his cake and had it, but that is as far of a fool I am going to allow him make of me. Instead, I dress up to the nines, making sure I look extra hot. No man has been able to bring me down since Eze, and he sure as heck won't do that now.

As I head towards the door, he walks out of his room, also dressed for work.

"You're going to work early?" I ask, trying to sound casual.

"Yeah…" is his hesitant reply. "Ezioma, did you hear what I said in your room this morning?"

I smile and give it a curt wave. "Oh that? Never mind. We don't have to make a big deal out of it. It's fine. I'm fine. Have a great day at work."

And with that, I walk out of the apartment before he has the big idea of sharing a cab with me. I don't know how long my façade will last, and I don't want to run the risk of imploding before him.

Upon getting to work, I am grateful I love my job enough for it to provide me a means of escape. I immerse myself so deeply into it, I don't even have time to come up for air. I am a hyper ball of energy, rolling from meetings to conference calls to document reviews to strategy sessions the whole day, and when the office empties out, I use the quiet time to respond to emails and read Info Memos and Term Sheets. By the time I walk out of the Goldman building to a waiting official car sent to give me a ride home, it is well past 11pm. Upon getting home, I am happy to see that Dili has already retired to bed, and this begins a regular pattern for me; leaving the apartment at the crack of dawn and not getting back till about midnight. By so doing, I avoid seeing him for that whole week, and even when the weekend comes, I decide to spend it at work as well.

After playing the avoidance game for another week, Dili surprises me by showing up at my office one day.

"What are you doing here?" I ask as I walk into the lobby after being notified of his presence.

"Should I move out, Ezioma?" he asks. "Rather than turn you into a workaholic ninja afraid of her own home, should I leave? If you really don't want to see me again, I could find myself somewhere else to stay."

"There's no need for that, Dili," I answer. "May will soon be here, and I'm sure your permanent card will be ready then."

"So why are we this way, Ezi? Why are we now like strangers?" he exclaims in exasperation. "How could we go from being deliriously happy to…to this?"

At that point, my carefully woven façade unravels, and I let my anger show. "You expect us to be 'business as usual'? After telling me that, at the end of the day, it's Onyeka you want?"

A few curious glances are cast our way, but I am past the stage of caring.

He nods slowly. "I knew you weren't fine with it."

"Okwudili, I'm not going to play this game with you," I continue, glaring at him with all the anger and hurt I have been nursing. "We've both had our fun. Let's just stick to the original script and forget all the other nonsense. You focus on your Onyeka, and I'll focus on my own life."

He remains standing there even after I have stormed off to the elevator that will take me back to my floor, but I make sure not to look back at him, lest, like Lot's wife, I turn into a pillar of salt…or in this case, a basket case of unrestrained emotions. Being in close proximity with him after so long has shown me I can't trust myself with him yet, not with the way he still makes my heart race and the butterflies in my stomach flutter. No, I have to stay as far away from him as I can possibly manage.

Back upstairs, I can barely concentrate and find myself absentminded, which is probably why I pay no attention to the caller ID on my phone when it rings towards the end of the day.

"Ezi?" comes that unmistakable New England accent.

I sit up in my chair. "Seth?"

"Hey, stranger! It's been a long time," my ex-fiancé says in response. "I thought you promised to stay in touch. We haven't spoken in, what, two years?"

I smile. "I'm so sorry. It's been pretty hectic. Work has been really busy."

"I hear you made Executive Director. Congratulations." He hesitates for a moment before continuing. "I also heard you got married."

I shut my eyes, my fake marriage biting me in the behind once again.

"Yeah. Yeah, I did."

"I'll be in New York for a family function this weekend. My cousin, Larry - you remember Larry - his son's Bar Mitzvah is on Saturday," he continues. "If your husband won't mind, will it be okay for me to crash in the spare room?"

I inhale deeply, wondering how I am going to tell Seth that my 'husband' actually sleeps in the spare bedroom. Even though it has been two years since he last asked, every time Seth is in New York, he has always found a roof over his head in the apartment he once co-owned. So, I feel bad having to turn him down now.

"Ezi, are you still there?" he asks. "Will your husband mind?"

I sit up, remembering the allegiance this same 'husband' of mine has sworn to another woman. Yes, the spare room might be occupied, but nothing stops Seth from sharing my own room the way he has the last few times he's stayed over. Even though we'd broken up then, anytime he was in New York and asked to stay over, we always ended up sleeping on the same bed and having great no-strings-attached sex. There's no reason why we can't do the same this time, Dili or no Dili.

"It's fine. You know you're always welcome." I answer with a smile. "When do you arrive? Thursday?"

"Actually Friday," he answers. "And I'll be out of your hair by Sunday."

"Great! I look forward to seeing you again."

"Me, too." There is a pause before he continues. "I've really missed you, Ezi. I sometimes wonder if I made a big mistake walking away from us."

We end the conversation on that nostalgic note, and I decide to close early for a change. Apart from there being no need to dodge Dili anymore, not after finally coming face-to-face with him this morning, I decide to while away my time daydreaming of Seth and all the things that could be.

"You're home early," Dili remarks as I let myself into the apartment. "I guess that means no more hide and seek games."

I ignore him as I take off my coat.

"How was work today?" he asks, trying to make small talk.

"Oh yeah, before I forget," I say. "Seth will be in town this weekend, and he'll be staying here."

A deep frown forms on Dili's face. "Seth, your ex-fiancé? Why would he stay here?"

I shrug nonchalantly. "He stays here when he's in town."

"Where is he going to sleep? On the living room sofa?"

"Don't be silly, Dili. The man used to co-own the apartment. I could never make him sleep on the sofa," I answer. "He'll be in my room with me."

"What?!" Dili retorts.

I don't dignify him with a response and instead head to my bedroom. But Dili is clearly not done with our conversation.

"Your ex is going to sleep in your bedroom with you?!" he bellows, following me into my room. "You are going to sleep with your ex?"

"Okwudili, what's it to you?" I yell. "Considering you are occupying the only other alternative, where would you have him stay?"

"In a hotel, I would think!" Dili yells back. "I don't see any rational reason for him to sleep here, when I'm sure he has a million other options in Manhattan!"

"He might have 'a million other options' but this is his best one," I retort. "This was his home for many years, an apartment he paid for with his sweat. Even when I bought him out, he didn't even sell to me at market value. So yeah, anytime he's in town, you can be darned sure I'll accommodate him."

"I thought all your people here think you're married," Dili demands. "Isn't that what he knows too? Yet, you still want to have him in your bed, with your husband under the same roof."

I laugh sardonically. "Married indeed! Yes, that's what he thinks. But I have every intention of filling him in on the truth when he gets here."

"I'll sleep in the living room," Dili says, his own frustration rising. "Let him have my room, I don't mind."

"What is this obsession you have when it comes to me and other men?" I exclaim, also frustrated. "That was how you almost burst a blood vessel when you thought I was going to sleep with Madufuro. You want me to stay here like a celibate fool, whilst you're there planning how to go surprise Onyeka for Valentine's Day?"

Dili stares at me, unable to come up with a suitable comeback.

"Okwudili, please leave my room." I say firmly. "You have no right to dictate who I do or don't entertain in my bedroom. Seth will be here on Friday, and he's going to stay here with me."

Defeated, he leaves and rather than feel triumphant, I am completely drained. I am sick and tired of Dili's possessiveness, when I know he is still cavorting with Onyeka. I am sick and tired of the mixed signals he keeps sending. It makes me even more determined to have Seth over to put paid to this hold Dili has over me…once and for all.

For the rest of the week, the atmosphere is tense in the apartment, with Dili and I barely speaking to each other. Our living room has turned into something of a ghost town as we have now resorted to having even our meals in our respective bedrooms. He is annoyed and, frankly, so am I.

On Friday, Seth calls me when his train arrives Penn Station from Durham, North Carolina, and I take a taxi to meet him there. Upon sighting his bright red hair, which he has grown out from the cropped style he had as an Investment Banker, into a messy quiff, I can't help but smile.

"You always are a sight for sore eyes!" he marvels, after we embrace. "You look amazing, Ezi. Marriage sure is treating you well."

"You don't look bad yourself!" I remark, choosing to ignore the marriage reference. "I see you let your hair grow out. Looking more like a College Professor! And why on earth did you opt for a twelve-hour train ride when you could have just flown?"

"Not all of us are making investment banking money," he answers with a sigh. "I can't believe I ever thought life would be easier in the academia. It's almost as hectic as being out here in Manhattan!"

I raise a brow. "Oh? Any regrets?"

He smiles and shakes his head. "Not one. Best decision I ever made. The only thing that would make it complete is if you were there with me. But I guess that's too late now. So…tell me about your husband. I hear he's also Nigerian. Where did you meet him? How long did you two date?"

I smile stiffly. "So many questions! Don't worry, there's lots of time to fill you in on all that," I answer with the hope it will kill off the conversation, for the time being at least. By the time we get to the apartment, and he sees he'll be sharing a bed with me after all, I'll have no choice but to come clean.

We chat about Goldman and Duke in the cab ride to the apartment, and I can see the shocked look on my doorman's face as we enter the building holding hands, and as Seth greets him heartily. I smile inwardly as I imagine Tomas' confusion. The poor guy must think me the most complicated woman he has ever met in his life.

Upon getting to the apartment, I am surprised to find Dili already there. At a little past 4pm, it is early even for him.

"Ah, you must be Seth!" he says with a warm smile, extending his hand in a handshake. "I'm Dili, Ezi's husband."

Seth smiles and shakes him heartily. "Very glad to meet you."

I watch in astonishment as Dili proceeds to engage Seth in conversation, asking him about his trip and life at Duke, before leading him to the guest room.

"What are you doing?" I snarl, grabbing Dili by the arm after he has left Seth alone to unpack.

"Giving the guy the room he should have," he snarls back. "Sorry if that ruins your plans."

"I hope you don't think you're going to sleep in *my* room!" I snap, enraged to my bones.

"Don't worry. I'll sleep in the living room," Dili mutters before walking away.

By the time Seth emerges from the guestroom shortly after, I have no choice but to go along with Dili's charade. The three of us chat through dinner and, long afterwards, and as Seth finally retires to his room, Dili remains in the living room under the pretext of watching TV.

My eyes are wide open as I lie alone on my bed. Deep in my heart, I am relieved I didn't go through with my plan of sharing a bed with Seth. It would only complicate things, especially as I can see from Seth's body language that he wants me back. As flattering as that might be, I'm not sure returning to him is the wisest thing for me to do.

After tossing and turning for hours, I head to the kitchen to pour myself a glass of juice. Walking past the living room, I stop and look at Dili's sleeping form on the sofa. He looks uncomfortable, and I marvel that he has put himself through that discomfort just to keep Seth away from my bedroom. And I can't control the small smile that forms on my lips.

The rest of the weekend is uneventful. Seth is away most of Saturday at his family function and returns too late for us to be compelled to have another night of conversation. And early Sunday morning, he takes the train back to Durham, leaving Dili and I alone to continue our acrimonious co-existence.

Later that week, I get a surprise email from Azuka, inviting me for their annual Christmas party the following Wednesday, the 23rd of December. I am tempted to turn it down but decide against it. Even though I am fully aware than Nnamdi would also have invited Dili, I am eager to get out and try to meet new people.

That Wednesday, I leave work early so I can have enough time to beautify myself. At about 7pm, I hear Dili leave the house and know he is on his way to Nnamdi and Azuka's apartment. It's ironic how, only a year before, we'd attended the party as the best of friends, our friendship untainted by sex and unrealistic expectations. Now, only a year later, we can barely stand the sight of each other.

I don't leave the apartment for another two hours and arrive at the party a little after 9pm. It is already packed to the rafters and in full swing. I exchange greetings with Azuka and a few of the ladies I recognize from the previous year, before taking a seat. I can feel several appreciative glances from some of the guys and I'm grateful I spent all that time getting myself dolled up for the night. Despite wanting to be oblivious of him, I scan the room for Dili, and I see him sitting alone at the far end of the room, nursing a drink. He looks anything but happy to be there, and it surprises me, considering how much fun he had the year before.

He looks up and our eyes meet.

I immediately tear mine away and smile flirtatiously at one of the men who has been checking me out. Ain't no way I'm going to dull myself tonight.

The guy moves closer to me and introduces himself as Iheanyi, a cousin of Nnamdi's. We are in the middle of chatting about how life as a Nigerian undergrad at UPenn compared to his own alma mater of Northwestern University, when Patoranking *My Woman, My Everything* stops playing abruptly. I look up, wondering what has gotten into the DJ, only to see Dili take a seat before the grand piano in the living room. My heart stops as his fingers strum the opening keys of John Legend's *Ordinary People.*

As he sings the song, his eyes are on me the whole time. Everyone in the party listens in rapt attention to him sing and play, and our eyes remain in a hold, neither of us able to look away. When the song ends, the room explodes in rapturous applause, but even that doesn't break our gaze. Because, through all that applause, our eyes and hearts have communicated words long left unsaid, and I realize several things. I realize that, despite everything going on in his life, he does love me. I realize I am still madly in love with him. I realize I still want to be with him. I realize it is better for me to have him, even if only for a few months, than to lose him forever now. I realize I am ready to accept whatever he can give me until the inevitable happens and he has to return to Onyeka. I realize I am ready to make do with that.

He makes his way over to me and I rise to my feet, Iheanyi in mid-sentence. Dili takes me by the hand, and we wordlessly leave the party. When we get home, the minute we walk into the apartment, I dissolve into his arms, and as my body, heart, and soul succumb to him, I know that this is the only place I want to be.

Later that night as he sleeps, I rise to my feet and walk to my workstation, wanting to release my feelings onto my keyboard.

***<u>Ordinary People (John Legend) – December 23, 2015</u>***

*Maybe we'll crash and burn.*

*Maybe we'll survive.*

*Whatever the odds, I'd rather spend a day with you than a lifetime apart.*
*I'd rather have you for a moment, than lose you forever.*

*I'm going to savour every minute of the little time we have left.*

*My love, this time we will take it slow.*

Returning to bed, he pulls me closer to himself. I close my eyes, basking in every beautiful moment of it. Yes, until he has to go to Onyeka, I will enjoy every minute with him.

Every single minute.

# CHAPTER TWELVE

## Me & Mrs. Jones

AND SO MARKS THE BEGINNING of the second phase of our relationship. Maybe because we are both aware of everything truly at stake and the limited time we have together, we enter it with everything we have, not holding anything back. And it is much more intense.

So, so much more.

We reach a level of intimacy that surpasses sex. We are content to just be in each other's arms, sometimes even in complete silence. If I thought I was in love with him before, in the weeks and months that follow the Christmas party, my feelings for him multiply in leaps and bounds. He becomes everything to me. And from the way he looks at me, holds me, wants me, I know the feeling is mutual.

With the dawn of the New Year, as grateful as we are to see another year, we are painfully aware that our time together is slowly coming to an end. Unless Dili chooses to lie to Onyeka when he gets his permanent Green Card, he will have no more excuse to continue this arrangement with me. In an ideal world, once that happens, the next thing would be to begin divorce proceedings, while he arranges to bring Onyeka over.

But we choose to live in denial. We don't talk about it, and we don't talk about her. We immerse ourselves headlong in our love, our beautiful love. We become each other's appendage, together from the moment we open our eyes, to when we shower, to when we have breakfast at the Starbucks down the block, to when we share a cab to work, to when we meet up for lunch, to when he stops by my office after work, to when we share a cab - or sometimes walk - home, to when we have dinner, to when we retire to bed.

We become each other's everything.

He must limit his contact with Onyeka to when he is at work because he doesn't call her when we are together. There are no more midnight phone conversations with them whispering sweet nothings. It seems like she is fading from his life, and when he makes no move to travel to Nigeria for Valentine's Day to 'surprise her', I can't help but feel somewhat victorious…and hopeful.

By the end of February, I start to really hope. Maybe Onyeka *will* soon be a thing of the past after all. Maybe what they have *will* fade naturally and uneventfully. Maybe she *will* be the one to back out of the whole thing after meeting someone else in Nigeria.

Maybe Dili and I won't have to divorce after all.

I have so many daydreams about what our vow renewal will be like. It will be a sharp contrast to the rushed ceremony at City Hall, for sure. I fantasize about wearing a beautiful wedding gown, very likely a Monique Lhuillier or Elie Saab in pink or blush tones, in a sunset ceremony on a rooftop with a panoramic view of the Manhattan skyline. I fantasize about having my sister, Ebere, fly in from London with her family, and my brother, Enyinna, from his base in South Africa. Dili's mother and siblings will also be there, as will our close friends here in Manhattan. Instead of just the two of us, we'll be able to share our special day with our loved ones.

And every time I think about this, my heart bursts with hope and anticipation…of what could one day be.

In March, he surprises me with a romantic trip to the Maldives for the Easter weekend. As we arrive the beautiful luxury resort, it feels like I am truly in heaven. With the chalets laid out to give the illusion of suspension over water, looking out into the vast expanse of sea from our veranda, it's like we are the only two people in the world.

"This place is pure perfection!" Dili says, as we lie in each other's arms. "I wish we could stay here forever!"

I nod in agreement. Staying here forever would dissolve to nothing the complexities of our lives that await us back in Manhattan. How wonderful that would be if it were possible!

"This is, without a doubt, my second favourite place on earth!" I say.

Dili looks at me with a raised brow and a curious smile. "Second favourite?"

"Nothing beats Friday Harbour in Washington State as my ultimate destination." I answer.

"You went there with Seth?" Dili asks, an edge in his voice.

"No, silly!" I giggle, tickled by his jealousy. "I went there alone shortly after our breakup to recharge. A colleague at work suggested it, and it was the best experience ever!"

"Really? I never would have imagined Washington State as the ultimate travel destination."

"I rented a waterfront house on Rosler Road, I'll never forget. Apart from the beautiful ocean, there were ponds on the property, and acres and acres of beautiful greenery." I sigh as I remember it. "I'm going to buy a retirement home there. On that same street, if I can. When I'm old and grey and ready to leave this world, that's where I'll retire. That's where I want to die."

"You won't get a retirement home in Umuahia, your hometown?" Dili teases. "What if your significant other has different plans for you?"

My lips curve in a smile as I look at him. "Well, does he?"

Dili shrugs and looks away, and it leaves me lightheaded, wondering if this is his way of telling me he has no plans to leave, that our love will stand the test of time, and that we will grow old together.

Later that evening as I lie in bed, I reluctantly pull out my iPad. Even though the last thing I want to do is write, my Editor has been breathing down my neck over the irregularity of my column and I know I need to do better if I want to keep the gig.

Dili is still on the terrace, reading a book. From where I sit on the bed, I have a great view of his beautiful profile, and for a moment I just stare at him, wondering how on earth I got so lucky.

With a smile, I select my song of the day.

***Me & Mrs. Jones (Michael Buble) – March 27, 2016***

***Me and Mrs. Jones***
***We got a thing goin' on***
***We both know that it's wrong***
***But it's much too strong***
***To let it go now***

"What are you doing? Writing your column?" Dili asks, startling me. "I need to find time to read it one of these days."

"I'd rather you didn't," I laugh, remembering some of my very salacious articles in recent times.

He takes the iPad from me and smiles. "*Me & Mrs. Jones*? Really?"

I grab it from him, suddenly embarrassed. "It seems apt, doesn't it?"

He is quiet for a moment and listens to the music still playing, as if hearing its lyrics for the first time. "Well, I'd rather not think of us that way, as two people sneaking around."

I look him in the eye. "Aren't we?"

It is the first time I have made any reference to Onyeka since our reunion. Even though his gaze doesn't waver, he says nothing in response, and I take his cue to drop the topic. No good can come from ruining our beautiful romantic holiday by bringing up Onyeka.

"I remember the first song I heard you write your article to," he says, smiling. "Keane's *Russian Farmer's Song*. You made me fall in love with that song. I don't know if I ever told you this, but I listen to it almost every day now."

"Really?" I exclaim, genuinely surprised. "I thought you called it 'white music'."

"*Good* music," he counters. "Every time I hear it, I think of you."

And with that, my article, Onyeka, and everything in between, are forgotten for the night.

We spend another magical day on the island before leaving the following Tuesday. Flying through Dubai, we are tempted to push forward our connecting flight to New York and spend some time in the city, but with work beckoning, we reluctantly do the right thing and continue our journey.

Our plane lands in JFK at 7pm on Wednesday. Dili and I are exhausted as we make our way through Immigration and as we get a cab to Manhattan. On the ride to our apartment, we power on both our phones which were switched off the whole time we were on holiday and, immediately, messages start to drop. I see a small frown crease his face and I wonder if they are perhaps messages from an enraged Onyeka unable to reach him for almost a week. But I don't ask. And he doesn't say anything. It does feel like a small victory, though, keeping him away from her for so long, but, better still, that he didn't even miss her at all.

It just serves to convince me she might soon be a thing of the past.

We walk into the apartment, and as is habit for me, I click on the answering machine to listen to our messages. The first few are from Ebere and her family, and some of my friends, wishing us a happy Easter. But it is the fifth message that changes everything.

***Obi'm, I can't get through to your mobile phone. Ebee ka ị nọ? Where are you?***

Both Dili and stop dead in our tracks at the sound of Onyeka's voice. We both turn to look at the answering machine like it is the woman herself.

***I'm sure it's the network. Anyway, how are you? And Sis Ezioma? I hope you guys had a lovely Easter.*** Then she giggles. ***Babe, I have a surprise for you! I didn't want to tell you until the thing clicked, but I sent my passport along with those of my colleagues going to the U.S. for training. I decided to try my luck, especially as I wasn't selected for the training in the first place. And guess what? I GOT THE VISA!***

As she giggles hysterically, my heart literally stops beating and I sit on the nearest chair, unable to fully process what I am hearing.

***Heiii! Chukwu Daalụ! Thank God! Can you just imagine this favour, after all this time we have been waiting for your Green Card? And they gave me a two-year visa! Chineke dị ukwuu oooo! God is wonderful oooo!***

I steal a look at Dili's face, but it is stoic and unreadable.

***And I have another surprise for you!*** She giggles. ***In fact, I wanted to surprise you by just showing up, but I decided against it only because it won't be nice to come without letting Sis Ezioma know beforehand. I've bought my ticket. I bought it from my savings. I told you I've been setting some money aside from what you send.***

*I've bought my ticket and I'll be leaving Nigeria on Saturday, to arrive in New York on Sunday.*

This time, Dili and I look at each other, the gravity of her words falling on us like a pile of bricks.

*Can you imagine? After four long years, God has finally done it! Chineke emeela ya! Nna anyi n'ekele gi! I hope Sis Ezioma won't mind me staying with you? But you said she's a nice lady, so I'm sure she won't. Biko kelee ya. Thank her for me o. Thank her for this wonderful thing she has done for us. Only God can reward her for her kindness.*

And then her giggles turn to tears.

*Can you believe we will finally see each other again, obi'm! N'oge na-adịghị anya ị ga-eji ịhụnanya gị! You will soon be with your love! After four long years! God is good! God is good! By the time your Green Card comes out, we can marry immediately, and you can file for me.* Then she giggles again. *Ewo, my airtime has finished. Biko kpọọ m mgbe ị nwetara ozi a. Call me as soon as you get this. I love you!*

And then silence pervades the room.

I look at Dili and small beads of sweat have formed on his forehead, despite the cool spring weather.

Neither of us needs a soothsayer to let us know the party is over.

# CHAPTER THIRTEEN

## *You Could Be Happy*

AS ONYEKA'S VOICE trails off, Dili and I stand there in silence. After a few minutes, as if on cue, we retreat to our separate bedrooms, neither of us saying a word.

What more is there to say, really?

Onyeka now has her visa and, come Sunday, will be reunited with her man. Her man who has warmed my bed for months, but who has always made crystal-clear his stance when it comes to her. True, in recent times, his stance hasn't been quite as resilient, but, if I'm to be honest with myself, I knew exactly what I was getting into.

And, well, here we are.

But that doesn't stop me from lying awake all night, staring at the ceiling. It doesn't stop me from being hopeful of hearing a light tap on my door. It doesn't stop me from longing for his familiar warmth beside me.

But none of these happen. In the morning, I leave the connecting bathroom door open, hopeful he will join me as usual. But he is painfully absent, and as I head to the door on my way to work, the first time I have had to do so alone in months, his door remains shut. I hesitate by it, wanting so much to knock, but common sense prevails, and I leave the apartment instead. I know I have no choice but to accept the abrupt end of our relationship.

Getting home that evening, Dili is in the kitchen making dinner. From his stiff smile and impersonal questions about my workday, I know we have reverted to our status quo. As we eat and make idle chat about work and President Obama's recent trip to Cuba, neither of us mentions the infamous message from Onyeka from the previous night, and neither of us makes any romantic overtures, either. And as we politely bid each other goodnight, it is almost difficult to imagine that, less than forty-eight hours before, we'd been an intensely passionate pair. I guess it is easier for us to adjust to our new reality than talk about it.

It isn't until Sunday morning that Dili finally mentions Onyeka.

"Her flight arrives this afternoon," he says, as we eat breakfast. We both know very well who *her* is.

I look up at him, wondering why he has chosen to offer me this piece of information.

"Will you come with me to JFK? To pick her up?" is his surprising question.

That is when I see, for the very first time, fear in his eyes. I realize he is frightened of his reunion with the woman he hasn't seen in four years. I recognize guilt in his eyes, and it dawns on me that he is ashamed of what transpired between us. I realize I am nothing but a mistake, a slip he wishes he'd never made.

And for the first time since we returned home on Wednesday, I can feel my heart breaking to little, tiny pieces.

"Sure," I answer. Whilst I am hurting from the realization that Onyeka is more important to him than I ever was, I am also curious to finally see the woman. Yes, I have seen several pictures of her and can probably make a sketch of her by heart, but that isn't the same as seeing her in the flesh, hearing her speak, observing her mannerisms and everything about her that has won the heart of the man I love.

At 1pm, we get a rental car and head to JFK. It takes us over an hour to get there, and we wait in expectation for the arrival of the *Air France* flight from Lagos. Even after the flight's arrival is finally announced, we anxiously await her emergence from Immigration and Baggage Claim.

"I hope you tutored her on what to say," I mutter. "Before she tells them she is here to join her husband."

Dili glances at me from the side of his eye. "She knows exactly what to say, Ezi."

I purse my lips and cross my arms, suddenly overtaken by jealousy and wondering what I am doing there, waiting to welcome my very own rival.

It's insanity.

When she emerges, it is like even the air in the room changes. Like a ray of sunshine, she stands out from everyone around her. Her skin, golden and flawless, doesn't even match the glow that radiates from within her, her mega watt smile stretching from ear to ear. Everyone around her turns to stare. She is so much more beautiful than even I expected.

She lets out a scream when she sights us, and in typical Hollywood - or Nollywood - fashion, pushes aside her luggage trolley and runs to her long-lost lover. I look to see Dili also run to her, and they are soon reunited in an emotional embrace. From a few feet away, I watch them, and I almost go crazy with envy. I see for myself the depth of the love they *both* have for each other. Nothing one-sided at all.

After what seems like forever, they pull apart from each other and she sights me. The smile on her face grows wider, and before I know it, she has enveloped me in a bear hug.

"Sis! It's so wonderful to finally meet you!" she says, looking at me like I am some sort of celestial being. "Thanks so much for everything! I brought you some lovely gifts from home. Even my mother sent you something!"

As she rambles on, I take in her beauty and see that she is more flawless up close. Even with her very minimal make-up, long hair cascading loosely down her shoulders, and very casual travel attire of a tracksuit and sneakers, she has paled me into insignificance, my cashmere Marc Jacobs sweater, Roberto Cavali jeans ensemble, and all. Even in only sneakers, she stands over six feet and her voluptuous curves are evident beneath her loose attire.

I have never felt more invisible.

Luckily, she is all talk as we head to the rental car, so I don't have to make any conversation, which is just as well, because my inferiority complex has left me tongue-tied. As I take the driver's seat, I observe how awestruck Dili is by her, listening to her mundane talk with rapt attention, and I realize I was a fool to have ever thought he'd choose me over her.

"But *obi'm, enweghị m obi ụtọ na gị*. I'm not happy with you," she says, as we approach Harlem. "My friend told me that with your temporary Green Card, you could have travelled out of the country. Why didn't you come to see me? Nkeiru was even asking if you came to surprise me for Valentine's Day. She said you told her you would. *Emere m ihere nke ukwuu!* I was too ashamed to tell her you didn't even mention it, let alone come. *Kedu ihe mere?* What happened?"

I feel Dili steal a glance at me, but my eyes remain on the road, unwilling to be roped into their discussion.

"*Ugegbe*, I've been so busy with work," he says lamely. "I really wanted to, but I haven't been able to get any time off."

I smile bitterly at the term of endearment he has used for her. *Ugegbe.* Radiating Beauty. Funny how he has never used any such endearment with me.

"*Eeeiyah!* If it's because of work, then I should be the one apologizing to you. *Biko,* we don't want to do anything to jeopardize this our fantastic job *ooooo*!"

As she giggles, I turn on the radio, cranking up the volume on Hot 97 FM. The less I hear of their conversation, the better.

"Wow! This is where you live?" she exclaims in amazement, when we get to my apartment building, and it makes me nostalgic as I remember Dili's identical reaction the first time he came here. "And you have been housing Dili here for free all this while? You are a real angel on earth, Sis Ezioma!"

Her awe and amazement remain all through the elevator ride to my floor, and by the time we get to my apartment, she is completely star struck. Dili takes the opportunity to leave the apartment under the guise of returning the rental car, and I can almost murder him for leaving me alone with her.

"Wow, sis! You are a real inspiration," Onyeka gushes. "I am so impressed by you. And it's not just because of this beautiful apartment. Whenever I go on your LinkedIn page, I doff my hat to you. You are simply amazing and have achieved so much already."

I smile modestly. "Thank you, Onyeka."

"My plan is to start a postgraduate program in a good school as soon as possible," she continues, taking a seat on the couch. "I'm thinking Columbia. As soon as Dili and I marry, that's what I'm going to do. No babies for the first few years, *biko*! I want to make big bucks and be as glamorous as you, sis."

"You're already glamorous," I say, more to shut her up than flatter her.

"But nothing like you," she gushes. "Just look how everything about you is set! Look at your apartment, your designer clothes! You are what they call 'complete package'! *Ha ga-abụ ndị ìsì ebe a!* They must be truly blind over here for a woman like you to still be single."

I laugh, amused by her choice of words. Blind indeed!

"But on a serious note, sis," she says, her voice dropping as she leans in. "I have something to ask you. You've been living with Dili for two years now. *Ọ nọ na nwanyị ọ bụla ọzọ?* Has there been any other woman?"

Beads of perspiration dot my forehead. I find myself suddenly unable to breathe as I try to work out if she knows about our affair or is merely asking an innocent question.

"I know you won't want to tell me, but I really need to know. *Biko,*" she pleads, mistaking my discomfort for reluctance. "*Ị bụ nwanyi dị ka m*. You're a woman like me. I'm sure you would want to know if you were in my shoes."

"But why has that thought crossed your mind?" I ask, trying to sound cavalier, when I am literally dying inside.

She shrugs. "These last few months, things were different. He stopped calling as frequently as he used to. Dili that could call me up to ten times a day before, suddenly would go days with no contact. Everything just seemed strange. My spirit told me something was wrong. In fact, if it wasn't because of my respect for you, my plan was to show up here unannounced and catch him red handed."

It is now my turn to feel guilty. "He hasn't cheated on you. It's probably been work that has kept him busy. There has been no other woman."

Except me.

The relief on her face is palpable and I feel sick to my stomach, nauseated at myself for the role I have played in hurting such a simple minded, innocent girl. When Dili returns home about an hour later, I leave them alone and retire to my bedroom.

But sleep and any form of rest elude me. Instead, I lie awake that night, tortured by images of them intimate in his bedroom. I even listen for telltale sounds, but, thankfully, there are none. But I am not naïve enough to think they are not having sex. After being apart for four years, I know that's probably all they are doing, ravaging each other's bodies. And the visual destroys me.

The next day, I leave for work early and spend the whole day bracing myself to face them, the reunited couple, later. Thankfully, I get through an evening of idle chatter with, all while trying to act normal. This continues for the rest of that week and into the next, all of us acting like one big happy family; me, my former lover, and his fiancée. What could be more complicated than that?

But rather than feel better, I am worse off with each passing day. Every time I see them stealing kisses or laughing over private jokes, it feels like a punch to the gut. I find myself now looking forward to Dili's permanent Green Card getting issued, so they can leave me alone in peace. It would be easier for me to mourn the loss of our relationship alone, than to have it shoved in my face every crying day.

What makes things worse is her adulation of me, which seems to multiply everyday. She worships the ground I walk on and hangs on to every word that comes out of my mouth. On her first weekend, I have to hide out at my office to escape her request to 'hang out'. After what she chose to discuss the last time we were alone, 'hanging out' is the last thing I want to do.

By the end of the second week, I can no longer hold it in and confide in Mia over drinks after work. She listens in rapt attention as I tell her the entire story.

"Oh, you poor thing!" she says, holding my hand sympathetically. "And you've been going through all this alone?"

"I didn't want to involve you in something illegal," I say. "It's not exactly the most straightforward of arrangements, marrying for a Green Card."

"But the chemistry between you two!" she exclaims. "Whenever you're together, your sexual energy is always so intense and overpowering!"

"We have a strong physical attraction, no doubt. I guess it was just the sex for him."

Even without my saying it, she can pick up on what I have not said. "But you fell in love with him."

I wipe away a tear. "I've been in love with him since I was five years old. How am I supposed to just let him go, and be happy he's with someone else?"

She puts a comforting arm over my shoulder. "Because that's what you gave him your word you'd do. From everything you've said, he never hid anything from you. You knew what the deal was from the beginning. Besides, you're too classy to fight over a guy, least of all with some young girl hot off the plane from Nigeria. You have to let him go."

I wipe away more tears and nod in agreement. Mia is right. The sooner I forget about Dili and fully release him in my heart, the better it will be for me.

"Do you have a picture of her?" Mia asks, and I pull up a few of Onyeka's pictures from her Instagram account. "She's pretty."

I nod in resigned agreement. "Yeah. She's even prettier in real life. She looks like a model!"

Mia shrugs. "But it's just vanilla pretty, though. Nothing I don't see every day walking down Fifth Avenue. You, on the other hand, have an unusual beauty that people don't come across very often."

I laugh, knowing she is only trying to make me feel better. "Oh really? Unusual beauty?"

"Yep!" Mia nods enthusiastically. "You're a 'Katie Girl'! Remember that episode of *Sex & the City*, when Carrie and her friends talk about that old Barbara Streisand and Robert Redford movie, and Carrie realizes she's a Katie girl and Mr. Big's fiancée, Natasha, is just a simple girl. That's exactly what this is. You're a Katie girl and Dili's lady is just a simple girl. You never should forget just how fabulous you are."

I smile, grateful for my friend's attempt to cheer me up. But as I walk down Broadway, headed to my apartment, I find myself consoled by her words. Yes, I might not be as beautiful as Onyeka, but I know that there are so many parts to me that make me the phenomenal woman I am.

Getting to the apartment, I find it empty, and remember Dili mentioned something about taking Onyeka out for dinner. And I am happy to have the house to myself.

After dinner and a shower, I pull out my laptop to write for the first time in days. And what I choose is to write an ode of release to Dili, the man I love. An ode of release…and a wish for happiness.

***You Could Be Happy (Snow Patrol) – April 15, 2016***

*The most painful thing in life is saying goodbye to someone you love. And today, that is what I am doing.*

*Today, I release you, my love. I release you to live your life exactly the way you want to. I release you to love who you want to…do the things you want to.*

*I release you to happiness.*

My lips quiver and tears roll down my face. I make no attempt to restrain them and instead give full rein to them, crying like a baby as I bury all the fantasies and desires I have ever nursed for Okwudili Dike.

I know it's time to let go.

# CHAPTER FOURTEEN

## Linger

AS THE WEEKS ROLL BY, the three of us settle into something of a pattern. Onyeka has taken to waking up early in the morning to prepare meals for Dili and I before we leave for work. I indulge her for the first few days, but soon have to break it to her that her heavy white bread sandwiches and even heavier meals of rice or potatoes are just too much for me. I leave the house as Dili is compelled to eat breakfast with his fiancée, and I don't see the pair of them until I get home from work. Sometimes, I hang around to chat, and other times, I don't. I no longer feel the need to pretend when I don't want to. The nights I feel like being alone, I politely excuse myself and retire to bed early.

Even though we have reached a congenial understanding, it inadvertently pushes Dili and I further apart, as we are unable to have any interaction, conversation or otherwise, that does not involve Onyeka. Which is just as well, because there really is nothing to talk about.

Not anymore.

Sometimes, I watch them. I watch to see how they truly are with each other, and the ease and fluidity of their connection is a stab to my heart. She fusses over him in a way it would never have crossed my mind to, and he seems to enjoy this adoration. In the end, I accept that she is a better choice for him.

But it still hurts.

Towards the end of May, after Onyeka has been with us for almost two months, I pay a frantic visit to Michelle, our Immigration Lawyer. Surely, Dili's permanent card should be ready by now.

"I'm afraid not, Ezi," is her frank answer.

"But you said it would be ready by our second anniversary!" I exclaim in my own exasperation. "We hit the two-year mark last week!"

"Remember I said *if* we were lucky, it would be ready by your second wedding anniversary. I also said it could be two years after the issuance of his temporary card, meaning it could be another year still," she refutes, making me want to throw up my hands in total and complete exasperation.

Walking the several blocks back home so I can clear my head, I have tears pouring down my face. How am I supposed to live like this for another year? How am I supposed to watch the man I still love frolic with the woman he has chosen, and still keep a smile on my face? Mia keeps telling me how strong I am, but the truth is I'm not. I'm not strong at all. I just want to return to how my life was before this whole mess started. I just want to forget Dili even exists. I am sick and tired of having to wear a fake smile on my face. I'm sick and tired of the pity I get from Azuka, who has taken to calling me weekly to 'check on' me. I just want to return to my life as carefree as it once was.

One Saturday in early June, I am having breakfast in the kitchen when I am ambushed by Onyeka.

"Sis, *i ga-arụ ọrụ taa?*" she asks, before suddenly clamping her mouth with her hands and looking around nervously. "*Chai.* And Dili has warned me about all this Igbo I speak. I meant, are you going to work today?"

For a moment, I'm tempted to lie, but decide against it. "No, not today. I just want to take things easy. And why doesn't Dili want you speaking Igbo?"

She shrugs. "He says he wants me to get used to speaking only perfect English, especially as I'll get a job as soon as he is able to file for me." A wide smile forms on her face as she grabs me by the hand. "Since you're free, let's spend the day together. Ever since I got here, you're always too busy. I know you have better things to do than hang out with a local girl from Nigeria, but I'd really love for us to spend time together."

"Don't you and Dili have plans today?" I ask.

"He's gone to the gym and said something about stopping at the office briefly," she answers sullenly. "*Biko,* Ezi. I'd really love to spend the day with you."

At this point, I know I can't tell her no. The truth is, even after she and Dili leave my apartment, if we're all in this same city, we might as well learn to be friends.

"What do you want to do?" I ask, forcing myself to look enthusiastic.

She squeals in excitement. "I want to buy an outfit for Frank's birthday tonight. Dili gave me some money for an outfit a week ago but having you with me to pick a bomb dress would be so much better!"

Ah yes, Frank's birthday. One of Dili's friends came visiting with his wife a few weeks ago and invited us, me included, for a night-out to celebrate his fortieth birthday. I know he only extended the invitation to me out of courtesy, and I have no intention of wasting a good Saturday night club hopping with a bunch of strangers.

After breakfast and a quick shower, Onyeka and I take a cab downtown. We start first with the normal high street shops before making our way to Saks Fifth Avenue, where I do most of my shopping.

I exercise all the patience I humanly can as she tries on outfit after outfit, before settling on a lime green BCBG Max Azria lycra dress that hugs her curves.

"You look stunning!" I can't help but exclaim. The truth is everything she has tried on has looked amazing on her. I guess that's the advantage of having a goddess-like body.

"You don't think my hips look too big?" she asks, twirling in front of the mirror with a perplexed look on her face. "*Heiii!* See my stomach oh. And my breasts! Everything just bulging!"

"Onyeka, that dress is perfect on you. Some of us wish we had the curves to carry off something like this."

"*Nne,* don't even say that o! You don't know how lucky you are to have small breasts. I'm sure you can even afford to go some days without wearing a bra!" she counters.

Rather than flatter me, I feel insulted.

"You don't have half the problems I do," she continues. "Everything always looks raw and sexual on me. But as for you, you can even be naked without looking vulgar."

"Well, they say African men prefer women with your kind of body," I retort.

She smiles in agreement. "True. But sometimes, you want to be taken seriously. I'm sure you don't have men staring at your chest at work, when you're trying to make a serious point. You don't have that problem. As for me, *na only my breasts and yansh they go dey look!*"

Tired of the conversation, I start browsing through the racks, looking for something for myself.

"What about this?" Onyeka says, pulling out a modest long-sleeved chiffon top. "Beautiful and classy, just like you. And age appropriate too."

Age appropriate?

My smile is stiff as I shake my head. "Not quite my style."

In the end, I don't buy anything. I have a closet full of clothes still with price tags, so don't really need anything new. But as we make our way through the other stores so she can buy shoes and accessories, I decide to follow them out tonight, even if it is just for her to see that I'm not a dry wallflower and can be sexy as well.

We make our way further downtown, and as we walk down West 20th Street, she stares longingly at the wedding gown clad mannequins in Kleinfeld Bridal's window display.

"I can't wait for the day I'll finally buy my dress!" she gushes. "Can we go inside and look around?"

"You need to have an appointment for that," I mutter, knowing one step into the bridal shop will push me completely over the edge.

"Soon and very soon," she says, a dreamy smile on her face. "I can't wait for when Dili and I get married. You'll come back here with me to get my dress, won't you, sis?"

I nod, even though I know there will be a higher chance of hell freezing over than me following her to pick the gown in which she will marry the man I love. Nope, no way that's going to happen.

"I really can't wait!" she continues when we are in a cab on the way back home. "You've been so good to us, but I can't wait for when Dili and I can finally move to our own place. My cousin in Atlanta says he can get a much better job there, so we plan to move as soon as he gets his Green Card."

Now this is news to me.

"What about his job here?" I ask, unable to mask the irritation in my voice. "Is he going to just give up everything and move to Atlanta?"

"No, sis!" she giggles. "He will get something there before he leaves New York. It's just what we're working towards."

I remain silent as she continues to chatter on, and when we walk into the apartment, she announces to a surprised Dili that I will be following them for Frank's birthday festivities after all. I can see in his eyes that this is not something he expected, and it buoys me even more to attend. Who knows, there might be a fine, eligible bachelor suitable for my almost thirty-nine-year-old self.

Later that evening, I am expertly applying my makeup when Onyeka taps on my bedroom door and walks in nervously. "Hi, sis. Sorry to disturb you, but are you sure the dress isn't too vulgar?"

"Onyeka, you're beautiful!" I say for the umpteenth time. "If we were the same size, I would have offered you a jacket to wear over it, but the truth is you don't need it."

She gapes at my walk-in closet, as if beholding the eighth wonder of the world. "If we were the same size, I wouldn't even need to go shopping. Your closet is a designer store on its own. Look at those shoes!" She walks closer, her mouth hanging open at my floor-to-ceiling shoe display. "*Nne*, you are fashion itself! I'm sure you could go two years without repeating a single outfit! You don't know how lucky you are to be so tiny. If not for the face, I'm sure I could pass for your aunty, with this my big size."

*If not for the face*. Wow!

She picks up a pair of my shoes from the floor. "You're a size seven? I'm sure you never have trouble finding shoes your size. Me and my size twelve feet are forever a problem. You saw how hard it was for me to get a decent pair today."

"Are you and Dili ready to leave? Give me a few minutes and I'll be done," I say, eager to change the subject.

"You don't have any problems at all," she continues, oblivious. "I'm sure you'll just throw on a simple blouse over one of your designer jeans, and you'll be good to go. You have no stress at all."

I glare at the door long after she has left the room, angered by her assertion of me being on the boring and predictable side of fashionable. A simple blouse over designer jeans was what I'd had in mind to wear, but now, I am determined to show her that I, too, can look sexy and desirable.

A few minutes later, I step out of my bedroom in a black spandex jumpsuit that leaves very little to the imagination. With a deep cut-out running down the middle, it enhances and amplifies my modest breasts, and pushes up my bottom to give me a round and pert derriere. Sky-high red stilettos complete my look, and I know that modest, decent, and boring are not words that can be used to describe me tonight.

As I approach Dili and Onyeka, I see in his eyes a look I haven't seen in a long time.

Desire.

I hear Onyeka go wild with excitement over my transformation, but my attention isn't on her. My attention is on her fiancé whose eyes remain fixed on me. And it gives me immense satisfaction.

The three of us head to the popular 40/40 Club, where we meet up with the rest of Dili's friends, including the birthday boy, Francis. Nnamdi and Azuka aren't there, and I am grateful for that. Typical Naija style, we settle in the VIP section, and the boys are soon popping champagne like it's going out of fashion. I am getting a lot of compliments about my look, and this only serves to embolden me further.

"Dance with me," I say, pulling Dili to his feet and leading him to the dance floor.

Rihanna and Drake's *Work* is playing and as we dance, I see in his eyes the same Dili who could not keep his hands off me, the one I used to make sweet love to from sun up to sun down, and I find myself suddenly determined to fight for him.

I move closer to him as we dance, so close there isn't even space for a whiff of air to pass through. I cross my arms behind his neck as I twist my hips around his, and I am pleased to feel his own arousal. I lean forward such that our foreheads are touching, and as we look at each other, it is like we are alone in my apartment as lovebirds all over again. It is like we are loved up in the Maldives all over again. He belongs to me, and I am not letting him go. Not without a fight.

I look over in Onyeka's direction and I see her watching us, a frown on her face. This propels me further and I run my hands all over Dili's chest and place his own hands firmly on my bottom, my hips still swirling erotically against him. Dili, who seems to be in some sort of trance, is unable to break away from my grip as our raunchy dance continues. It isn't until Onyeka suddenly rises and walks out of the club that he recovers himself, pulls away from me, and chases after her.

Luckily, the other members of our party have not noticed what happened, or are pretending not to have, as they continue dancing and merrymaking. Not wanting to pursue Dili while he is chasing Onyeka, I have another drink and continue dancing. But even as I dance and give off the impression of being carefree, deep inside, my heart is burdened. All I want to do is go home and talk some sense into Dili's head. Surely, he can see that we still have magic. How can he want to give it all up? How can he want to give us up?

After thirty minutes, I leave the club and hail a cab to take me back home. Getting to the apartment, I see Dili sitting solemnly in the kitchen. He doesn't even look up when I walk in. I stand silently at the kitchen door for a few minutes, watching him.

"Where is Onyeka?" I ask.

"She's locked herself in the bedroom," Dili answers, rubbing his temple.

I pull out my phone and set John Legend's *Ordinary People* to play.

"Remember this song, Dili?" I ask him. "Remember you sang this song to me at Nnamdi and Azuka's Christmas party, only a few months ago?"

He sighs deeply. "Ezioma..."

"*'Girl I'm in love with you'? 'We're right in the thick of love'? 'And though love sometimes hurts, I still put you first and we'll make this thing work...?*" I remind him of some of the lyrics. "If you don't love me, why did you sing me that song? If we're not meant to be together, why did you sing it to me, trying to win me back?"

"Ezi, it's not as easy as that," a deflated Dili responds.

"Tell me you love her like you love me! Tell me what you have with her is even a fraction as good as what you had with me!" I demand, getting more frantic.

"Yes, Okwudili," comes Onyeka's voice by the door. "Why don't you tell her?"

Dili looks up at the sound of her voice, but she has already retreated in the direction of their room. He looks at me, his face a mix of frustration and anger as he chases after her.

And I finally have my answer.

I return to my bedroom and sit on the bed, trying to process all that has happened that evening, trying to process how Dili could go from desiring me one minute, to chasing after Onyeka the next.

I am still sitting in that position when my door opens and Onyeka walks in. I sit up straight, not knowing or trusting her motive for being in my bedroom, especially after all that has happened.

"When I was in your room earlier tonight and you sprayed your perfume, I wondered why it was such a familiar smell," she says, her voice calm and steady. "It wasn't until I got back to the house from the club tonight that I realized that's the smell that's all over Dili's bedroom - on his clothes, his sheets, his furniture. Everywhere in that room is your smell," she laughs and shakes her head. "You know, my friends in Nigeria warned me. They told me there was no way Dili wasn't having a sexual relationship with you, a woman he's been living with for two years. But I told them it could never be, and it wasn't because I trust him. I didn't think you were the type he would go for. Physically, he would never have looked at someone like you when he was in Nigeria. It just goes to show that men will always be men, and no matter how wonderful a meal is placed in front of them, sometimes they will still want to snack on dry, old suya."

I smile at the dig but choose not to say anything in response.

"No wonder you dressed like this tonight. In your mind, you were hoping to continue from where you stopped, *okwiya*? Don't you have any shame? At your age? A man younger than you?"

"Only by a few months," I answer, looking at her brazenly. "And yes, I have no shame. I'm not ashamed to admit that what Dili and I had was beautiful. I'm the reason he stopped paying you any attention earlier this year. That was me. So I guess he must like his 'dry, old suya' after all."

Onyeka laughs and claps her hands. "*Ọ bụrụ na agwọ adịghị egosi anụ ya, ụmụ ntakịrị ga-eji ya na ịkụ nkụ*. If a snake fails to show its venom, little kids will use it to tie firewood. *Nne,* you must think me a pushover. I might be young but if you think I'm going to cross my arms and hand you a man I have loved for almost a decade, *ị bụ egwuregwu oh*! You're a real joker!" She laughs again, but there is little humour in her laughter. "If Dili wants you so much, why has he been on his knees since we got back from the club, begging me? Why?"

This time, I look away, unable to maintain eye contact lest she sees the hurt in my own eyes from the realization that, again, Dili has chosen her.

"*Nne*, you've done enough for us *o*! You've tried. But it ends tonight," she continues. "First thing tomorrow morning, Dili and I will be out of your house. I'm going to make sure you get divorce papers within the week. Enough is enough, *biko. You don try*!"

"Dili and I can't get divorced until he gets his permanent card," I mutter in response.

"That is trash! I've been speaking with my people in Atlanta, and they say there are ways around it," she snaps. "Thank you for housing us, *Sister* Ezioma. We are grateful for everything." With that, she turns and leaves the room.

About an hour afterwards, Dili himself comes into the room.

"Ezioma," he calls out.

I look at him, finally, fully, and truly deflated, and with no words in response.

"Ezioma, why did you have to behave the way you did tonight? We were all doing just fine…" Dili says, equally deflated.

"Onyeka says you're leaving in the morning. Is it true?" I ask, finally finding my voice.

He nods. "She insists we'll not spend another night here. She'd leave tonight if she could."

"Where are you guys going to go?"

He shrugs. "A hotel, maybe. But we'll have to get an apartment soon."

"And the divorce? She says you'll be sending papers soon."

This time he sighs. "I've already told her that might take a little while."

I nod and we remain there in silence, me sitting on my bed and him standing awkwardly at the door, neither of us knowing what to say.

"I didn't want it to end this way," he finally says. "You've been so wonderful to me, Ezioma. I really didn't want it to end this way."

"I just want to know something," I say. "All that time we spent together, did it mean nothing to you?"

Our eyes lock and I see him struggle for words. "I will always cherish the time we had together, Ezioma…"

"But?"

"But we always knew we didn't have forever," he continues, now unable to maintain eye contact. "I'd already made a promise to Onyeka. We both knew that."

I smile sadly and nod. "I guess we did. So I guess this is where we say goodbye and good luck, right?"

He makes as if to take a step forward to me but decides against it. "Thanks for everything, Ezioma."

I give him a thumbs up sign and he walks out of my bedroom…and out of my life.

Unable to stand the thought of tossing and turning all night, I take a sedative and soon fall into a deep, dreamless sleep. By the time my eyes finally open, the sun is shining bright and it is almost mid-day.

I rise to my feet and walk to his bedroom. I open the closets and see that all his clothes are gone. His books are gone from the shelf and his *New York Yankees* cap is no longer hanging on the door. I lean on the wall to steady myself, the finality of it all hitting me hard. He is really gone. Dili is really gone. It is well and truly over.

I walk like a zombie to the living room, to my workstation, hoping that the pain will go away if I can write it all down. Maybe writing about it will be a form of release for me. I select ***Linger*** by The Cranberries and try to put my emotions into words.

***Linger (The Cranberries) – June 06, 2016***
***Is that the way we stand?***
***Were you lying all the time?***

Rather than help me write, the song only breaks me further, and I am soon sobbing like a baby. I go back to his empty bedroom and collapse on the floor by his bed, weeping over his pillows, drinking in his familiar scent. My heart is broken in a way I could never have fathomed, in a way I could never have prepared for.

I remain in that kneeling position, crying into his pillow as day eventually turns to night.

I have lost everything.

# CHAPTER FIFTEEN

## Sunday Morning

I EVENTUALLY FIND MY WAY TO MY BED and I do not get up from there for the next few days. I ignore my ringing phone and only venture out of bed for urgent toilet breaks. I do not eat, I do not sleep, I do not even think. I just lie there, the emptiness I feel weighing on my chest like a boulder.

It isn't until Wednesday, when Mia and a few friends from work somehow find a way to sweep past the doormen and bang on my door, that I manage to get out of bed. I am tempted to ignore them at first, but when I overhear them making plans to get the Building Superintendent to force the door open, I reluctantly give in.

Letting them in, the girls are sympathetic about my supposed illness, but one look at Mia and I know she has figured out what has really happened, especially with Dili conspicuously absent. She stays back after the others leave, after which I break down in her arms. She remains with me for the rest of the day, forcing me to eat my first meal in days.

"I don't want to leave you alone." she says, when she is still with me at midnight. "I could call Todd to let him know I'll be here a few days?"

I smile and shake my head. "I'm fine. I just needed to mourn for a little bit, to get it out of my system. I'll be at work tomorrow."

"You know you don't have to. I could let Pierre know you're feeling unwell, and I'm sure you could get at least another week off."

"I need to get out of this house," I answer. "I can't keep lying on my bed, crying over something I never had. I need to get busy again."

Mia envelopes me in another hug. "I'm here for anything you need, babes. If you ever need company, I'm only a phone call away."

I am grateful for her concern, but when I am alone in my apartment again, I almost wish I had taken her up on her offer, the silence and emptiness hitting me with a potency renewed. Standing at my door, the still and quiet of the apartment taunts me. Walking down the hallway, my eyes fall on Dili's empty bedroom, the door still ajar, and it is a fresh stab in my heart. In the living room, there is an outline on the coffee table where his laptop used to be. Sitting on the couch, I can still smell him in the room. It is the most gut-wrenching paradox; having him absent but so present.

I allow my mind wander to what he could be doing at that very moment. I wonder where he and Onyeka are staying, if he is happier finally being alone with her, if he misses me, if he even thinks about me at all. I imagine them hunting for a new apartment. I wonder if they will decide to remain in Manhattan or move to the suburbs, or maybe even Atlanta like Onyeka said. I wonder if he will proceed with the divorce, regardless of not yet having his permanent card. I wonder how soon they will get married after the divorce pulls through. A year? A few months? A couple of weeks? The same day?

As fresh tears roll down my face, I decide I can no longer live like this. I will no longer waste tears on him. I must revert my heart, my mind, my body, and my soul to how they were before he blew into my life like an ill wind. I need to eliminate every and any thing that reminds me of him.

The next day, I decide against going to the office, but this time have the decency to call my boss. He is sympathetic about my feigned illness and agrees to give me some days off.

But instead of continuing to lie in bed and wallow, I go on to purge my home of every trace of Okwudili Dike. I strip the sheets in his bedroom and mine, and rather than throw them in the washing machine, I bag and trash the lot. I fish out my older sheets, even those already laundered and folded, and trash them as well. I trash towels, throw pillows, anything that could have his scent. When I am done, I attack the furniture with odour eliminating sprays, literally dousing a whole canister on the living room sofa alone. But when, even after all the spraying, I can still smell his annoying signature Davidoff scent, I know I must make more permanent changes.

I call a U-Haul truck and when it arrives, I have the movers take out almost every stitch of furniture in the apartment; the sofas in the living room, Dili's bed, my bed, even the coffee table in the living room, and the dining table and chairs. Riding with the movers down the utility elevator, I have no idea where they will be conveying the furniture to, but getting downstairs and sighting Tomas, I decide there couldn't be a better recipient than my dear doorman.

"All of this for me?" he exclaims. "Are you moving?"

"Just making a few changes," is my cheery answer to him. I find this act of purging therapeutic and can finally almost see the rainbow at the end of this very dark storm.

"Wow! Thank you so much!" Tomas says, beside himself with emotion. "Camila will be over the moon!"

"Consider it a late wedding gift!" I say, smiling at him.

"You and Mr. Dili already gave us a lovely gift, Ma'am."

At the mention of his name, my good mood evaporates like the wind.

"Were you here when he left on Sunday?" I ask.

He nods. "I helped call a cab for him and his sister."

Ah yes. We had introduced Onyeka as Dili's 'sister'.

"Did he tell you where they were going?" I probe further.

"He did ask me to recommend a good hotel," Tomas answers, unable to hold my gaze. "I suggested a nice one in SoHo that Camila likes a lot."

I restrain myself from asking any more questions, knowing I gain nothing from knowing where Dili and Onyeka are lodged. What use is ridding myself of almost all my expensive furniture if I keep my mind fixated on him?

Returning to my apartment, the consequence of my impulsiveness stares me in the face as, save for the window drapes, it is just about as bare as the day Seth and I bought it.

So I pack a small bag and head to The Hyatt, where I book a luxury room for a few days. That night, I order new furniture online and don't return to my apartment until they are delivered the following weekend. But even with lying on a brand-new bed in brand-new sheets, Dili's presence is still as strong as ever.

I manage to go through the weekend and return to work the following Monday. Being back there is good for me, as it finally gives me the escape I need. I throw myself headlong into it, slaving away till late at night, and when I return home, I don't even turn on the lights, desperate to keep thoughts of Dili at bay. I work weekends as well, leaving my apartment as early as 8am on both Saturday and Sunday mornings. Unlike the past when my long hours away were me running away from Dili, this time I am running away from my own thoughts and memories which, when I am alone, are so strong and overpowering, they almost drive me crazy.

The weeks roll by, and on July 11th, my birthday, I awake with the cold and stark reminder that I am thirty-nine years old, only a year separating me from the grand old age of forty. I am in no mood for the office banter and festivities that accompany birthdays, especially as I know there will be jokes about it being the last year of my 'sexy thirties', or how I am on the cusp of middle age. So I decide to stay home instead. Thankfully, my apartment no longer feels like a haunted house, and I enjoy a few hours of mindless morning television.

Later that afternoon, I decide to take a stroll to our…*my*…favourite patisserie and perhaps order a few cupcakes to binge on, if only for today. As I put on my wig, I am struck with a sudden wave of awareness, wondering why I have been hiding under purchased human hair for years. In another wave of impulse, I drop the very expensive head of hair in my bin and take out my cornrows. My hair is bushy and overgrown beneath, so I tie a scarf before leaving the house.

My first port of call is an Afro-Caribbean hair salon a few blocks away, where they proceed to treat and trim my unruly natural hair, taming it into a short and manageable afro. Cupcakes forgotten, I prance around Manhattan for the first time in…ever, in my own natural hair. And it feels liberating.

After wandering around aimlessly for a few hours, I return to my apartment, and I am shocked to find Seth waiting for me in the lobby, bunch of flowers in hand.

"Happy birthday, Ezi!"

I gasp in amazement. "What are you doing here? You didn't tell me you were coming!"

"I wanted to surprise you. I've already been to the office and was told you didn't come in today."

"But you've never surprised me on my birthday!" I say, still surprised to see him there. "I can't believe you rode twelve hours on a train just to do this."

"It turns out it's only two hours by plane," he teases, his eyes twinkling. "Are we going to chat here, or are you going to invite me up?"

Riding up to the apartment in the elevator, we make small talk and I find myself pleased to have his company. As liberating as my afternoon activities have been, it feels good to have someone around.

"I love your hair," Seth says, as I open the apartment door. "I'm glad you finally decided to ditch your weaves."

Seth always said he preferred my natural hair to wigs or weaves, but I'd never taken him seriously, thinking he knew just as little about black women's hair preferences as I did about his baseball addiction. Since I had no intention of learning about the latter, I ensured he also didn't encroach on the former.

"Thanks," I say, smiling from ear to ear. "It feels good not to have that weight on my head. Literally."

"You changed the furniture?" he remarks as he walks into the living room.

"Yeah," I answer. "It was time."

He nods in understanding. "Mia told me you and your husband broke up. I'm sorry to hear that."

I shrug, trying to appear nonchalant, unwilling to be dragged into any conversation about my fake husband and fake marriage.

"Actually, I'm not sorry," he suddenly says. "In fact, I'm downright pleased. When Mia told me, I got on a plane almost immediately."

"You mean this isn't just you surprising me on my birthday?" I ask, my brow raised.

"It is," he answers. "But it's also me trying to fix one of the biggest mistakes I ever made. Losing you was my worst mistake, Ezi. My life has no meaning without you."

"Seth, we've been over for four years," I mutter, not quite knowing what to say.

"Four of the worst years of my life!" he says, taking my hands. "I love you, Ezi. I want to be with you forever. Come back with me. Come back to Durham with me."

I stare at him and realize I'm not scandalized or flabbergasted by his request. Instead, the idea takes root in my mind, the idea of a change of environment not sounding bad at all.

And then I make the most spontaneous of decisions ever.

"Okay," is all I answer.

His eyes light up in what I realize is surprise. He clearly didn't expect me to agree so easily. "You'll come to Durham?"

"Yes, I will," I answer, even more certain of my decision. "I could even enroll in a graduate program, or something. I've always wanted to study Creative Writing."

"I could get you a Teaching Assistant position," he says, his shock becoming excitement. "Oh my goodness, Ezi! Are you serious?"

Nodding, I feel the same lightness I felt after cutting my hair that afternoon, the thought of leaving town and starting my life somewhere new sounding like the logical way to move on from the Dili fiasco.

Seth and I spend the rest of the evening making plans, and that night, lying in his arms in my bed, even though it is not as earth shattering as it was with Dili, it feels comfortable and familiar. And I realize that is just what I need now.

Comfortable and familiar.

He spends another day with me before leaving for Durham, and we agree I will join him at the end of the month. The hardest part is giving my notice at work, where my bosses engage me in a series of back-to-back meetings trying to make me change my mind, and even offering to double whatever I have been offered elsewhere. When I convince them I am not leaving for a rival firm but Grad School, they offer me sabbatical leave instead, which I accept.

Time passes in a whirlwind, with several farewell lunches and drinking sessions with different groups of friends. But as bittersweet as saying goodbye is, I am excited about starting a brand-new life. I pack up my designer clothes, send them to storage, and replace them with clothing more appropriate for my new life in the academia. But one thing I refuse to give up is my apartment. I refuse to even let it out, instead deciding to keep it as a getaway for whenever I'll need it.

On my last night, as I prepare to write my final article for the *Manhattan Buzz,* I look at my suitcases around me, all packed and ready for my morning flight to Durham, and it feels bittersweet. I know I will miss my lovely apartment and my wonderful Manhattan life, but the time has come for me to make a change in my life.

For my song for the day, I decide on the same one I used for my very first article, Maroon 5's *Sunday Morning*.

***Sunday Morning* (Maroon 5) – July 30, 2016**

*And so, my friends, we have come full circle. With this song, we said 'Hello', and now we have to say 'Adieu'.*

*I remember the day I wrote my first article, my relationship with ex-fiancé was unraveling and I was hoping for something that would lead me back to him. Well, today, four years and a broken marriage later, the ex-fiancé is no longer an ex. He's no longer a fiancé, either. For now, he's just a boyfriend, but yes, life has led me back to him.*

*But today, he is not the reason for this song. This song, I dedicate to all of you, my wonderful readers. You have been amazing, and I hope life does lead us back to each other, even as I trade my Manhattan stilettos for loafers and moccasins in Durham, North Carolina.*

*I will continue to document my musical journey of life, but this time on my personal blog, www.thesoundtrackofmylife.com. Stop over if you can.*

*Peace…and Love!*

*Miss E.Z.*

I sit back in my chair when I am done writing, allowing the wave of nostalgia cover me. But even through the nostalgia, through the bitter sweetness of it all, as I listen to the lyrics of the song as it begins playing a new cycle, my mind wanders to the one person it shouldn't.

Immediately, I shake my head vigorously, forcefully ridding my mind of any lingering thoughts or memories of Dili. Come tomorrow, my life begins anew; in a new town, with new experiences and opportunities, with a man who wants to be with me.

And *that* is what I should be fixated on.

# CHAPTER SIXTEEN

## Drive

MOVING TO THE UNIVERSITY TOWN of Durham is everything I hope it will be. Seth receives me like royalty, and I am touched to find he has readied his lovely residential quarters for me, with personalized towels, throw-pillows in my favourite colours of red and purple, and a desk by the window where I can write. Coming from being with someone who couldn't even declare me to the world, this immediately feels like an enormous step up.

I am disappointed to find that the university doesn't have a Creative Writing program, and that, with it being early August, I am too late to apply for a Master's degree course. But Seth convinces me to start a certificate program in Philosophy, Arts & Literature, with the plan for both of us to move to Yale University next year, where he will accept an offer he has been considering, and I can start a Master's degree program in Comparative Literature. It sounds like a great plan, especially as it will see us moving to Connecticut and closer to home…or what home used to be; New York City.

By the time the academic year is in full throttle at the end of August, I have fully settled into my new life. Just as he promised, Seth secures me a Teaching Assistant position in his faculty, which helps keeps me sane. The money is less than what I would use for lunch back in NYC, but in the small town of Durham and with my toned-down lifestyle, it is more than enough to tide me over without my having to touch my plush savings. Yes, I might still have my job at Goldman, but you never know what could happen tomorrow.

As for Seth and me, even though there are no sparks anymore, he is more loving and devoted than he was the first time we were a couple. I am finally able to understand the saying of a person having 'enough love for two people'. Seth definitely has enough love for us both, and even though it is nowhere as heady and intense as what Dili and I shared, it is nice, familiar and comfortable. The only glitches occur when he tries to talk marriage or other long-term plans. Somehow, the mere mention of that makes my heart race…and not in a good way. By the middle of September, he has proposed to me twice…and I have turned him down twice. I'm happy with the way we are now. Relatively happy and with no strings attached. Why can't it stay this way forever?

But at nights, even as Seth and I cuddle to sleep, I am unable to shake off thoughts of Dili. Though I manage to refrain from thinking about him during the day, late at night when I close my eyes to sleep, there he is. I see him as vividly as if he is lying there beside me. I remember his touch as if his fingers are tracing my body like they used to. I feel his breath as if his face is mere inches away from mine as it used to be. And I hate myself for still thinking of him this way.

However, at the end of September, all that changes when I get a phone call from Michelle, our Immigration Lawyer.

"Dili got his permanent card last month," she says. "He says he tried to get in touch with you to let you know but found out you'd moved."

"Oh, that's nice," I answer in the most aloof tone I can manage. "I guess it's time for me to send him divorce papers. I'm surprised he hasn't done that already."

"That's why I'm calling," she says, and from her tone, I know I'm not going to like what she says next.

"I recommended a divorce lawyer, Alex, to Dili and his girlfriend," she continues. "I thought they were getting along fine, until Alex told me a few days ago that Dili's girlfriend started asking him some very leading questions. She wanted to know if you'd been married long enough for Dili to file for spousal support, and she also asked a lot of questions about Equalization Payment. Either she's been doing a lot of reading, or someone somewhere has been pumping her with a lot of information."

My blood starts to boil. "Equalization Payment?"

"Ezi, you should have signed a Prenup when I told you to," Michelle sighs. "As it is, if they can establish that you have a higher Net Family Property value than Dili does, which you obviously do, you could be mandated to split it with him 50:50."

"And is he in on this as well?" I ask, my body quivering in my anger, unable to believe what I am hearing.

"Well, when I called him to ask him about it, he seemed genuinely surprised. He sounded like he was hearing about it for the first time, and when I asked Alex, he confirmed that Dili wasn't with his girlfriend when she asked him the questions," Michelle answers. "Alex declined working with them after that, and when I spoke with Dili earlier today, he told me they were looking for another lawyer and would be in touch soon."

I am so angry, I am literally seeing red. Even though Michelle has exonerated Dili from being a part of Onyeka's scheme, I still hate him for it. How dare they, after all the help I have rendered them! If it weren't for me, he would have been deported to Nigeria ages ago. How dare they repay my kindness with this act of treachery!

"You need to lawyer up," Michelle continues. "Who knows if the lady will succeed in getting into Dili's head. You need to be prepared so you can fight off whatever they come at you with. I'm going to send you the number of one of the best Divorce Attorneys I know. She doesn't come cheap, but she's a monster and will crush those guys if they try anything stupid."

She leaves me with the Divorce Attorney's details; Samantha McNeil, a name I have heard many times from some of my colleagues at work. When it comes to Divorce Attorneys, there are very few better than her in the city of New York. Michelle and I agree that the best thing is for me to establish contact with Samantha now, and then wait for Dili and Onyeka to make their move.

As Samantha and I have our first conversation, and as she sends me a tentative bill, I am angered anew that the thanks I am getting for my help is court time and a big hole in my pocket.

But as September rolls into October, then November, and then the end of the year, but still with no word from Dili and Onyeka, I start to get anxious. Could this be a strategy? To delay and prolong things for as long as they can? Michelle says she hasn't heard from Dili in just as long, and is equally as in the dark as I am. By February 2017, I am insistent on kick-starting divorce proceedings, but she remains adamant that I wait to see what they have up their sleeve. We agree that if we still have not heard anything by June, a year after our separation, then I can go ahead to file first.

As frustrating as the delay is, I nonetheless use it as an excuse to ward off Seth's proposals which, by March 2017, have reached seven. But am now less anxious about the thought of being married to him and start to contemplate actually telling him 'yes' the next time he asks.

The last weekend of March, I am invited for an old family friend's wedding in Chicago. I know it will be a reunion with several familiar faces both from Naija and America, but what scares me most is the prospect of running into Dili and Onyeka there, as his late father was just as close to the groom's as mine was. My first instinct is to send my regrets to Obida, the groom, but I change my mind in annoyance. I absolutely will not spend the rest of my life running away from Dili and Onyeka! In fact, I want to look them both in the eye and challenge them for daring to conceive whatever it is they are plotting. The ingrates that they are!

As I leave for Chicago on Friday evening, I restrain myself from running to the stores to buy the slinkiest and sexiest dress I can lay my hands on. I will make no special effort for Dili, or anybody for that matter. I am going for that wedding as Ezioma of today, and not the frivolous and flashy girl of yesterday. If Onyeka shows up looking like she just stepped off the runway, which I'm sure she will, well then good for her. This new Ezioma, this Ezioma that is comfortable in her own skin, is too self-assured to be intimidated by anybody.

These are the words of affirmation I repeat to myself all through the two hours and fifteen minutes it takes to get to Chicago. I book a hotel far from the venue of the wedding reception to avoid the chance of running into Dili and Onyeka, and the next morning, I head to the ceremony in a simple peach dress with a small rose in my afro. Unlike the past when I would have spent hours painting, moulding, and contouring my face, this time, a single sweep of light foundation, mascara, and tinted lip gloss are enough for me. I am no longer desperate to make up for whatever beauty handicaps I might have.

Or so I thought.

Walking into the reception after the church service, I find myself so nervous, I feel faint. Dili and Onyeka were not at the church service, which is no big surprise. As I walk into the Lakeshore Hotel where the reception is holding, I slow down my walking pace, lest my quivering legs send me crashing to the floor. I am grateful to be distracted by a few aunts and cousins, who barrage me with questions and soon lead me to their table, making me glad I had the presence of mind not to invite Seth along, as their questions would have been a lot more probing if I'd shown up with a white guy. Maybe even more tragic than still being single a few months to my fortieth birthday.

As I am laughing over a very crude Igbo joke one of the ladies cracks, very reminiscent of the kind of thing my late Mom would have said, I see him. Dili is walking up to our table with a smile on his face, and the one on mine vanishes completely.

"Hi, Ezioma. I knew I'd see you here. I've been looking all over for you," he says, after politely greeting the older women.

Not wanting to give the women a show, I force a smile. "Hello, Okwudili. How are you doing?"

He shrugs. "Okay, I guess," he looks at me in appreciation. "You look lovely. I always said you look best this way, beautiful and natural. It really suits you."

"Onyeka *nko*?" I ask, unable to mask the hint of sarcasm in my voice. "She's not here with you."

Something flashes in his eyes before he shakes his head. "No, she isn't. Ezi, can we talk?"

"If you want to talk, *nọdụ ala*! Sit down here," I retort, my irritation rising, wondering what he could possibly want to say to me.

"Ezi, darling, we see some people who just came in that we'd like to greet," one the older ladies says, as they all rise to their feet, their eyes twinkling with mischief.

I am both angered and anxious as they leave the table, all too aware of how much of an impact Dili still has on me several months later. Standing there in his navy-blue suit, I am so aware of his body, of his familiar smell, it is killing me inside. I am afraid to look him in the eye lest I melt to butter at the sight of them, so I keep my eyes and attention focused on my drink.

"Ezi, I've really missed you," he says, sitting beside me. "It feels like a part of me died last June. I haven't been the same since then."

"And Onyeka? What about her?" I mutter, still not looking at him. "Did a part of her die as well?"

"It didn't work out with us," he says. "We kept fighting over so many things. She was convinced I was still in touch with you, and there were some things she did that I didn't quite agree with."

"Like try to squeeze me for spousal support or equalization payment?" I snap, glaring at him.

From his deflated look, I know I have hit the nail on the head. "Michelle told you. I swear to you, I didn't have a part in any of that. I almost lost my mind when I heard about it. I don't think I've ever yelled at anyone the way I yelled at Onyeka that night. I was so angry she could even contemplate something like that."

"And so you broke up with her?" I retort sarcastically.

"No. I had to find a way to forget about it somehow. It changed my perception of her, no doubt, but I'd made her a promise and I had to swallow my feelings and see things through," he answers. "What broke us up was less dramatic. She went to Atlanta to spend Thanksgiving with her family there, and she never came back. Apparently, her cousins, the same ones who pushed her to demand those things from our lawyer, introduced her to a rich Nigerian Web Developer over there. According to what she told me over the phone, I just wasn't a sharp enough guy. From what I hear, she's pregnant for the dude now. I guess they'll be marrying soon."

I look at him, filled with both anger and...well, anger. "You are both lucky you didn't try any mess with me, because you would have regretted ever even knowing my name if you had." I laugh mockingly. "So she was the one to leave you in the end. Who would have ever thought?"

"To be honest, it was a relief," he says, taking my hand. "Ezioma, I didn't know what love truly was until you happened to me. With you, I understood what it was to fall in love with your best friend. I was just as happy being in bed with you as I was sitting beside you in the living room arguing politics. You were a slow burn for me, and like all slow burns, the flame remains, burning a little brighter every day. I don't think words will ever be enough to tell you how much in love with you I was…and that I still am." He pulls out his phone and smiles wistfully. "I made a playlist of all the songs that remind me of you. Every day, when I'm home alone, I listen to them and it's like having a piece of you back."

He hands me the phone, and, true enough, there is a playlist called ***Ezioma,*** with such songs as *Russian Farmer's Song, Ordinary People, Me & Mrs. Jones, Knocks Me Off My Feet,* the *Moonlighting Theme Song,* and even *You Get What You Give.*

"*Russian Farmer's Song* is the one that really brings you closer to me," he continues, a smile and faraway look on his face. "I listen to it, and it's like you're right there next to me. I love you, Ezioma. I still love you."

"But yet, you left me for her," I answer tartly, a lump forming in my throat. "Tell me something, Dili. If she hadn't left you for another man, you'd probably still be with her now, wouldn't you?"

He stares at me for a few moments. "What choice did I have, Ezi? I couldn't do otherwise. I could never hurt a woman the way my father hurt my mom. And I'd made a promise to her. She flew to the U.S. just because of me. I could never have been the one to end the relationship. Not even when I was dying inside, missing you."

"Well, newsflash. You did hurt a woman in just the same, maybe even worse, way your dad hurt your mom." I say, looking him in the eye. "You didn't want to break Onyeka, but you broke me. You broke *my* heart."

He has nothing to say in response, and we sit in silence, the weight of my words bearing down on us both.

"I hear you got back with Seth," he finally says. "I ran into Mia once, and she told me you'd quit your job at Goldman and left for North Carolina to be with him."

I sit up straight. "Yes, I did. We're back together now."

"And you're happy?" he asks, looking at me, his eyes probing. "Being back with him is what you want?"

I laugh sardonically. "You think I would have given up my whole life in New York if it isn't."

He moves so close to me, I can feel his breath on my face. "Look me in the eye and tell me you're truly happy with him."

I look away, unable to lock eyes with him for fear that all the emotions I have caged for months will break loose. I don't want him to see in my eyes that I have loved nobody the way I love him. That I never have, and probably never will.

"I'm very happy with Seth," I manage to answer. "And we're getting married as soon as you and I can get our divorce sorted. So I'd really appreciate it if you could speed that up."

Dili nods and I am surprised to see his eyes water. I am almost tempted to take back my words, to tell him I am a horrible liar, and that he is all I want...all I will ever want.

"I'll work on that as soon as I get back to New York," he answers, before a sad smile curves his lips. "If you're happy, then I'm happy."

"Thank you," I answer. "We're moving to Connecticut in August, so I can start a postgraduate program. He also got a job offer there."

"Yale?" Dili inquires.

I smile and nod in forced enthusiasm. "I can hardly wait! I love this new life of mine. I really do."

Another sad smile from him. "I'm glad to hear it, Ezi." Then he rises to his feet. "It was wonderful seeing you again. And I'm happy to hear that you're happy."

As I watch him walk away, I'm dying inside, my soul crushed anew, and my heart ripped out of my body all over again. A part of me wants to chase after him to tell him he's right, and that there will never be anyone else. But instead, I remain seated like my ass has been glued to my chair. As I watch him walk out of the hall, tears I didn't even know were gathering pour down my face.

I can't help but feel that this time, I have lost him forever.

Lying in my hotel room later than night, I am more determined than ever to finally accept Seth's marriage proposal. Maybe being married will permanently exorcise me of this Dili obsession. Maybe it will get rid of all these wanton feelings I still have.

Maybe.

I return to Durham the next day and make a big show of fussing over Seth. I am more affectionate than I have ever been, and I am eager for us to finally take things to the next level. I decide that if he doesn't propose again, I'm going to bite the bullet and propose to him myself.

"Are you busy later today?" I ask, as we prepare to leave the house the next day, Monday.

"Not really. I have a Faculty Meeting later this afternoon but should be done by 6. Why? What's up?"

I smile, coy. "How about we have dinner at The Fairview? My treat."

"The Fairview? Fancy much!" Seth laughs. "What's the occasion? Did I miss a birthday, anniversary, or something?"

"Let's just say it's a surprise," I wink at him. "All you have to do is make sure you arrive well dressed."

We kiss each other goodbye, and as I go through my day, I practice the words to tell him that I am ready to commit my forever to him…again. The more I think about it, the more convinced I am that this is the right decision, the best decision for us to make. With any luck, Dili and I should finalize our divorce in a couple of months, and maybe Seth and I could be married before we move to Connecticut in the fall.

I am having lunch at a diner near campus when my phone rings.

"Hi Ezi. It's Naomi. Do you have a minute?"

Naomi is a Medical Doctor and one of the friends I have made in Durham.

"Sure. I just drove out to town to have a meal at Charlie's. I was craving a bacon and cheese wrap," I answer. "What's up?"

It is only for the shortest of minutes, but I notice that she hesitates. "It's about some of the tests we ran, Ezi."

Every year for the past decade, I get a comprehensive medical check-up. This being my first year in Durham, I even convinced Seth to get it done with me, and we spent a few days getting thoroughly tested and checked out.

"What about them?" I ask, not wanting to get unnecessarily worked up.

"We saw a suspicious shadow in your mammogram," she continues, picking her words carefully. "I had several of my colleagues look at it, and they all agree that it looks suspicious. Like a mass."

"A mass?" I repeat, my heart racing. "But I don't have any lumps or anything."

She is quiet and I know she is trying not to say the wrong thing. "I don't want us to jump to conclusions, Ezi. Could you come over to the clinic tomorrow, so we could run some more tests? An MRI scan? Maybe even a biopsy of the mass, if we can?"

I agree to return to the hospital the next day, and after the call is over, I remain seated at the diner, the implication of what Naomi has just said weighing heavily on me.

I might have cancer. Just like my mother and sister before me, I might have cancer.

I remain in that sitting position in the diner as day turns to night. I ignore Seth's phone calls, knowing he is probably waiting for me at the restaurant.

I am like someone in a trance.

As The Cars' *Drive* plays from the diner's old juke box, its lyrics have never rung truer than they do now.

*Drive (The Cars) – March 27, 2017*

***Who's gonna pick you up***
***When you fall…***
***…You can't go on***
***Thinking nothing's wrong***
***Who's gonna drive you home tonight?***

There's no point being delusional or unrealistically positive. If they think it could be cancer, it most probably is cancer. It killed my mother…my baby sister…and now…

It's here for me.

# CHAPTER SEVENTEEN

## Bohemian Rhapsody

STILL SITTING IN THE DINER, I am catapulted all the way back to 2005, when I got the worst phone call I'd ever received in my life. It was from our family doctor, Dr. Kowano. I'd almost not taken the call, as that was the time a lot of fraudster calls were coming from Nigeria, and I wasn't sure if the strange number was one of them. Thankfully, I'd answered it on the second ring, and what I went on to hear forever changed my life.

"Ezioma, I'm so sorry to bother you like this," Dr. Kowano had said after we exchanged pleasantries. I was still trying to process his surprising call and my brain was already running all sorts of scenarios in my head.

But none the numerous scenarios prepared me for I heard next.

"It's your mother," he continued, his voice grim. "I'm so sorry to call you like this, but she has left me with no choice. I know I shouldn't be breaking patient confidentiality this way, but I feel I owe it to your late father, who was so wonderful to me."

"What's the problem, doctor?" I asked, my heart racing a mile a minute.

"Your mother has cancer, Ezioma. Stage Four breast cancer. And she has refused to proceed with any more treatment."

Till this day, I clearly remember the impact of his words on me. It was about 4pm of the Friday before the July 4th Independence Day weekend, and the office had already emptied out. I'd just been promoted to Associate from Analyst and was trying to earn extra brownie points by working through the holiday. But as he spoke, even though I was sitting at my desk, it felt like I was caught in a hurricane, and everything was spinning all around me. I grabbed the edge of my seat to steady myself as his words sank in.

Cancer? From where? How?

I was on a plane to Nigeria the following Sunday. With Ebere still in Germany at the time, and Enyinna having just relocated to South Africa, Uchechi, our youngest sister, was the only one with our mom in Nigeria, and even she was in school most of the time. It was no wonder our mother had been able to hide her condition for so long.

Getting to the house, one look at her and I knew she was in a bad way. She didn't seem surprised to see me. It was like she'd even been expecting it.

"That *yeye* Chike!" she said, referring to Dr. Kowano. "I knew he couldn't keep his mouth shut!"

I went on to confront her about her decision not to undergo further treatment, but she remained adamant. Apparently, she'd discovered the lump in her breast as far back as two years prior. It was a small one and the first few doctors she'd seen hadn't thought much of it. It wasn't until the lump got bigger that she decided to go to the Teaching Hospital, where she'd been diagnosed with

Stage Two cancer. She'd been told she didn't need chemotherapy, and quietly underwent a lumpectomy and a few sessions of radiotherapy, after which she'd been given the all-clear. Unfortunately, earlier that year, two years after being declared cancer free, another lump revealed this time Stage Four cancer, which had already metastasized to her bones. She had one session of chemotherapy, but had such a bad reaction to it, she decided to pull the plug. Which was why Dr. Kowano chose to take matters into his hands by calling me.

"*Nwa'm*, going through that chemotherapy treatment is hell on earth," my mother said to me. "I can not live my life that way. That treatment is a fast track to death, and I am not going to put myself through that again."

Nothing I said could change her mind; not me threatening, not when Ebere and Enyinna flew into town after I co-opted them to help convince her, not even when I threatened to quit my job back in America so I could sit with her in Lagos forever. My stubborn mother remained unmoved and instead chose to depend on some Naturopathic Medical Practitioners, who propagated natural herbs as treatment for cancer. Even though she continued to steadily decline, I couldn't remain in Nigeria forever, and had to return to work after over a month away, as did Ebere and Enyinna. Alas, the natural herbs did not work, and she succumbed to her cancer a day after her birthday in November of that same year. As we buried her, I hated myself for not being more persistent. I hated myself for not forcing her to undergo the necessary treatment. As a matter of fact, we all did, my siblings and I. In different ways, we blamed ourselves for our mother's death. Thank God for Seth, whom I'd just started dating, and who held my hand through the healing process. If it weren't for him, I might have had a nervous breakdown.

Somehow, I got over it. The following year, just while I was still riding the wave of excitement from another promotion at work, I got an email from Uchechi, a seven-worded email.

*I found a lump in my breast.*

The first thing I did was to call her, and she confirmed that she'd found a small lump on the side of her breast the day before. Not wanting to repeat my mistake from the previous year, I flew to Nigeria the very next day. Ebere was newly divorced from her first husband and was also back home in Nigeria. We rallied around and took Uchechi to South Africa for better medical care. It was there she underwent chemotherapy. Having to watch my baby sister suffer through the horrible effects of the treatment was the hardest thing I ever had to do. Seeing her degenerate and in so much pain when I was too helpless to do anything about it, broke me.

After seven grueling weeks of intense treatment, we took her back to Nigeria. I returned to the States almost immediately and made it a point of duty to check on her daily.

Just before Christmas of that year, 2006, Uchechi started complaining of a persistent shoulder pain. After several trips to different doctors, she was told it was nothing to worry about and that it was likely nerve damage from the radiotherapy. She was sent for physiotherapy and given painkillers. I didn't take it too seriously, advising her to rest over the Christmas holidays, assuring her all would be well.

But the pain worsened in the New Year, and it got so bad that she was unable to cope in school. Even though she'd been desperately trying to catch up on the schoolwork she'd missed during her cancer treatment, the pain she was suffering soon became unbearable. That was when I started to worry. That was when I instructed Ebere to take her to see a better doctor. After routine examinations showed alarming abnormalities in her blood levels, she was diagnosed with pneumonia. With her history in mind, I organized for Ebere to take her back to South Africa for further medical attention. It was in South Africa that we were hit with the worst bombshell. Uchechi's cancer had returned and metastasized to her lungs. Within a few days, I had joined them in Johannesburg, but no sooner had I landed did her doctors realize the cancer was also in her liver. While we were discussing a logical mode of treatment, it was discovered to be in her brain as well, which was when the doctors advised us to opt for palliative care, as there was nothing they could do for her. Hearing that our baby sister had only weeks to live shattered us. We were devastated.

We pondered over where she would get the best palliative care; there in South Africa or back home in Nigeria. It was Enyinna who'd been able to shake off his own emotions and advised that we take her back to Nigeria, as it was 'more expensive for a corpse to be taken home than for her to fly on her own accord.' So, we took her back home.

On Sunday, April 8th, 2007, Easter Sunday, lying on her bed and surrounded by us - her siblings and her nurse - my beloved Uchechi died. Burying her was worse than burying our mother, and I cried myself ragged every single day, even after I'd returned to New York, cancer having done its worst for the second time in two years.

Which is why, siting in the diner, I know that a cancer diagnosis is as good as a death sentence for me.

I finally leave the diner just as it is about to close for the night. Driving home, it is like I am in a trance. I don't hear the music playing from the radio or even notice any other drivers on the road.

I can't have cancer. I just can't.

I get home to a very upset Seth, but after I make up a lie about getting held up in a meeting, he seems pacified and satisfied by my excuse. But that night, lying in bed with my back to him, my mind races all night, wondering what the outcome of my tests will be. Morning simply can't come soon enough.

By 6am, I am already showered, and before it's 7am, I am on my way to the clinic. Naomi is waiting for me, and I am soon ushered to see an older doctor, a silver haired man with a kind face. He performs a physical exam, and when I see a frown cross his face, I know I might be in trouble.

"Do you feel anything?" I ask.

"There's definitely a mass there, underneath the fatty tissue," he answers.

I am sent off for several scans, followed by a painful biopsy to remove fluid and breast tissue for testing, but I am gravely disappointed that none of my results will be ready soon, and that I will have to wait a few more days for the verdict.

I go through the rest of the week like a zombie, unable to focus on anything other than the possible outcome of the tests. As the week draws to an end, just as I am about to lose my mind, I finally get the phone call I have been waiting for.

"I'm sorry, Ezi. It's cancer," comes Naomi's sober voice. "All the tests confirmed it. But the good news is that we caught it in time. It's Stage Two. Thank God for last month's routine exams. If we'd waited for the tumor to manifest through a lump, it might have become Stage Four and much harder to treat. We also found a small mass in your other breast, but if we move quickly, we could beat this thing."

I want to cry and laugh out loud at the same time. I want to strangle her for daring to raise my hopes by telling me nothing but lies. We could beat what? The same cancer that killed my mother and sister? How do I tell her that, in my family, we don't come out on top when it comes to cancer? How do I tell her that, in my family, cancer wins every time?

I go straight home, not knowing what to do with myself. With Seth not home, I am happy for the peace and quiet, and choose to write in my blog, something I haven't done in a long time. Now that I am no longer paid to write, I only come on the blog whenever I feel like it.

And today, it is the only outlet I have to release all my pent anger and frustration.

*Bohemian Rhapsody (Queen) – April 05, 2017*

***Too late, my time has come***
***Sends shivers down my spine, body's aching all the time.***

I am struggling to write words of my own when droplets on my keyboard are an indicator that I am crying. But the more I wipe them off, the faster the tears rush down in torrents, and it doesn't take long before I am bawling my eyes out.

I have cancer. I'm going to die.

And there's nothing anyone can say or do about that.

# CHAPTER EIGHTEEN

## Sailing

SITTING IN NAOMI'S OFFICE the following day, it feels like I'm having an out of body experience as the words *lumpectomy, mastectomy, chemotherapy,* and *radiation* keep flying about. I look at her as she talks, my eyes as dead as I feel, not knowing what to make of what is going on.

Are we really seated in her office discussing cancer treatment? For me?

"Is that fine for you, Ezi?" Naomi asks.

"Huh?" I respond, jolted out of my reverie. From the distressed look on her face, whatever question she has asked is a serious one.

"Because of the size of the masses in both breasts, Dr. Cooper thinks it would be best to have a double mastectomy," she repeats kindly. "And I agree with him. It's best to get all the affected tissue out ASAP."

I nod, as what she says sinks in. A double mastectomy. Meaning I will lose my breasts. Both of them.

"Of course, you can always have reconstructive surgery," she continues, trying to make me feel better. "Get you a nice C or DD cup, ehn," she adds with a grin and wiggle of her eyebrows.

I don't even crack a smile.

"Of course, that will have to be after your treatment," she goes on. "We need to get you an appointment with an Oncologist immediately. The sooner we begin, the better."

I nod like a zombie. Oncologist. God knows my attachment to that word is anything but pleasant. I heard it more than enough times when Uchechi was ill. Now, I'm the one who must see one?

This can't be happening.

"But if you're thinking of having kids later on, you might want to consider freezing your eggs," Naomi says pensively. "We might have to start with that first. Meaning we really must make decisions right away."

"Can I…can I call you tomorrow, Naomi?" I ask. "I need a minute to think about all of this. I need time to process it and decide what to do."

Naomi nods and reaches for my hand. "Have you told your family? You need a good support system now more than ever."

I smile stiffly. Tell my family? How? Ebere fell to pieces when our mother and sister went through this. Or is it Enyinna, who spent the next years after Uchechi died battling the chronic alcohol addiction he only kicked a couple of years ago? I could never put my siblings through that again. Not after what we went through watching our parents and sister die within a few years of each other. I would never be so callous as to rope them into this journey with me, when we all know how it's going to end.

Getting home, Seth is already there and as I listen to him go on about his workday and how much he is looking forward to our move to Connecticut in the fall, I realize I do not want to go down this journey with him, either. It will not only not be unfair to him, but it will also be unfair to me. I don't want to spend my last days with a man I do not love.

That is when I finally own up to the bitter truth. I do not love Seth. Being with Dili showed me that whatever Seth and I have is not love. It probably never was. It doesn't even scratch the surface. It is a beautiful friendship at best, with fairly decent benefits. It would have been fine for a quiet and unexciting life, the kind we have now, and what we would have if we do get married. But now that I can literally count the end of my days, it would be a disservice to both of us to continue.

The truth is I would rather retreat somewhere to die alone. And there is only one place that comes to my mind to do that.

My favourite place on this earth.

So I listen to Seth talk, adding the perfunctory nod and smile to show some interest. When he reaches for me in bed that night, I lie that I am on my period. As soon as he is asleep, I reach for my laptop to see if the quaint cottage in Friday Harbor is available. It is, so I lease it for a full year. As I have every intention to at least give this disease my best fight, I search for hospitals in the area and pencil down a few to consider. By the time the sun rises, not only am I still awake, I have mapped out my entire plan. I will leave for Friday Harbor as soon as I can, sign up for every treatment possible, and, when my body finally fails, die lying on a hammock in a backyard facing the ocean.

I might not have chosen this disease, but I sure as heck am going to choose how I will succumb to it.

Naomi is surprised when I show her the list of clinics I am considering. "Washington State? You have family there?"

Not wanting to go through the trouble of convincing her why I think it's the perfect place for me to quietly fight this illness, I simply nod and smile. "Yeah."

"These two are good centers," she reluctantly concedes, pointing at the first two names on my list. "I could make some inquiries to find out which of them has better Oncologists." With a deep sigh, she looks at me, her exasperation evident. "But are you sure, Ezi? We have some of the best doctors in the country here. Are you sure you want to go all the way to Washington State?"

As she asks the question, I realize I have absolutely no doubt in my mind that it's what I want to do. What I *need* to do. My decision to move has been the only thing that has given me any form of comfort since my diagnosis, and I am more certain than ever that it's the only hope I have of, if not beating it, living decently for the remainder of my life.

That night, I decide to tell Seth, not about my cancer, but my decision to leave. I take him to the same restaurant we were meant to have dinner last week, and it is only when he arrives looking more dressed up than is normal for him that I realize coming there was a mistake and has probably sent all the wrong signals to him.

But it is what it is.

"I'm leaving, Seth," I say, right after our appetizers and before our entrée.

He looks at me, momentarily confused. "What do you mean 'leaving'?"

"I'm leaving Durham." And then I finally bring myself to look him in the eye. "And I'm leaving you. It's over."

He stares back at me, stunned. "Is this some kind of joke, Ezi? We're about to start a whole new chapter of our lives! We have only a few weeks before we move to Connecticut…"

I shake my head. "I won't be going to Connecticut, Seth. I'm so sorry."

He shakes his head and laughs sadly. "This can't be happening. I thought you brought me here because you're finally ready to accept this." He brings out the black velvet box with the engagement ring he has been carrying about for months. "Ezi, is it anything I did or said? I promise I'll change. Whatever it is, I'll change."

"It's not you, Seth. It's me," I say, hating myself for using the cliché phrase. "I have a lot I'm dealing with, and I need to be alone now."

"Are you going back to Manhattan? To Goldman? To your ex?" he asks.

"No," I answer. "I need somewhere to clear my head and Manhattan isn't where I can do that. I'm going to my favourite place in the world. Somewhere quiet and peaceful. And I'm going alone."

"I know this is my punishment for leaving you and coming here," Seth says after a while. "I know you never did forgive me for it. No matter what you say to the contrary, I know that's the real reason."

I don't have the energy to argue with him. If that's what he chooses to believe, I've decided to let him.

"What about your program? Aren't you going to at least finish it? You only have a few weeks left," he asks.

"I'll finish it some other time," I answer, knowing I can't afford to hang around for the extra few weeks it will take to complete it. From the look of things, with the timer on my life already ticking, it's unlikely I'll be alive to even need it.

We eat the rest of our meal in silence and drive home in silence. That night, rather than sleep in our bedroom, he opts to sleep on the couch. The next morning, as soon as he has left for school, I leave immediately. I pack my things, call a cab, pass through the hospital to confirm Naomi will send my medical records as soon as I decide on a doctor, and head straight to the airport. I am on the 9pm flight out of Durham and land in Seattle a little after 5am the following morning. It is another five-hour drive to Friday Harbor, and I do not alight from the taxi until about 11am later that morning.

But standing there before the quaint building, the sound of the ocean as a backdrop, I know I have made the right decision. The Caretaker is there to hand me the keys to the house and, walking in, I am relieved to see that it looks even better than I remember it; welcoming, serene, tranquil. This is truly the best place for me.

I spend the next few days settling in and getting re-acquainted with the town. But it is more to avoid making a trip to any of the clinics I identified. It isn't until Naomi sends a frantic message inquiring about my progress that I accept I cannot hide from it much longer. I cannot hide from the fact that I am not in this lovely town on vacation…but to get treatment for my illness.

The following Tuesday, almost a full week after I my arrival, I see a doctor, Dr. Pickens. He reviews my test results from Durham, and the first thing I notice as he scribbles are the underlined words on the notes on his desk – *Grade Three*. I immediately freak out, wondering what this means especially as I was told my cancer is Stage Two. He calmly tells me not to panic, and explains that, yes, the cancer is Stage Two, but it is also Grade Three, meaning more aggressive.

He goes on to confirm I will need a double mastectomy, plus the possible removal of some lymph nodes, which will be accompanied by chemo and radiotherapy. But unlike what I was told in Durham, the mastectomy will be after I have undergone chemotherapy, not before.

"Doesn't it make more sense to take out the breasts before treatment?" I counter.

"That's what happens in some cases," he answers patiently. "But your tumours are a significant size and there's also the high chance that your lymph nodes are already involved. Shrinking them before the surgery will give us a better result."

As I let that sink in, he drops another bombshell by telling me the breast reconstruction will not happen the same time as the mastectomy, but later, meaning I have at least two major surgeries in my future, not to mention any procedure I'll need to remove my lymph nodes.

We proceed to talk about my desire to freeze my eggs, and he refers to me a fertility specialist, Dr. Mendes. I see her the following Thursday and we discuss all my options. Because of my age and the urgency of treatment, she places me on a short protocol, which will see me taking daily injections to stimulate egg production from day three of my next cycle. With my current cycle ending, I am back at her office a little over a week later, thus starting a daily routine of self-injections.

On any given day, this act alone would have tipped me into full-on depression. As if my looming cancer treatment is not enough, I have to contend with this invasive act of retrieving eggs from my body. But every night as I sit on my front porch, with the soothing sight, smell, and sound of the ocean, the injections don't seem quite so bad after all. A few times, I do wonder why I am even bothering. I do wonder why I am saving my eggs when the odds are high that I will not be alive to use them. But regardless, I soldier on, determined to see it to a logical end. Even if I don't get to use the eggs before I die, I could always donate them to another couple, meaning there is the slimmest of chances that I could leave behind offspring after I go.

After four weeks of injections and monitoring, my eggs are collected. In the days following, I am allowed to recover before returning to my doctor, and I am faced with the cruel reminder that the hardest part of this journey still lies ahead.

Returning to Dr. Pickens' office a few days later, we have a more detailed discussion of my treatment plan, and I am scheduled for a CT scan the next day, followed by a bone scan. The next day, I am at the hospital, bright and early, feeling a lot less cheerful than I have forced myself appear. I am made to drink a large glass of white liquid, lie on a bed for a baseline scan, and then have a line fitted for them to pass in their dye. Even though I'd been warned, the rush of warmth through my body as the dye courses through is so intense and overwhelming and, for the first time since I started my treatment, hot tears roll down my face as it dawns on me that, intense though this may be, it is nothing compared to what lies ahead.

I am back in the hospital two days later for my bone scan, which, thankfully, is not as traumatic as the previous one. My results later that week show that the cancer has not spread to my lymph nodes or bones. It is a relief to me as, considering what happened with my mom and sister, I'd been expecting it to have already spread. But I know better than to get carried away. After all, Uchechi's cancer didn't metastasize to her organs until after the chemotherapy and radiation she endured. So there's a high likelihood that it will still happen to me later.

Dr. Pickens explains that I will have six cycles of chemotherapy, followed by the mastectomy and then radiotherapy. He books me in to see an Oncologist, Dr. Chambers, and we schedule a date for my chemotherapy to start.

Goodness. Chemotherapy. For me? It feels so surreal.

Shortly before my start date, I have a minor procedure to insert a porta-cath, which will make the administration of the chemo drugs easier. Though not a painful procedure, it isn't the most pleasant either.

"Don't you have someone to take you home?" Dr. Chambers asks, as he sees me struggle to the door on my own.

I smile and shake my head. "I came here alone."

A frown creases his forehead. "But you have someone to take care of you when you start your treatment, don't you?"

Not wanting to attract any undue sympathy, I nod and answer. "Yes, I do." But as I walk out of the building, I have a large lump in my throat and my heart aches over the fact that I am truly doing this alone. I thought I was strong enough, but now that it is staring me stark in the face, the loneliness and despondence I feel breaks my heart.

That night, I sit on my porch, staring at boats sailing in the horizon. For the first time in weeks, I log into my website and start writing.

***Sailing (Christopher Cross) – May 30, 2017***

*Life is full of paradoxes, constant contradictions.*

*Saving money by spending it. Knowing one thing but knowing nothing. A jumbo shrimp. A wise fool. Being cruel to be kind.*

*As I sit here, staring out at the most beautiful ocean, imagining myself on one of the gorgeous and colourful boats sailing by, I am in, without a doubt, the most beautiful place in the world.*

*But also facing the ugliest experience of my life.*

I stop writing as my tears threaten to choke me. No. I can't break down. I've come too far to break down now. I'll go through the chemo. I'll go through it alone. And I'll either come out stronger…or dead.

Both outcomes I am prepared for.

I hope.

# CHAPTER NINETEEN

## One Last Breath

I AM GIVEN A SMALL BREAK before starting chemotherapy, and I savour every moment of it, spending all my time thinking and meditating…and preparing myself for what lies ahead. Several times, I wake up in the middle of the night, sweat pouring from my body as I vividly remember Uchechi's chemotherapy ordeal, the visuals so clear, it feels like we are back with her in South Africa all over again.

Unable to stop myself, I call Ebere to ask questions about what I might have forgotten about our sister's treatment.

"Before Uchechi started chemotherapy, were her lymph nodes already affected?" I ask casually.

"Which *kin* question are you asking me after all these years, *biko*?" she retorts. "Anyway, no they weren't. I'm surprised you've forgotten, especially considering how glad we were when her doctor told us."

I do remember. I'd only hoped I wasn't remembering correctly. Uchechi was also told her lymph nodes were clean, but her cancer had metastasized aggressively anyway. I guess this means I shouldn't be screaming from the rafters just because mine hasn't spread yet. Just because it hasn't done so now doesn't mean it won't eventually.

It's high time I accept that, eventually, this cancer is going to kill me. Whether I like it or not.

"Have you considered scalp hypothermia?" Dr. Chambers asks. "You have such lovely hair and I'd be sad for you to lose it."

My hands reach for my afro, which I haven't even been taking great care of. I remember Uchechi's hair falling off, starting the morning several clumps detached from her scalp as she showered. I remember how broken we all were by that experience and how it had brought to reality the cancer beast. If anyone had doubted Uchechi's diagnosis before then, losing her lustrous hair had been the clincher.

I decide to take Dr. Chambers advise and try the cooling cap therapy, to preserve my hair. On the day of my first session, I take painkillers as Dr. Google suggests I do, and when the cap is strapped to my head, I brace myself for the 'five to ten minutes only' of intense pain. Except the pain lasts longer than 'five to ten minutes', but for the entire thirty-minute duration. And the cold feels a whole lot worse than 'taking ice-cream on a very hot day'. Rather, it is nothing but unpleasant, and I am in the worst agony of my life as the intense cold attacks every atom of my brain. It is the most debilitating experience ever, and as I leave the clinic, I know I will not be returning.

That night, I take matters into my own hands.

With a pair of clippers from a drug store, standing in my bathroom, I shave off my hair. I know I will never have the motivation to return for another cold cap session, but I also know I can't allow myself suffer the heartbreak of watching my hair fall out. I am determined to retain control of as much of this journey as I can.

When I am done shaving my hair, I stand there, staring at my bald reflection in the mirror, and for the first time since all this started, I see the Ezi everyone probably does; the one who has cancer. I run my hand across my neck and see for the first time how frail I look. My clavicles are more pronounced, and my t-shirt is already hanging loose on my petite frame. It looks like I have lost at least twenty pounds…and I haven't even started treatment yet.

The night before my first chemotherapy session, I sleep well, which is surprising, considering all my anxiety. In the morning, I have enough of an appetite to eat a hearty breakfast of oatmeal and fruit, following which I even go for a run.

Getting to the hospital, one look at me and a deep frown forms on Dr. Chambers' face. I don't know if it's my bald head or the fact that I am, once again, unaccompanied. Luckily, he dwells on neither and instead introduces me to my nurse, a pleasant looking Asian woman called Penny. As today is the first treatment cycle, everything is doubled for the loading doses, as we don't really know how my body is going to react. Will it hurt when the infusion is connected to my porta cath? Will I get any, all, or none of the possible reactions to the drugs? It's anybody's guess, really.

Penny is very cheerful and chatty, maybe a little too chatty. She settles me into a cozy small room with walls painted a soothing aqua colour. She points out the location of the toilet, which she is sure I'll soon need, considering the amount of fluid to be pumped into my body. She checks my blood pressure and temperature, talks me through the process, and even asks if I would like to listen to any particular type of music. For someone whom music plays a big life role, I surprise myself by answering with an indifferent shrug. Lying on the reclined chair, music is the last thing on my mind, and when a Yanni CD starts playing, I tune off.

Finally, I am hooked up for the infusion. Penny draws some liquid and blood from my port, to make sure everything is working, before connecting a bag of saline.

"So, this is how the process goes, Ezeeoma," she says, and I am amused by her mispronunciation of my name. "There'll first of all be a saline flush, then comes the Herceptin, then another saline flush, then the Pertuzumab, then another saline flush, the Docetaxel, and a final saline flush."

I nod in understanding, having already heard this a thousand times from Dr. Chambers.

During the first saline flush, Penny offers me a cup of tea and I accept, partly in amazement. As I lie there, sipping tea while having the flush, I am amazed by how far things have come in the decade since Uchechi had her treatment. For the life of me, I don't recall her being this relaxed during any of her sessions.

After the saline, Penny connects the Herceptin.

"Are you sure you don't have someone who can accompany you next time?" she asks. "This can be a very dull procedure."

I smile politely and shake my head. "It's fine. I'll nap if I get too bored."

As the drug passes through, I start to feel really cold. Not even when Penny adjusts the room temperature does this make a difference. There we are, in the middle of summer, and I am shivering like I'm naked in Antarctica. Penny takes my temperature and sees it has fallen dramatically.

"It's probably because the drugs are refrigerated for storage," Penny says, cranking up the heat and wrapping me in a thick blanket.

I don't know if it's the cold, but I suddenly start to feel off. Not sick or anything like that, but just not quite right. I realize that the drugs are finally starting to take effect in my body, and my heart races in fear at the very thought. The infusion is slowed further, and I gradually start to warm up, although not enough to throw off the blankets. At one stage, I actually do fall asleep very briefly, awakening when Penny puts in the saline flush.

The second and third infusions last for almost three hours but go considerably well. Overall, the whole process takes about five hours, and by the time it's over, I still feel very much like myself.

Once all the infusions have gone through, Penny checks me again and gives me my Filgrastim injection with an ice pack. The chemo will, no doubt, hammer my white blood cell count, so the Filgrastim is to stimulate my body to produce more white blood cells. I'll have to administer it myself, but thanks to my experience with the egg freezing, self-injections are no longer novel or scary to me.

"You're really a strong one!" Penny remarks, as I tie my headscarf and carry my bag. "Your first cycle of chemo and you look like you just went to the mall."

"I feel perfect," I remark, excited. "In fact, I think I'm going to go for a run as soon as I get home. Or maybe even a swim."

"Don't push it, though," Penny reprimands. "You need to rest. Sometimes, these drugs come with a delayed reaction."

I nod, convinced there will be no such delayed reaction for me, not with how fantastic I'm feeling.

"Your next cycle is in exactly a fortnight, on the 28th," she goes on. "And try to come with someone next time, okay? You might not be as strong then."

I am smiling smugly to myself. If I have come this far alone, why will I need anyone next time?

I call for an Uber, and when I get home, I make myself a bowl of pot noodles and settle in my sofa to binge on Netflix. At some point, I fall asleep.

The nausea jolts me awake.

I don't have enough time to rush to the bathroom before I throw up everything I have eaten, and then more, all over my living room floor. So weakened am I by the violent bout, I am only able to crawl away from where my vomit lies, but I move only a few inches before throwing up again. At this point, I am unable to move any further, and just collapse right there on my vomit, adding more to it as night rolls by. When the sun rises the next morning, I awake still lying in my vomit, and as I peel myself from the floor, I am weeping. Even though I have no food at all in my system, I manage to get out a mop and go on to clean the mess I have made. Because I am so weak, it takes thrice the time it ordinarily would, but I am determined not allow myself wallow in the stew of my vomit. After furiously scrubbing and mopping the hardwood floor, I get into the shower and furiously attack my entire body, desperate to rid myself of the pungent smell. I am barely able to throw on a t-shirt and a pair of shorts before I crawl into bed with a big bowl by my side. A part of me is ravenous and desperately wants to eat, but a bigger part of me is appalled by the mere thought of food. So I lie there, drifting in and out of sleep, the sleep punctuated by several wet and dry heaves into the bowl beside me. By the end of the day, I am weakened not just by hunger, but from having expunged everything in my body. The next day, I manage to drag myself to the kitchen to nibble on some dry bread, but no sooner have I eaten a few slices do I find myself rushing for the toilet bowl to throw up. In the end, I give up and just lie on my bed, waiting for hunger to kill me before the chemotherapy can. It isn't until several days later that I start to feel human again.

And I realize I have underestimated this process.

By the time my next chemotherapy session comes around, it is with fear and trepidation that I make my way back to the clinic. I am tempted to forgo the whole process and just wait for the cancer to kill me, but I eventually decide to just take the bull by the horns and go anyway.

From the sympathetic look on Penny's face, I know I must look as bad as I feel.

"You had a rough time?" she asks.

I shrug, still trying to be brave. "Just a few days when I couldn't stomach food. But I'm fine now."

She nods in understanding, more understanding than I give her credit for, before she proceeds to hook up my line and start the process all over again. Maybe because I now know what to expect, the minute the fluid hits my bloodstream, I start to have something of an anxiety attack. My heart races and I am short of breath. I want to throw a stone at the speaker softly playing Michael Bolton's greatest hits. I want this over. I want it all to be over now.

The five-hour session seems like ten this time, and the nausea doesn't even wait for me to get home before it begins. Sitting in the Uber on the way home, my head is spinning, and I am praying I don't throw up all over the back seat. Thankfully, I manage to restrain myself till I get home, and as I rush to the toilet, I can feel the indications of an extremely bad stomach. I remain in the toilet for the rest of the day, with violent diarrhea and even more violent vomiting. I am afraid to leave the toilet, for fear that I will mess up the rest of my house. When I am too tired to sit on the toilet seat for much longer, I slide down to the floor, where I remain as day turns to night.

It is another rough few days, and this time I feel even worse than I did after my first treatment round. I have a burning sensation in my fingers and toes, and painful sores have formed in my mouth. When I finally gather the strength for a shower, I catch my reflection in the mirror and cannot recognize the painfully thin woman looking back at me.

"Uchechi…" I call out at the reflection, because it looks just like her at the tail end of her life.

That is when I know that I am going to die just like she did.

That night, I manage a meal and sit on my porch. I know I am in the last lap of my life. I know there is no way I can survive four more cycles of chemotherapy, let alone radiation. I know I am only inches away from being six feet under…from my very last breath.

Maybe I shouldn't bother with any more treatment. Maybe I should just lie here on my front porch and wait for death to come and get me.

Because come and get me, it will.

I turn forty the day before my third chemo cycle. Sitting on my living room sofa, I can't help but feel saddened about where life has brought me on this landmark occasion. As a child, I'd envisioned myself almost a grandmother at the age of forty. A few years ago, I'd seen myself as married, at the very least. A few months ago, I would have been content to just be in good health.

But here I am, forty years old and none of these.

I allow the day to go by without fanfare. I just want it to end quickly. Except that it's ending will signal yet another day of chemotherapy.

It feels like being caught between the devil and the deep blue sea.

I make no pretenses as I leave for my chemo the next day. I throw on an old t-shirt and tie a scarf loosely on my head. I make no effort to hide my sunken eyes and drawn face. This is what two cycles of chemotherapy have done to me.

This cycle feels even worse than the earlier two, and as I ride back home in my Uber, I decide it will be my last session. I now understand why my mother vehemently refused more treatment. She was right about it being hell on earth. No, I'd rather live decently…until I don't. Not like Uchechi who suffered so much, only to suffer even more when death came calling.

Getting out of the cab, I see someone by my gate holding a bouquet of roses. As my eyes focus, I stop dead in my tracks.

Dili?

He looks at me, clearly not sure I am the same person. "Ezioma?" he calls out.

"What do you want?" I demand, angry he is seeing me in this state, bedraggled and haggard. "How did you find me here?"

"I went to Durham to surprise you for your fortieth birthday," he says, his eyes probing deeper into mine as his concern rises. "I've spent the last year doing nothing but think about you and I've decided to fight for what's mine. You're still my wife, Ezioma. We're not divorced yet."

I step back as he makes to come closer, and I look away from him, unable to make eye contact, unwilling for him to get an even closer view of me looking the way I do.

"Ezi, are you okay?" he asks, reaching for me.

"And how did you locate me here?" I retort, moving even further out of his grip.

"I saw Seth. He told me you'd left," he answers. "He said something about you going to your 'favourite place in the world'. I remembered you'd told me about a little cottage on Rosler Road in Friday Harbor. Remember? When we were in the Maldives? So I got on a plane here. I was worried I wouldn't be able to find the exact cottage, but, somehow, this happens to be the only leased property on the street."

"You need to leave. Now!" I say, my voice quivering as I start walking to my door extra fast. "I don't need you or anyone here. I'm not your wife. You need to go back to your life in Manhattan."

"Ezioma, what's going on?" he demands, his voice high in his panic. "You don't look like yourself."

"Just go away!" I yell, my back to him, as I fumble to open my door, my hands quivering. "Please, just go!"

"I'm not going till you tell me what's going!" he exclaims, and from the quiver in his voice, I know he is on the verge of tears. And who can blame him. I reckon he didn't expect to see me bald and weighing less than a hundred pounds.

I don't know if it's the feel of his hand on my shoulder, or the expected reaction from my chemo session, but my head starts to spin.

As I lose consciousness, I hear him shout in panic as he catches me as I fall. I hear him kick my door open, place me on the couch and dial 911.

And everything goes completely blank.

# CHAPTER TWENTY

## Love Is Stronger Than Pride

I REGAIN CONSCIOUSNESS in what I realize is a hospital bed, but I am too sedated to open my eyes. I can hear Dili's prayers as he sits beside my bed, and the doctors and nurses as they hover around intermittently. I am aware when one of the doctors informs Dili that their tests have shown I am undergoing chemotherapy, and I hear Dili's anguished cry as he repeats the dreaded word.

"Cancer?" he exclaims, his voice heavy with pain.

"She's had a few cycles of chemotherapy, from what we see," the doctor answers. "We're checking all the clinics around to try to find where she's being treated."

I am aware as Dili returns to my side, this time tearful. I am aware as he holds my hand, drenching it with his tears. I am aware when they finally identify my clinic and when Dr. Chambers walks into my room. I am aware of all of it. But my eyes remain closed, even when the sedatives have worn off.

I am aware as Dili engages Dr. Chambers in conversation, asking him questions about my treatment.

"I'm sorry, but I can't discuss a patient's confidential treatment with you," Dr. Chambers answers him warily.

"I'm her husband," is Dili's response. "I had no idea she was all the way across the country, let alone fighting…" his voice breaks, and I know he is probably crying again. "Let alone fighting cancer."

"Her husband?" Dr. Chambers exclaims, clearly surprised. "She has a husband and she's been going through all this by herself? I came so I could make arrangements to move her to a hospice from here. She needs care and can't go through this kind of treatment on her own."

"Well, there's no need to move her to any hospice," Dili answers, his voice firm. "I'm here now, and I'll take care of her."

At this point, I am tempted to open my eyes. Dili wants to take care of me? Dili wants to leave his life in New York to take care of me all the way here in Washington State?

Later that evening, I do open my eyes. Dili sits up the moment he notices and grabs my hand again. "Ezi. Thank God you're awake."

"I heard you telling my doctor you'll take care of me," I struggle to say, even though my mouth feels parched and my throat aches. "You didn't have to lie to him."

"I didn't lie to him, Ezi," he answers, leaning closer to me. "I'm your husband and I'm not leaving your side."

"What about your life in New York? You're going to leave your job and everything else to babysit me here?" I ask incredulously.

"None of those things matter, Ezioma," he says firmly. "You are more important than anything!"

And that is when I recognize it for what it is.

Guilt.

It isn't love that has moved Dili to give up everything to take care of me. It is guilt over the way he treated me. But rather than confront him about it, I close my eyes again. If he feels the need to put himself through this kind of penance, let him. I won't be hanging around too long anyway.

The next day, I am discharged from hospital and Dr. Chambers' clinic sends Dili a long list of instructions for my care. I am wheeled from the hospital straight to a waiting taxi, and when we get to my house, Dili carries me out of the car. I make no argument and instead rest my head on his chest, enjoying every moment of the pampering. He carries me like a baby to my bedroom and settles me in bed like delicate cargo.

As I drift in and out of sleep, I hear him take what is probably his first shower since he arrived Friday Harbor, and from the slightest opening of my eyes, I see him take position on the sofa in my bedroom.

"I have a spare room," I mutter. "You don't have to inconvenience yourself by sleeping on the couch."

"I'm not letting you out of my sight, Ezioma," he answers. "Not again. Look what happened the last time I did. I shouldn't have let you go so easily after seeing you in Chicago."

"Oh, you think I wouldn't have gotten cancer if you hadn't 'let me go'?" I ask sarcastically.

"At least I would have been here with you from the beginning," he answers.

He kills the lights, and we lie silently in the dark for a while.

"Why did you come all the way here without telling anyone?" he asks, breaking the silence. "Do Ebere and Enyinna know?"

"No, they don't, and I want to keep it that way," I answer tersely. "As for why I came here, isn't it obvious? I want to die in the place I love the most in the world."

"Don't you dare talk like that, Ezi," he says, sitting up. "I spoke at length with your Oncologist, and he seems confident that your treatment will be successful."

I smile to myself in the darkness. Of course, he would say that. Uchechi's doctors also sang us the same tune; how she was responding so well to treatment and how they were confident she would pull through.

Bla, bla, bla.

But she died. Uchechi died the same way I, too, am going to die. I choose to save my energy and not argue with Dili on the subject. He can delude himself if he likes. I know better.

"I think you should call your siblings. They don't deserve to be in the dark," he says, after a few minutes of silence.

"You are in no position to decide that!" I snap. "You weren't there when I had to piece them back together after we lost not only Mom, but Uchechi, too. Hearing this will break them. I know how long it took us to get Enyinna's alcohol problem under control. This is the last thing either of them needs."

I know he doesn't agree with me, but he says nothing more on the topic.

"I've decided to discontinue my treatment," I say. "The chemotherapy is killing me, and I can no longer put my body through it. Let me just die in peace."

"But you're already halfway through your chemo!" Dili exclaims. "Your doctor says you have only three more sessions to go."

"And what about the radiotherapy that comes after that?" I snap. "And the mastectomy? Did he tell you that I'm going to lose both my breasts? Did he?"

That is when Dili rises from the couch and comes to lie beside me on the bed. As he pulls me closer to himself, I have no strength to fight him. I am comforted by the familiar feel of his body. My eyes close as I bask in his presence once again.

My Okwudili. The love of my life.

"We'll get through this, Ezi," he says. "No matter how long and difficult the journey ahead may be, we'll get through it together. I'm not going anywhere."

And he makes good on his promise.

In the days leading to my next chemo session, Dili treats me like a queen. He awakens me to breakfast in bed, sees to it that I take my medication, carries me to the bathroom where he bathes me himself, and carries me back to bed where he brings me the rest of my meals. During the day, sometimes he carries me to the porch, where we have our meals and watch sailboats go by. Other times, he makes me watch mundane, light-hearted programs on Netflix.

"When did you start watching foolish programs like this, Okwudili?" I tease him, as we binge on *RuPaul's Drag Race*.

"It's a guilty pleasure, I won't lie," he laughs back. "I discovered it one day I was home alone, feeling lonely, and I got addicted."

I am happy for this addiction, as the lighthearted show makes me forget my own problems, if only for a little while.

On another occasion, as we are sitting on the front porch, I am moved to ask him about his job. "Did you quit to be here with me?"

"I'd already quit before coming here," he answers. "I got a great offer from Bain & Co."

I raise my brow. "How great?"

"Treble my former salary great," he answers. "I've called to let them know I have a personal emergency to take care of. They've promised that if the job is still open when we return to New York, it's mine."

"But what if it's not?"

He shrugs. "Then another one will come. That's secondary. *You* are my primary concern."

"What about your folks back home?" I ask. "Don't you send money to your mom monthly?"

He smiles. "I have enough in reserve to continue doing that, Ezi. I wasn't spending everything I earned. Don't forget the lecture you gave me about saving my money. I reckon it's why you've been able to sequester yourself here in Washington without a job. Decent savings."

I can't help the smile that forms on my lips. "I'm glad I taught you well."

"When we get back to New York, you're going to move in with me," he says, as we lie in bed on another occasion. "I bought this nice terrace house in Brooklyn. It's much bigger and more appropriate for us to raise a family."

I tense upon hearing this, for a number of reasons. I am tempted to ask if he bought that house with Onyeka, but now that she has left him, he has to settle for sloppy seconds. Even more so, I am tempted to ask him why he is so confident he will not return to New York with my ashes in an urn. But instead, I remain silent and listen to all his daydreams about what we will do when we are back in New York, and how he'll make sure I don't miss Manhattan at all.

All too soon, the day of my next chemo session arrives. I reluctantly agree to go, and Dili ensures I wear comfortable, loose clothing. He also applies a numbing cream to the area of my port, and packs a bag full of popsicles and minty sweets.

"I read that it's good to keep your mouth cool, to prevent mouth sores. The mints are to get rid of the aftertaste of the meds," he explains.

I can't help but smile. "Someone has been doing their research."

"I want to make this less unpleasant for you," he answers.

It is a quiet ride to the clinic, and as we walk inside, I am enveloped with the dread that is now familiar for me anytime I am there, because I know I will not leave in the same condition I have entered.

Penny is pleased to see me with company this time, and the smile on her face when Dili introduces himself as my husband almost splits her face in half. But as we get down to business, my hands quiver as she hooks me up to the line through which the meds will pass, knowing fully well the devastating effect they will have on me afterwards.

"So, what do you want to listen to? I read that listening to music during chemo helps and, knowing you, I'm sure you come with a full playlist every time," Dili teases.

"She refuses to," Penny remarks. "She just listens to whatever garbage that's already playing."

Dili looks momentarily surprised, before he pulls out his phone and small speakers. Obviously, he came prepared.

"Okay, I'm your personal DJ today," he says, trying to make light of things. "Name a song, any song."

I shut my eyes, unwilling to be drawn into the foolery of pretending my chemo session is some sort of disco session, and not the incredibly unpleasant experience it is. "I don't want to listen to anything, Okwudili."

"Just name a year, any year, and I'll pull up something you like," he persists.

I peer at him from my half-closed eyes. "1989."

He scrolls through his phone, and I can't help but smile when De La Soul's *Me, Myself and I* starts playing. I have a very vivid picture in my head of a twelve-year-old Okwudili rapping along to the song at his birthday party.

*"Mirror, mirror on the wall, tell me, mirror, what is wrong? Can it be my de la clothes or is it just my de la song?"* he raps along, and I giggle. From the side of my eye, I can see Penny beaming like a proud mom.

"What next?" Dili asks. "Name another year."

"1998," I answer, wanting to push the envelope further, considering we weren't in each other's lives at this point.

"Easy!" he says, as Busta Rhymes *Dangerous* comes on.

I squeal in delight, remembering some of the fun times I had with with other Nigerian undergrads at parties back in UPenn.

"Even if you were living in Timbuktu, I don't think there's anyone on the planet who didn't rock this song back then!" Dili beams.

As I bob my head to the music, I realize that I am less aware of the fluids being passed into my body. The next few hours roll by the same way, with Dili serenading me to Patra's version of *Pull Up to The Bumper* from 1995, D'Banj's *OliverTwist* from 2012, Rufus & Chaka Khan's *Ain't Nobody* from 1983, Drake's *Hold on We're Going Home* from 2013, and Beyonce's entire *Lemonade* album from 2016. For the first time since I started treatment, the session goes by rocket fast and is soon over. Yes, there are times it feels uncomfortable, but it is nothing as bad as what I experienced the last three times.

I leave the clinic in high spirits, and Dili and I still banter about music all through the ride back to the cottage. But when we're home, the nausea shows that it is no respecter of a little bit of musical relief. Without any warning, I heave and throw up violently the minute he lays me on the bed. I throw up not only all over myself and my sheets, but his clothes as well. Without flinching, he lifts me and carries me to the bathroom to clean up. He is midway through it when the diarrhea starts. I don't know if it is the intensity of both the vomiting and diarrhea, or just the shame of it all, but I am soon barely conscious. All I do know is that the vomiting and diarrhea do not abate until later the following day, and that Dili not only cleans me up each time but ensures that I stay hydrated. And when the nausea gives way to the worst and most painful pain in my fingers and toes, he spends all night massaging them, wiping my tears as I cry in anguish.

Dili is truly everything I could have ever hoped for and more, and there are a few times I am tempted to hope against hope that this is all for real, that he is here with me because he loves me. But all it takes is for me to catch a glimpse of myself in the mirror to realize I am only fooling myself. I weigh about ninety pounds now and look like one of those pictures of malnourished children from war torn countries. My bald head sits atop my skinny frame like a drum balanced on a stick, and I know that attraction is the last thing he must feel towards me.

No…what he feels is pity. Nothing but pity.

But at this stage of my life, I am ready to take it that way. If I'd been alone for this fourth chemo session, I probably would not have survived the aftermath. Ironic, because I know I won't survive the experience, period. Dili or no Dili.

After a while, I start to feel better, and we have a few uneventful days before it is time for my next chemo cycle. Instead of playing music, Dili surprises me by having us watch one of our favourite movies as kids, *The Last Dragon*.

"My goodness! I haven't seen this film in almost thirty years!" I exclaim. "We watched this every time we came to your house to visit."

"It was my favourite movie, especially as I looked so much like Leroy!" he says, with a wiggle of his brow.

"You wish!" I giggle, thinking how much better than the lead actor he still looks.

As we watch it, we recite some of the movie's iconic lines, bringing back so many wonderful memories.

*"Who's the Master?!" "Sho'Nuff!" "I AM the Shogun of Harlem!" "Don't hurt that face, baby! Don't hurt that face!"*

By the end of the movie, we are laughing so hard, I don't even notice when the session finally ends. Upon getting home, this time we are both prepared for the usual aftermath, and he tackles my vomiting and diarrhea like a champ, making sure I have bowls and a bedpan handy.

About a week later, when the aftermath has subsided, as we lie in bed, I am surprised when he says to me. "I read all your old articles with the *Manhattan Buzz*. Every one of them, from your first to…to the ones when we were still together."

I am not sure how I feel about that. "I hope you weren't too scandalized by all the salacious stuff!" I say, trying to make light of it.

"Not at all. As a matter of fact, I was humbled. I never knew how much you loved me, Ezi. Reading those articles opened my eyes," he says. "I truly hope there is still a little bit of that love left, and that I haven't sabotaged it all with the horrible mistake I made by leaving you for Onyeka."

I tense and grit my teeth. I want so badly to tell him I feel absolutely nothing for him. That it all died the moment I left Manhattan for Durham. But deep in my heart, I know I love him just as much as I ever did then. If not even more.

So, I say nothing.

"I also follow your blog, but you don't update it as frequently as you did your column," he continues.

"Gee…I wonder why."

"To be honest, it was one of your last posts that gave me the confidence to come looking for you. The one where you wrote about being happy, but sad. I figured you were having issues with Seth, so I got on a plane. It also helped that it coincided with your fortieth birthday, so I had more of an excuse to come find you."

I remain silent, not knowing what to say in response.

"I love you, Ezioma. You are the love of my life, and I will spend the rest of my days proving that to you," are his last words before he falls asleep.

I remain awake as he sleeps, and after about an hour, I pull myself out of his embrace and get out of the bed. Sitting on my porch, can't deny the strength of my feelings for him, even though I that killing them would be best for me…best for both of us.

I don't have the strength to write anymore. Instead, I close my eyes, wondering how I am going to insulate my heart from Okwudili Dike. I know that, contrary to what he thinks, he is not in love with me. He only feels indebted. And that can only last for so long.

But then I realize I don't have to worry myself about it. In a matter of months, maybe even weeks, I will be dead. The cancer will kill me. And it will put an end to all of this.

In the meantime, I am going to continue enjoying him; his presence, his attention, his 'love'. If these will form my last memories on earth, then it's not such a bad deal.

I guess.

# CHAPTER TWENTY-ONE

## Gravity

MY RECOVERY AFTER this fifth session proves more difficult than previous ones. Even after the nausea abates, the pain persists, and I am so weak I can't even get out of bed. I rely on Dili for everything. He carries me from the bed to the toilet. He bathes me. He feeds me. He does everything for me. And not once does he look angry or irritated about it. Instead, he is full of endearing words. He makes sure I don't slip into my typical melancholic mood by always cracking jokes or playing nostalgic music he knows I like. Even in my sad and sorry state, it is impossible for me to be depressed, not even when I try my hardest to.

For my sixth and final chemo session, I see the concern in Penny's eyes as Dili carries me into the room. I've never had to be carried in before, and it is evidence of the fact that I am fast deteriorating. Dili's music choice that day is less nostalgic and more romantic, as if he, too, is desperate to prove his love to me before I go away for good. That day, his playlist consists of songs from Stevie Wonder, Luther Vandross, John Legend, and Brian McKnight, with him singing along to every one of them.

"No piano to back you up this time?" I manage a joke, my voice barely a whisper.

He smiles at me, his eyes glistening. And that is when I see, for the very first time, the fear in them. I know I look like death itself.

"I don't know how to play all the melodies," he answers, kissing my frail hand.

I close my eyes, enjoying the feel of his lips and the beautiful lyrics of Brian McKnight, and I know that if I die this very moment, I will die happy and content.

Once the session is over, I am even weaker than when I got there, and, again, Dili carries me to our waiting cab and into the house. Thankfully, apart from a few dry heaves, there is no more vomiting, and I can manage to get to the toilet before my diarrhea hits. It is just as well, because my body would not be able to survive that kind of ordeal. Not in this state.

I am given a month after that last cycle to regain my strength before my surgery. Dr. Chambers has decided I will have radiotherapy after my mastectomy, and not before. Once that is completed, we can discuss my reconstructive options.

By the third week after my last cycle, I start to regain my strength. As I have been advised to exercise to try to regain some fitness before my procedure, Dili ensures we take long walks down the coast every evening. As we walk holding hands, I know we must make a very unusual and odd sight. A handsome Adonis of a man and a wasted, skeletal excuse of a woman. But I no longer care. I know that, despite this surge of energy, I will still succumb to this sickness. Uchechi also experienced this boost of energy after her treatment and had been strong enough to return to school. But where had she ended up in the end? Six feet under, that's where. And I am all too aware that will be my own destination.

A lot sooner than we think.

So, because of that, because I know this is only temporary, I ride this wave with Dili. I play along with his belief that I am, indeed, his true love. Sometimes, as we walk, I nestle my head on his shoulder as his arm rests on my waist. I am ready to enjoy this little bit of heaven before God takes me to the one up in the skies.

After all the love I have showered on Dili in the past, surely, I deserve this.

On the day of my surgery, I wake up feeling surprisingly calm. It is Dili who appears nervous, as he patters all over the house, trying to remember the things we have been instructed to bring with us. But I sit there, cool as a cucumber, not because I am overly confident about the procedure, but because I am so ready for death, I don't care if it is on this operating table, another one, or even in my bedroom at home. I have made peace with the fact that my life is fast approaching its grand finale.

We get to the hospital at 7:30am, and I am wheeled into the theater at 9. The last thing I see before I succumb to the anaesthesia is Uchechi's face, and I wonder if she has come to get me. I wonder if I will awake in heaven, with my parents and sister. I wonder if this journey will end this very day, on this very table.

But it doesn't, and I awake in a recovery room at about 1pm, still groggy from the procedure. Dili is there with me through it all, even when I am moved to a private room later in the day. I manage to give him and the medical personnel monosyllabic answers to their questions, as the sedatives and painkillers have completely knocked me out. And the following day, the intense pain I awake to explains why I was put on medication so strong.

The pain is so extreme, I simply cannot move. I lie still to avoid feeling it. Even when Dili talks to me, I don't move. With each passing hour, the pain seems to quadruple, and I am soon screaming and crying in anguish. There are four drains under and above where my breasts used to be, stitched into my skin. With even the slightest of movements, the drains pull and feel like knives poking me from the inside.

It is the worst pain I have ever felt in my entire life.

Except it isn't.

No, the real pain comes when I finally make it to the bathroom, and I see what remains of my womanhood. As I stare at my heavily bandaged chest, I am all too aware that beneath the bandages no longer lie my pert B-cup breasts. They are gone forever.

And I slump to the floor, wailing like a baby.

Dili rushes to the bathroom and joins me on the floor, taking me in his arms as I weep. He says nothing and rocks me as I cry, knowing I need that release. After about an hour, he carries me back to bed.

"I can't wait for when we can go back home to New York," he says from his position next to me on my bed. My head is on his shoulder and his fingers are caressing my hairless head. "We'll have a proper wedding this time, maybe even go to church. Our families will be there, and we can do things the right way this time. And then after that, you can help me decorate the house the way you want it. You can sell your apartment if you want, it doesn't really matter. Don't worry, by the time you see the house, you're the one who'll be excited about leaving Manhattan."

I drift off to sleep as he talks, trying to stay detached and disconnected from what he is saying. I know I will die soon, but even if I don't, I'm not that foolish not to recognize that this 'love' of ours can only exist here in Friday Harbor, where any kind of romance can thrive. Back in New York, back in the real world, he will only be able to keep up this farce for so long.

Before I am discharged, I ask Dr. Chambers why I wasn't given the temporary balloon or saline expanders I have read most women who undergo mastectomies get.

"Because of the size of your tumour and how much of your breast tissue and muscle we had to remove, we decided to give your breast cavities enough time to heal on their own. Hopefully, by the time you are done with your radiotherapy in about a month, you'll have your reconstructive surgery."

"And I get to pick any breast size I want?" I ask, with a sly wink.

Dr. Chambers smiles and pats me on the hand. "One step at a time."

We get home, and I am surprised to see that Dili has found time to have the apartment cleaned spotlessly. It is clinically sterile, and I know it has everything to do with the doctor's directive to reduce my risk of getting an infection. I am so touched by this gesture and as we eat dinner, I find myself beginning to wonder if I might be wrong after all. I start to wonder if what we have could be real after all. I start to wonder if maybe, just maybe, Dili isn't being driven by guilt or a feeling of indebtedness after all…but instead by love. Three months is a long time to put up a charade.

I slowly start to warm to the idea, and even the sight of the jagged lines across my chest where my breasts once were no longer depresses me. Instead, I fantasize about getting my new breasts, getting my hair back, regaining the weight I have lost. I dream of the life Dili and I could make together, and I even imagine what our wedding…or vow renewal…would be like. I can see the happy faces of our siblings and his mother, and it gives me all the motivation I need to fight my pain…and to fight this disease. Death loses its appeal to me, and, instead, I want nothing more than the gift of building a beautiful life with Dili, the forever kind.

Radiotherapy soon commences, and even though it is nowhere near as harrowing as the chemo, it is no walk in the park, either. The sessions are short and painless, no more than fifteen to twenty minutes, but the stinging after-effect is harrowing, with Dili having to rub my chest with soothing ointment to stop my skin from peeling. Over the four-week period, I deal with debilitating blisters and extreme fatigue, but what keeps me going is that at the end of it all, there is a high chance that we would have beat this cancer, and that I will have reconstructive surgery to make me feel like a woman again.

Finally, the day comes. November 2nd is the day of my final radiotherapy session, and I am given the all-clear by my doctor. The fact that this falls on All-Souls Day isn't lost on me, and I wonder if this is a sign from my departed family, cheering me on for being the first one to overcome this dreaded disease.

"So, when can you schedule me for my reconstructive surgery?" I ask the doctor, my grin spreading from ear to ear. "My husband and I would really love to be back in New York before Christmas."

Rather than give me a definitive date like I expect, his face clouds over.

"What's the matter, Doctor?" Dili asks, his concern making his voice rise. "Has her cancer spread?"

"Oh no, not at all," Dr. Chambers answered. "We caught it just in time."

"So why the long face?" I ask.

"We had to cut a lot deeper into your breast cavity than we wanted to, because of the size of both tumours," he answers. "I've spent the last few weeks evaluating your case with my colleagues, and we think your cavities might not be able to support any implants."

My heart crashes to my feet. "Any implants? Not even small ones? I don't mind a downgrade to an A-cup." I make a lame attempt at a joke.

He shakes his head. "I'm afraid not, Ezioma. But what we could do is construct a small flap, maybe even with a nipple, just so that you're not left with two scars running across your chest."

"A flap?" I repeat, not believing what I'm hearing.

"I still have to run it by a Plastic Surgeon friend of mine in California, but from what we can see, that's the only option we're looking at…"

He continues to talk, but I don't hear a word of what he says. I hear Dili engage him with questions of his own, but I have no interest in listening. The bottom line is that I have lost my breasts. Forever. And my consolation prize is some sort of flimsy skin reconstruction to cover my shame.

"Let's go," I say standing up, cutting Dr. Chambers off mid-sentence. "I think we've heard enough."

"I know it's a lot to take in," he says sympathetically. "I've already made an appointment for you to meet with our Counsellor later this week…"

"It's fine," I interject. "Thank you for everything, Doctor."

"About when you can leave for New York, I would recommend at least another month here, so we can monitor you. I can't discharge you until I've kept an eye on you for at least that long."

"No problem," I say, before looking at Dili, who is still sitting down and looking bewildered. "Let's go. Or do you want to sleep here?"

I stalk ahead of him to the waiting room, where I call for a taxi. I rebuff Dili's attempts at conversation, and we ride home in silence.

"Baby, I don't know why you're so angry about what the doctor said," Dili mutters as we walk into the house. "So what, about implants? I'm just relieved you've been given the all-clear."

"Oh, so you don't care that I won't have implants?" I snap at him. "You want to look me in the eye and say that me not having breasts won't be a problem for you?"

"No, Ezioma! It won't!" he snaps back. "What matters more to me is that you're alive, and that you'll be alive for us to plan our lives together…"

"Oh, please spare me the bullshit!" I shout. "When I had two breasts complete, I wasn't good enough for you. You still left me for Onyeka. Is it now that there is hardly any difference between me and a man that you won't do the same thing when we get back to New York?!"

"Are you kidding me?" Dili says, flabbergasted. "I can't believe you're implying that my love for you is because of your breasts! Ezioma, I love you for *you*. I love your mind, I love your heart, I love your spirit, and, yes, I love your body too…thin or fat, short or tall, bald or with hair to your ankles. You mean the world to me, with or without breasts!"

I glare at him, angered by his patronizing words, angered he would dare lie that it doesn't matter to him.

And I realize I was right all along.

His guilt has brainwashed him to the extent he believes this garbage of loving me unconditionally. If he couldn't love me unconditionally before, is it now that I have effectively been rendered unlovable that he will?

"I need to lie down," I say. "I'd prefer to be alone, if that's okay."

A beaten and defeated Dili shrugs. "I'll be here if you need me."

Without another word, I walk to the bedroom where I strip myself of my clothes. Even though I have started regaining a little bit of weight and there is a small fuzz on my scalp indicating possible hair regrowth in the near future, they take a back seat to the scars on my chest. A tear rolls down my face as I imagine the clothes I will no longer be able to wear and the questions I will now be forced to answer. Dili might declare unconditional love now, but can he truly tell me it won't be a turn-off for him when we finally have sex? Can he honestly say it won't bother him when I get curious stares from passers by or, worse, his friends…his colleagues…his family?

No. This won't work. Not like this.

Somehow, I find the strength to change into warm flannel pajamas. I reach for my laptop and cue on the one melancholic song that best fits my equally melancholic mood, John Mayer's *Gravity.*

As I listen to the song, a lone tear rolls down my face. I am unable to even log into my blog, let alone write anything. It feels like my world is over.

It would have been better if I'd died.

The only way I can recover from this blow is to return to my life the way it was before Dili showed up. This farce has to end. Now.

And there is only one way to make it.

I reach for my phone and dial a number I haven't called in months.

"Hello, Seth." I say, as soon as he answers his phone. "This is Ezi."

# CHAPTER TWENTY-TWO

## In My Place

I WALK INTO THE LIVING ROOM early the next morning, where I find Dili asleep on the couch. The TV is still on, and I know he must have slept off accidentally. Even with all my doubts about him, I know he would not have stayed away deliberately.

"Wake up," I say, tapping his foot lightly.

His eyes open and just like I guessed, he is surprised to find himself lying on the couch. "I must have fallen asleep watching TV. How are you? Are you feeling better than you did yesterday?"

"You have to leave," I answer, keeping my voice even. "It's time for you to go, Okwudili."

He sits up and looks at me like I've gone crazy. "Why would I leave without you? We have just one more month before your doctor discharges you…"

"Dili, stop all this pretense," I snap. "We both know the real reason you're here. You feel guilty about the way you treated me last year. You feel indebted to me for giving you the 'American Dream' and think you need to repay me. That's the real reason you've been doing all this."

He is speechless for moments, seemingly lost for words. "You think I've been here for four months because I feel…indebted to you? Are you being serious right now? I'm here because I love you, Ezioma. I'm here because you mean everything to me," he says when he finally finds his voice.

"Oh, spare me that, please!" I exclaim. "Where was this love when you left me high, dry, and heartbroken in Manhattan? If Onyeka hadn't left you for someone else, would you be sitting down here, declaring love to me? Let's not kid ourselves, Dili."

He rises to his feet, shaking his head. "I don't believe this."

"The last thing I want is to hear, for the rest of my life, how you gave up four months of yours for me. How you gave up the job of a lifetime for me," I continue to rant.

"I have never said anything like that to you, Ezioma!"

"But I'm sure you're thinking it," I answer. "Can you honestly tell me that you haven't regretted giving up your dream job just to be here with me? Can you honestly say you haven't wondered if you made the biggest mistake of your life walking away from everything?"

"Not for one second," Dili answers firmly, his eye contact with mine unwavering.

I shake my head and laugh sadly. "You're lying and we both know that."

"What has gotten into you, Ezioma?!" Dili asks in exasperation. "Is it still this issue with your implants? Is that the reason you're talking crazy all of a sudden? When did we go from planning our vow renewal to…to this crazy talk?"

"I've always known this, Dili. From the very beginning, I've known your real reason for being here. I just thought I'd be dead soon, and your true motive wouldn't matter," I answer. "Anyway, Seth is on his way here as we speak. So, really, you can leave now."

"Seth? Your ex, Seth?!" he exclaims.

"I never told you Seth and I broke up. I only left when I found out I had cancer because I didn't want to put him through the heartbreak of watching me die," I retort.

"So, now that you're cancer free, he's on his way here?" Dili retorts. "Well, I have news for you both. I'm not leaving! He might still be your 'boyfriend', but I'm your *husband*. We are still legally married, and I have every right to be here. You can call the cops if you want to because I'm not leaving this house."

I glare at Dili, my own emotions torn. I want so badly to believe all he's saying, to believe his love for me is unconditional, even if I have to live the rest of my life with no breasts. But my fear of getting heartbroken again quashes all that hope.

I walk away from the living room, return to the bedroom, and proceed to have a shower. Less than an hour later, Dili walks into the room with my tray of breakfast. Guilt overwhelms me when I see all the trouble he has gone through to prepare my healthy, organic breakfast of almond oatmeal with fresh blackberries and flaxseed, as prescribed by my doctor.

He places the tray before me and, without saying a word, walks into the bathroom for his own shower. Afterwards, from his casual jogging pants and t-shirt, I can see he has no intention of going anywhere. Which could pose a problem as Seth is truly already on his way here.

Last night, I told Seth about the reason I'd left Durham - my cancer diagnosis and my desire to either heal or die in my happy place. He'd been understandably emotional and said he'd be on the first flight over to see me.

The way it is looking, Dili will still be here when Seth arrives.

I have no plans to reunite with Seth. I just figured his re-emergence in my life would be the only catalyst for Dili to exit it. But right now, even that is not looking likely.

I take my tray to the kitchen before Dili has a chance to. The more he caters to and pampers me, the worse I feel. Despite his motivation, despite his driving force, there is no denying that he has been extremely good to me. If he hadn't shown up when he did, I am certain I would not be alive today. He has cared for me more than any parent or sibling could, and I am not ungrateful enough not to acknowledge that. But cruel as this may be, it is best for both of us. How long before he starts feeling trapped by our situation? How long before the sight of his wife and her flaps becomes a complete turn off? How long?

No, this is for the best.

I return to the bedroom, and I fall asleep again, mentally, and emotionally fatigued. A few hours later, I am nudged awake.

"You have a visitor," Dili says, his eyes bloodshot and his voice flat. "I thought you were joking this morning. You really asked him to come?"

I sit up, realizing Seth must be here.

"Why, Ezioma?" he asks. "Why would you do this? Why would you do this to us, after everything we've been through?"

His words take me all the way back to the previous year, the night we'd come back from the nightclub, and I'd begged him to choose me over Onyeka.

But he hadn't.

This memory hardens my heart and I sit up straight. "So that you would know exactly what it feels like to be rejected. So you'll know how it feels to have someone chosen over you!" I retort. "You chose Onyeka, and now I am choosing Seth."

"Is that what this is? Revenge?"

"Not revenge. More like karma," I answer. "Thanks for everything you've done for me, Dili, but my man will take over from here."

As I make my way to the living room, I feel sick to my stomach, and I pause in the hallway as tears pour down my face. I hold my mouth with both hands to keep from screaming aloud, hating myself for the hurtful words I have hurled at Dili, the only man I have ever truly loved. But as painful as this may be for both of us, it is for the best.

It is for the best.

After recomposing myself, I walk into the living room with a forced smile. Seth is sitting down, looking very uncomfortable.

"Wow!" he exclaims when he sees me, rising to his feet to hug me. "I didn't know what to expect. You look like you've been through a lot."

"This isn't even the worst of it!" I laugh. "I've put on a bit of weight now. Only a few weeks ago, I weighed less than a hundred pounds!"

Seth's eyes widen. "I'm so sorry, Ezi. I wish I'd known earlier," his eyes wander to the door. "You didn't tell me your ex-husband was with you."

"He's been taking care of me. But he's leaving now," I answer, hoping he is wise enough to discern this is a topic I will not discuss further.

As we make small talk about Durham and his decision not to leave for Princeton after being made an Associate Professor, Dili walks into the living room. He is now fully dressed, and I can see his bags beside him. My heart falls as I realize he is leaving.

"Can I speak with you?" he says to Seth, who in turn looks bewildered. "I want to talk you through her meal plan and administering her medication."

Seth rises to his feet, still looking confused, and walks towards Dili, who then leads him to the kitchen. I can hear their voices as they discuss the timing and dosage of my drugs, and all the food I need to abstain from. When they are done, Dili walks out of the house without saying goodbye to me. I peep through the curtains and see him board a waiting taxi. Rather than feel relieved, I feel dead inside.

"Why did you ask me to come here, Ezi?" Seth asks.

Seth is no fool. He is an incredibly intelligent man who has figured out exactly what is going on.

"Something tells me he's the reason you wanted me here," Seth continues. "And I guess mission accomplished, right?"

I look away, unable to answer him.

"Did you ask me to come because you still love me? Because you want us to be a couple again?" he asks. "If the answer is yes, I'm ready to roll up my sleeves now and pick up where your ex-husband left off. And as soon as you're released by your doctor, we can go back to Durham and get married."

I look at him, unable to lie to him. "I'm sorry, Seth."

He nods in understanding, comes over to hug me, and then walks out the door, his bags in hand.

And I am left sitting there, well and truly alone.

I rise to my feet and walk to the kitchen. Luckily, Dili wrote down the medicine and food instructions for Seth, so this will act as a guide for me, as I've had no idea about any of these. It dawns on me how heavy my reliance on Dili was, and I am hit with a deep sadness anew.

But it is better to go through pain now, than debilitating heartbreak later. If I'd lost the zeal to live the first time Dili left me for another woman, I might not survive it the next time he does.

Brushing it off, I get into the full swing of taking care of myself once again. After all, I did it before Dili showed up, in even worse condition than I'm in now. At least now, I am regaining my health and strength. Taking over my own care shouldn't be a big deal.

I do just that for the next few days, until a shrill ring of my doorbell intimates me that I have a visitor. I am shocked to see none other than my sister, Ebere.

"I swear, I would beat you black and blue if I could!" she yells as I open the door, her eyes bloodshot and her face puffy. "So it's true? You came here to die, *okwiya*? You had cancer and you didn't even tell me?!"

I reach out to embrace her, and she holds me so tight, it is like she is afraid of letting me go. The cold winter breeze soon pushes us inside the house, and as we sit beside my fireplace, she tells me she got a call from Dili a few days ago, telling her everything and asking her to come to me immediately.

"He said he was here with you, but left when your boyfriend showed up," she says, her eyes scanning the living room. "Where is he? Seth *abi*?"

"He's gone," I answer, not offering any more explanation.

"*Ehen*! Dili was right!" she exclaims. "He said he didn't trust the guy to hang around, which is why he asked me to come to you," she glares at me, her anger renewed. "But how could you not tell me something like this, Ezioma? *Chineke,* look at you! Look how wasted you look! It's like seeing Uchechi all over again. Is that how I would have lost you just like that? Is that how I would have gotten a phone call one day, with a stranger telling me you're dead?"

"Ebere, I'm so sorry. I didn't want to upset you and Enyinna."

"*Ị bụ onye ọjọọ!*" she weeps. "You are very wicked, Ezioma! You came to this remote place to die? Your plan was to leave Enyinna and I alone, *abi*? *Ị chọrọ igbu anyị*? You wanted us to die along with you?"

I hold her as she cries, and I spend the rest of the day telling her the whole story, starting from the day I got that horrible phone call from Naomi. I tell her about my decision to come to Friday Harbor, and how tough the first few months were.

"I thought I was going to die," I say to her. "In fact, the day Dili came, I'm sure I would have died right there on my doorstep!"

"*Eziokwu?!*" Ebere exclaims. "Hmm, we thank God. How long was he with you? "

I shrug, trying to appear nonchalant. "He came a day after my birthday."

"That's since July. Four months. Four months, Ezioma!" she exclaims. "I don't understand you. Isn't this the same Dili you have been crazy about since we were kids? The same one you married under the guise of 'helping him', when we all knew it was because you still had feelings for him. That's the same person you sent packing, after he gave up everything to look after you in sickness?"

"I won't accept pity love, Ebere!" I snap at my sister. "The only reason he was here was because he thought he owed it to me after what I did for him."

"What exactly did you do for him, *biko*?" Ebere demands. "You married him, and he got papers. *Ehen?* Big deal. Ten Thousand dollars would have gotten him the same from a stranger. If he wanted to pay you back, he could have written you a cheque for five or ten times that amount. Do you have any idea how much money he lost, sitting here taking care of you?"

I look away, unwilling to continue the conversation.

But Ebere isn't done. "If you can't remember how *hard* it was taking care of Uchechi, I sure do. And that was with three of us doing it. Dili was the only one taking care of you, cleaning your shit and vomit, feeding you, massaging you, and you say he did it because he felt he had to? *Nne,* he didn't have to do *nada* for you. He could have simply called me back then in July and zapped, the way most guys would have. The only reason he did all that is out of love for you. Surely, you're not too blind to see it."

"But look at me now, Ebere!" I yell, ripping open my shirt and exposing my scars. "Look at me now. You think he can love me like this? A woman with no breasts? You think he will stay faithful to me forever, when the sight of me will always turn him off?!"

Ebere stares at me, long and hard, before shaking her head. "Ezioma, you mean this spirit of low self-esteem is still chasing you? You mean you haven't changed after all these years?" she says, her voice sad. "Right from when we were kids, you always cried and complained about not being the 'pretty' one in the house, always failing to remember that *you* were the one our parents boasted about the most. I don't remember Daddy ever bragging about 'Ebere, his beautiful daughter'. It was always all about you, but even then, you were too blind to see it. Not even when you were the only one out of all of us to smell an American University did you recognize how special you are." She shakes her head again. "If you can't understand that it is possible for a man to love you just for you, then I don't know what to say to you. If I were to be disfigured by acid burns all over my body, and my arms, legs and even breasts were to be chopped off today, I know Chinedu would still love me. Love is more than just skin-deep. I thought you'd be wise enough to realize that by now."

At this point, I break down crying. "I can't go through that pain again, Ebere. When he left me last year, it broke me. I won't be able to handle it if it happens again."

Ebere comforts me silently and thankfully says nothing more.

Later that night, when she is fast asleep, I sit awake on the sofa in my bedroom, staring into space. My heart still aches from how badly I treated Dili, and I still long for him desperately. But despite Ebere's words, I am convinced I have done the right thing…at least for me.

But that realization doesn't stop it from hurting so, so badly.

I reach for my laptop, cue in a song, and start to write.

***In My Place (Coldplay) – November 09, 2017***

*Lost am I without you.*

*Scared am I without you.*

*Underprepared am I without you.*

*But without you is what I have to be.*

*For both our sakes.*

I stare out of the window into the beautiful horizon outside, as the moonlit night illuminates the ocean, and I know I can't afford to keep on mourning Dili's absence. I have to channel all my energy into fully recovering from the disease that almost claimed my life.

# CHAPTER TWENTY-THREE

## Live to Tell

EBERE ALMOST MAKES ME NOT feel Dili's absence, as she takes care of me almost as delicately and intimately as he did.

Almost.

Nothing is quite like the magical time I spent with Dili as he nursed me back to health. And nothing will ever be.

"Won't you go back to London to take care of your children?" I tease, after she has been with me a week.

"They have a father, *abeg*!" is her tart reply. "I told Chinedu that, unlike him and his polygamous family, I only have two of you and I can't play when it comes to either of you. I will be here for as long as I need to. So you better get used to seeing my face."

Later that week, I finally return to the clinic for my follow-up appointment with Dr. Chambers. It's not something I have been looking forward to, considering his last offer for me to speak with a Counsellor. I neither want to be counselled nor do I want to discuss these flaps he wants to give me in place of breasts. But I can't afford to skip the appointment, so I mentally prepare myself for all of it.

Walking into the clinic, the first person we see is Penny, who embraces me like a long-lost daughter.

"Oh, Ezeeeoma! Just look at you. You look so good! I'm so happy for you!" she beams happily. "Where is your husband?"

Ebere and I exchange a glance.

"He had to go back to New York," I answer politely. "This is my sister, Ebere."

"Nice to meet you," Penny beams at Ebere, before turning back to me. "Please give your husband my best regards. In all my years of being an Oncology Nurse, I have never seen a spouse as committed to making the process as bearable for their partner as he was. In fact, that first day he was here, playing you all that music, I cried like a baby when I got home. It was the most beautiful thing I'd ever seen my whole life. I haven't been able to stop talking about it. Even my husband knows all about my patient, Ezeeeoma, and her wonderful man."

I nod and smile before quickly make my way out of the room. I take care to avoid eye contact with Ebere. The last thing I need is to see the judgment in her eyes after hearing from a third party just how wonderful Dili was to me. What's done is done, and the sooner we can all move on with our lives, the better.

Dr. Chambers is very happy to see me and commends me on my improved appearance. I introduce him to Ebere, and he, too, spends the next few minutes raving about my wonderful husband.

"I'm glad you're here today, Ezioma." Dr. Chambers finally says. "There's someone I'd like you to meet. Remember I mentioned my Plastic Surgeon friend from California? Well, he's here and we've had some very interesting conversations about you. Would you mind if I invited him in for this consult?"

I shrug, not sure what another doctor would have to say about my dire case.

I am soon introduced to Dr. Harrison, a much younger doctor than I'd imagined, an African American man who looks no older than forty years old. He examines me briefly, all the while asking me questions about how my wounds are healing.

"It's just like I thought," he says, after the examination. "When Matt and I were talking and he told me about you, I didn't think it would be possible for there to be no chance of giving you proper breast reconstruction. Feeling your breast cavities, yes, they have been made pretty shallow, but we could deepen them by an inch or two, and they should be able to carry up to 300cc saline implants."

Ebere gasps but I am only able to stare at both doctors with an expressionless face, not quite able to assimilate what he is saying.

"It means you can get your implants, Ezioma!" Dr. Chambers exclaims. "You might even be able to get the C-cup you wanted!"

I still sit there, not knowing what to say. On the one hand, I am overjoyed by the fact I will be able to get new breasts, but on the other hand, it saddens me because this was the reason I ended my relationship with Dili. And it all feels like an anti-climax now.

I finally muster the required excitement and enthusiasm, and Ebere and I throw plenty of questions Dr. Harrison's way. By the time we leave the clinic, I have been scheduled for surgery on the 5th of December, which is, ironically, Dili's fortieth birthday.

In the days leading to my surgery, I am filled with both excitement and sadness. I am excited about getting breasts again, but sad about not being able to share the experience with Dili. And when the day arrives, as I am wheeled into the theatre, all I can think of is him, and what he is up to on his milestone birthday. A part of me wants desperately to call him, but another part of me has no idea what to say to him. I still love and miss him with all my heart, but I know that my actions were unforgivable, and he won't be blamed for never wanting to hear my voice again.

By the time I regain consciousness after surgery, the overwhelming pain temporarily relocates my desire to reach out to Dili, but as I begin to feel relief from the painkillers, the desire returns. But that is when I realize that, even though it is 10pm here in Friday Harbor, it is 1am in New York, and no longer his birthday.

I take that as a sign from God and decide to focus on my healing instead.

I am discharged after a few days, and Ebere continues to take care of me. The week before Christmas, her husband and kids arrive to spend the holidays with us, and on Christmas Eve, so does Enyinna and his fiancé, a lovely South African girl called Iminathi. Even though I endure the same scolding from Enyinna, of keeping my illness a secret, we all eventually settle down to a beautiful family Christmas celebration.

Being with my family reminds me how blessed I am to be alive. A few short months ago, the thought of dying was appealing to me. Maybe because, deep down, I thought I had nothing to live for. But looking at my lovely sister, who has given up two months of her life to be with me, her husband who worships her, their three beautiful sons, and my dear brother who is my father's spitting image not only in looks but character, and now about to get married to a lovely woman, I realize I have so much to live for. So, so much. That I am loved by all these people is proof enough to me that life is beautiful, with or without romance. I might not have a man, but I do have a wonderful and loving family. And that is all that really matters.

I am discharged by Dr. Chambers on January 8th, and it is an emotional farewell at the clinic, with these people who have been like family to me for the better part of a year. By the end of that week, I return the keys of my cottage to the Caretaker, and Ebere and I make our way back to New York. As our plane lands in JFK airport, my heart soars and it feels like the homecoming it is. As our cab rides through Manhattan, I feel like getting out and kissing the ground. Having been gone almost two years, I had no idea how much I missed the place, and when we get to my apartment building, I feel like kissing my doorman, Tomas, on the lips. Such is my joy about being back home.

But the sad look on his face reminds me that I am not the same Ezi he bade farewell to two Augusts ago.

"Welcome back, Miss Ezi!" he says, hugging me gently. "I'm so glad you're back. How are you feeling now?"

The smile on my face wanes as I wonder how he knows I have been ill. Yes, I might be leaner, but I am far away from how skeletal I was at my worst. I also have considerable regrowth on my scalp for it to pass as an intentional haircut.

Ebere and I go up to my apartment, and, walking inside, I am surprised it doesn't smell as musky as I'd feared it would. I look around and see that the place is as clean as a whistle. No dust anywhere. I see that my vast collection of scented candles has been removed and even my potpourri bowls have been emptied. Opening the fridge, I find it not smelling as stale as it should after so many months of inactivity, but instead stocked with healthy food items. Even my pantry has been stocked with organic cereals and snacks.

It has Dili all over it.

I look at Ebere. "Was Dili here?"

She shrugs. "I told him we were coming back this week and he said something about coming to get your apartment ready for you. I didn't know he'd do all this. But hey, good for us *abi*? At least, we don't have to go to the supermarket today."

"I didn't know you were still talking with him," I say, surprised.

"Why wouldn't I talk to him? Why would you think that?" she retorts.

Before I can answer, there is a soft knock on my door. I open it to see Tomas.

"I'm so sorry to disturb you, Miss Ezi, but Mr. Dili asked me to give you these," he says tentatively, as he hands me a bunch of keys and an envelope.

I recognize Dili's house keys, but when I open the envelope, my heart sinks to my feet.

Divorce papers.

Seeing them saddens me and I pinch my nose to stop myself from crying. But what else did I think would happen after my horrible behavior? Of course, divorce is the logical next step for us. Logical, yes, but it doesn't stop it from breaking my heart.

"What was that?" Ebere asks when I return to the kitchen.

I shake my head and force a smile. "Nothing. Just a neighbour saying hello," I lie. "When you speak with Dili, tell him thanks for cleaning up and for the groceries."

Ebere stays with me for another couple of days before she returns to London. Finally alone in my apartment, I start to feel more like my old self again. I get my things out of storage and allow myself bask in the luxury of my old designer clothes. As the new week dawns, I tidy my hair into a trendy, albeit short, haircut, and I return to my old office to see everyone.

Mia is emotional when she sees me. "Oh my God, Ezi!" she exclaims. "Dili told me. I ran into him a few weeks ago, and he told me all about it."

I embrace my old friend and give her a detailed account of all that has transpired since I left New York. We are both emotional, she more so, as she realizes just how close I'd been to losing my life.

Seeing the rest of my team, my former boss reminds me that my job is waiting for me anytime I'm ready, but as I leave their expansive West Street office, I realize that going back is the last thing I want. That evening, I get into touch with a former boss of mine who left Goldman a few years ago, to oversee a small private equity fund, and who has been wooing me to join him ever since. Two years ago, leaving Goldman for such a small fund would have been unheard of for me, but today, I am more than willing to explore that possibility.

We meet up the next day, and after a brief chat, he makes me a firm offer, which I happily accept. I am surprised it is as well-paying as Goldman, but with considerably less stress and agro. By the end of January, I am fully settled into my old life, and even have my old column with the *Manhattan Buzz* revived. It is like I never left.

Except I did.

I feel Dili's presence everywhere. In March, when the tenth season of *RuPaul's Drag Race* starts, I can't help but remember the times we would watch it in Friday Harbor, squealing and laughing over RuPaul's many phrases. Watching this new season alone, and not having Dili to giggle with over RuPaul telling the queens '*The time has come for you to lip sync for your liiiiiife!*' makes me miss him even more. Even the mundane task of making my breakfast of almond cereal reminds me of him. Four months after our final separation, I feel him as keenly as if we were together just yesterday.

But I know I must find a way to release him…forever. The divorce papers still sit in their envelope on my kitchen table. I will get to them, but not now. Definitely not now. I need to be stronger before I can go along with the process of severing our relationship for good.

But that doesn't stop me from feeling melancholy, and I find myself only writing about sad, melancholic songs in my newly revived article.

***<u>Live To Tell (Madonna) – April 04, 2018</u>***

*In this beautiful city of Manhattan, we all walk around looking happy, content, satisfied, and whole.*

*But the truth is almost all of us has a secret…a common secret…the secret that we are broken on the inside.*

*Beneath all the Louis Vuittons and Manolo Blahniks, we are often little more than patched up dolls, doing the best we can to look like we have it all.*

*When the truth is that we have nothing at all.*

# CHAPTER TWENTY-FOUR

## How Can You Mend a Broken Heart?

AS THE WEEKS ROLL ALONG, I settle into my old pattern, whatever the pattern was before Dili came into my life four years ago. I redecorate my apartment, rediscover my love for good food and fine dining, and throw myself into social activities with my friends. My new job is great, and I am amazed that I get so much fulfillment from it while still having time for a life as well. The cherry on the cake is that get around to completing the certificate program I was pursuing at Duke University remotely, so the time I spent there wasn't in vain.

I am grateful that, after being on the brink of death, I am blessed to have my life, my very good life, back again. I am no longer so skinny that I draw curious stares from passersby but have instead filled out pretty nicely and am back to my pre-sickness size 4. My hair has regrown, and my skin has lost the discolouration from all the medication. I have treated my already rich wardrobe to some eye-popping new additions, and I am back to feeling like my normal fashionista self. The old Ezioma is back.

The old Ezioma who has it all.

So why then do I still feel this painful hollowness inside? Despite anything I do to fill the ache in my heart - immersing myself in client briefs, dinner dates with Mia and my other girlfriends, shopping till I drop every weekend - the emptiness remains. And it is worse when I lie alone in bed at night. No matter how long I try to delay this by staying up late writing my article, or watching reruns of *Sex & The City*, the moment I shut out the noise, I am overwhelmed by a deep and intense sadness.

A sadness like only one thing I have felt before; the heartbreak I suffered after Dili left with Onyeka. It is ironic, because this is the feeling I was trying to avoid when I let him go, when I let our relationship go last year. But here I am, feeling just as broken as if I were experiencing that heartbreak all over again. It is one Sunday morning as I sit alone in a café near my apartment that I realize that, despite everything I have done to prevent it from happening, my heart is broken, but this time not by Dili...but by my own insecurity.

I recall the words I said to him that horrible November morning, and I feel sick with regret. I remember the beautiful four months we'd had prior to that day, and I can finally see that everything Dili did for me was out of love...and nothing else. My eyes water as I remember how tenderly he would carry me, bathe me, clean me, feed me, all while constantly declaring his love for me. Not for one day, not for one single day, did he ever show anger, impatience, or disgust over my condition...which is not something I can boast of when I was my sister's caregiver.

I realize that what I have desired for the better part of my life was handed to me on a platter of gold... only for me to throw it away, breaking it to pieces.

The comprehension of my mistake sends me into a deeper depression, one that doesn't even go away when I do things to distract myself from it. It is with me from the moment I open my eyes in the morning, when I pass the café Dili and I frequented as a couple, when I think I smell his perfume waft past me, when I see someone like him walking down the streets of Manhattan. I see him every morning as I make my breakfast of organic oatmeal or Greek yoghurt with fruits. I see him everywhere...and in everything. But where I see him the clearest is in my heart, anytime I close my eyes.

And I accept that the love I have for Dili will never go away. No matter what I do, it will never go away.

On the first Saturday of May, sitting at my kitchen window and basking in the first warm hint of summer sunshine, I decide to do what I should have done ages ago. Before noon, armed with a bag containing our favourite pineapple upside-down cake, I am on the Number 2 train headed to Brooklyn, to pour my heart to Dili, to try to get back the only man I have ever loved. I found his address in the divorce documents still lying on my kitchen table five months after my return home. It took a lot for me to finally open them, and as I flipped through the pages for his address, seeing the other contents – irreconcilable differences as the grounds for divorce, November 3rd, 2017, as our date of separation, and zero spousal support for either party – made our pending divorce not just a theory but a reality.

And I knew I had to fight for him.

Through the forty-five-minute train ride, I choose not to fixate on the divorce papers and instead fantasize about us tearing them up when we are reunited...hopefully tonight. I close my eyes and daydream about being intimate with him again. While we were in Friday Harbor, apart from being too sick for either of us to contemplate sex, I didn't think he would find me sexually attractive, not with the way I looked - bone thin, bald, and breast-less. But while I had been fixated on the fact that we weren't having sex, his love for me had transcended anything physical or carnal. He showed me the meaning of true, pure love.

But I was too blind to see it.

I walk from the station to the Park Slope area of Brooklyn. Some former colleagues from Goldman moved to this neighbourhood after getting married, and it is easy to see why. With the trendy Brownstones and town houses lining its streets, it is almost as upscale as living in Manhattan, but with the added benefit of more space and serenity.

As I approach Dili's townhouse, my heart is racing fast and beating so loudly, I can hear it in my ears. With shaking hands, I press his doorbell and stand back, praying he answers the door. Just when I start to wonder if he's home, the door opens and surprise flashes on his face when he sees me.

"Hi, Dili!" I exclaim, trying to sound cheerful, a lot more cheerful than I feel. I toy with the idea of lying that I was 'in his neighborhood' but realize he will see through that immediately. "Long time no see."

"Hi, Ezioma," he says tentatively. "What are you doing here?"

"Happy belated birthday!" I say, raising the cake like a trophy.

But he is not impressed. "My birthday was five months ago."

"I thought I'd stop by to say hello, why the frowny face?" I laugh, unnerved by his coldness. "You love Franco's Pineapple Upside Down Cake!"

He doesn't look convinced. "Thanks," he says, taking the cake from me.

"Is that all you're going to say?" I exclaim. "Won't you even let me in after I came all this way?"

He hesitates for a moment, before stepping back to allow me into the house.

"Wow!" I exclaim. "Very nice place. The décor is lovely. Did Onyeka decorate it?"

"I bought it last February, long after she left," he answers, his voice flat.

"Oh really? I thought you said you two moved to Brooklyn almost immediately…"

"We rented an apartment," he answers impatiently. "Why are you here, Ezioma?"

"Why? Do you have a hot date?" I respond, with a wiggle of my brows.

He doesn't smile.

"How have you been? What do you think about this season of *RuPaul's Drag Race*? Those queens are on another level this year," I say, knowing I'm rambling but unable to stop.

"I don't watch it anymore," he answers coldly.

"Really?" I exclaim, genuinely surprised, considering how much he loved the show. "It's really good. I ran into Sharon Needles at a bar in Manhattan a few months back. Remember how happy we were when she won Season Four?"

He shrugs and I can see that his patience is fast dissipating.

"And how did it go with Bain? Was the job still waiting?" I ask, desperate to keep our conversation flowing.

"It was, but I got a better offer from Verizon. I started with them in February."

I clap my hands happily. "That is amazing! Wow! Up you, Okwudili! You've really done good for yourself."

He shrugs again and I know I am minutes away from being thrown out of the house.

"Meanwhile…surprise!" I exclaim, pointing at my breasts. "I got the implants in the end!"

"Yes, I know. I spoke with Ebere the day of your surgery," he answers.

I look at him, surprised my sister didn't even mention it. "That was your birthday."

He smiles sarcastically. "Wow, I'm flattered you remember."

"When did you speak with her?" I ask. "She never said anything to me."

"I spoke with her daily while you were at Friday Harbor. The day of your surgery, we spoke every hour," he answers.

I am filled with both anger that my sister kept this information from me...and a deep regret over the way I cast away a love so beautiful. "Thank you. I really do appreciate the concern."

He shrugs again. "I was just trying to finish what I started, which was making sure you left Friday Harbor alive."

I nod, understanding the hidden meaning of his statement, that he didn't do it out of any romantic emotions...but out of duty.

"I hope you had a great day, though!" I say, forcing a smile. "Welcome to the land of forty! You're officially an old man now. What did you do? Did your friends take you out?"

"I was in Nigeria," he answers. "I spent the whole of December with my mom. She and my siblings threw me a small party."

"Oh, that's nice," I say. "Did you tell her about me? About us?"

He shrugs again. "There was nothing to tell."

His words stab me in the heart like a knife piercing through.

"I'm sure all those Naija babes were all over you," I tease. "Fine American boy!"

"Ezioma, what exactly are you here for? Is it the divorce papers? Did you bring them?" he asks, clearly eager for me to leave his home.

That is when I know I have to come clean...or risk losing him forever.

"I acted really badly in Friday Harbor," I finally say. "I allowed my insecurities and fears cloud my thinking, and I did and said things I didn't mean."

He crosses his arms without saying anything, waiting for me to continue talking.

"You know I've been in love with you almost as long as I have been alive," I say, my eyes starting to water. "I loved you when we were kids. I loved you the moment I set eyes on you here in New York City. I loved you all the while you were all over Onyeka..." My voice breaks with my rising emotion. "I loved you even when you left me. I loved you when you came to Friday Harbor like my knight in shining armor. And I love you now. I love you, Okwudili. You are the only man I have ever wanted. The only man I have ever loved."

He looks at me, his face expressionless. "You didn't seem to remember this 'love', when you replaced me with Seth, or when you kicked me out of your house after I'd served my purpose."

"It's not like that, Dili," I say desperately. "I was just reacting after hearing about my implants."

He sighs deeply. "Look, Ezioma. You got what you wanted. You got your revenge. For months after I left you, I was broken in a way I have never been before. Even while I was in Nigeria, I was a mess. It has taken me months to get over you. I have only just started picking up the pieces of my life. You made me feel what you must have felt when I left with Onyeka. So, I guess we're even now."

The tears are now pouring fast down my face, but from the set expression on his, I know our conversation is over. There is nothing more to say. I have lost the love I had hoped and longed for all my life.

"Thank you for everything you did for me," I say, through my tears. "Thank you for being there for me, for taking care of me. I will never be able to truly thank you enough."

He shrugs and looks away.

"And thank you for clearing out my apartment and stocking my fridge before I got back. That was very kind of you."

"It was no big deal," is his curt answer.

I nod sadly. "Well, thanks anyway," I reach to touch his arm. "Bye, Dili."

He steps away from my touch like it is a ball of fire. "Please sign the divorce papers when you can. I don't want to rush you as I'm sure you haven't regained your strength a hundred percent. But try to anytime you feel able."

I nod again and even manage a small smile. "Sure. I'll do that."

He sees me out of the house, and I walk like someone in a trance to the train station. The tears start anew and continue non-stop through the long ride home, the reality of my loss hitting me hard with each stop. This time it is even worse. This time, I am the architect of my pain. This time, I am the reason for my heartbreak.

As I emerge from the 57th Street Subway station and make the short walk to my apartment, it feels like I am bleeding from every orifice, when in fact, it is only my heart that is hemorrhaging. For the first time since I moved into my building, I do not acknowledge greetings from the doormen and instead breeze past them like a ghost, a zombie. When I get to my apartment, I sit in silence on my living room sofa. By this time, my tears are spent, but I am still weeping sorrowfully on the inside.

I remain in that position for hours, as daytime turns to night. It is my article-writing alarm that jolts me out of my trance, and I rise from my crouched position.

Opening my laptop, my broken heart is unable to think up a banal topic to write about. Not only is my heart broken, but so is my spirit…my soul.

I cue on Al Green's *How Can You Mend a Broken Heart,* and as the melancholic song plays, tears start to pour from my eyes anew. And I know I can't give up. I just can't.

***<u>How Can You Mend a Broken Heart (Al Green) – May 05, 2018</u>***

*Di'm. Obi'm. Last year, in Friday Harbor, you told me you read every one of my old articles, here and on my private blog. I wonder if you still read it…my column. You probably don't. You probably gave it up the same time you gave up on loving me.*

*But here I am, writing you this letter still. Hoping you'll read this. Hoping your heart will long for mine again.*

*Do you remember this song, obi'm? From our favourite scene in the Sex & the City movie when Miranda and Steve reconcile. As I sit here, my keyboard wet from my tears and my heart aching with love for you, with my whole heart, that is what I long for with you.*

*Remember how Miranda thought she could never forgive Steve for what he did to her? Remember how all the anger and pain disappeared like vapour when they saw each other on that bridge? That is what I pray for, for all the pain, heartbreak and sadness from the last two years to disappear…allowing us love each other…forever.*

*The way we are meant to.*

*You are the love of my life, di'm. Nobody else. You are the only one my heart knows, the only one my heart wants. And that is why I am here, giving you my heart anew, here on my Manhattan Buzz column. Wishing…hoping…praying that you open yours to me again.*

*Give us another chance, my love. Give our love another chance. Remember how good we were together? How we were like two peas in a pod? Let's not throw that away. Please.*

*Please.*

*Just like in the movie, I'm going to wait for you in a place that means something to us. Remember the Starbucks where we met? The one on West 23rd Street? I'm going to wait for you there tomorrow, Sunday, the 6th day of May. I'm going to wait for you, and just like Miranda hoped Steve would show up, I'm going to hope that you do, too. And if you don't show up tomorrow, I'll be there at noon every Sunday until you finally do.*

*I will wait for you forever, my Okwudili.*

*I will wait for you forever if I have to.*

I stare at my screen, feeling bare and naked for writing such a personal article. But before I can change my mind, I publish it, sending it into the public domain before I can do anything to stop it.

As I retire to bed, I know I am just grasping at straws. Dili won't even read my article, lest of all meet me at the café we haven't returned to since that April morning four years ago. But as hopeless a situation as it is, it is the only choice I have.

The next day, I leave my apartment in good enough time to get to the café before noon. I sit on the same table I sat that spring morning years ago, watching people file in and out, staring eagerly at their faces. Male and female, young and old, black and white, happy and sad, the sea of faces is as varied and endless as they come, but I keep my eyes on the door, peeled for the one - the only one - that is of interest to me. It occurs to me that quite a number of the people entering the café could have read my article and might be wondering if the woman in the red knit shirt and blue jeans is Miss E.Z, the writer of the *Soundtrack of my Life* column, waiting for her man.

I start to lose hope after waiting almost an hour. Gazing out of the window my table faces, I accept the painful fact that he won't show up. Not today. Maybe not ever. I wonder how long my broken heart will allow me endure the pain of coming here to wait in vain for a man who has probably already moved on.

At 1:53pm, I push away the cup of coffee I am nursing, the third since I got there, my hopes and dreams dashed. Taking a deep breath, I reach for my bag and, before rising to my feet, look out of the window again.

And I see him.

I take in a sharp intake of breath as he appears at the door, my heart pounding, wondering if it is just my eyes, my senses, my heart playing tricks on me. But it is really him. Walking in, Dili spots me where I sit, and he walks in my direction, his steps tentative. As his eyes hold mine, I recognize in them the same fear and apprehension he must also see in mine.

I rise to my feet, and we are soon standing before each other; two wounded souls broken by love…broken by each other.

"I wasn't sure you'd come," I croak. "I didn't even know if you'd read my article."

"I almost didn't." he answers.

"Read the article or come?"

"Both," he answers. "I thought I'd gotten over you but seeing you again yesterday…" he shakes his head. "Before I went to bed, for the first time in months, I decided to check out your article…and then I read your note."

I nod, grateful he did, scared he did.

"I'm afraid, Ezi," he continues, his eyes holding mine. "I'm afraid of losing myself to you again, only to be hurt once more. I'm afraid of loving you."

"That makes the two of us. I'm also afraid," I echo, my heart slamming against the walls of my chest.

"But the emptiness and loneliness I feel without you is far worse than the fear," he says, his eyes damp with tears. "I love you, Ezioma. And I want to make us work."

He takes a step forward, which is all the prompt I need to leap into his arms, finally reunited with the love of my life.

Forever.

# CHAPTER TWENTY-FIVE

## Ribbon In the Sky

"I STARTED FALLING IN LOVE WITH YOU almost from the very beginning," Dili says to me, as we lie in each other's arms in his bedroom in Brooklyn. "When we were on our fake honeymoon in Long Beach."

I look at him, surprised by this piece of information. "But you were always raving about Onyeka. Every sentence you made had her name in it."

"I didn't really understand my feelings. It was the first time I'd spent that kind of extended time with you, the first time I got to know the real you. I loved all our time together; the jokes, the laughter, the fun conversations," he continues. "I didn't recognize it as anything other than just enjoying your company. But on our last night there, when I walked in on you writing your article and listening to *A Russian Farmer's Song*, I was so intrigued by that side of you. And after I left you for my room, you were on my mind the whole night. That was when you began to make your way into my heart."

"And there I was thinking it was because the sex was so hot," I tease him.

"Well, that too," he chuckles.

"So how come you did nothing about it?" I ask him, all laughter gone. "How come you kept on going on and on about Onyeka? And how come you tried to fix me up with Madufuro?"

"I didn't want to admit it to myself," he answers. "The last thing I wanted was to be like my father, hopping from one woman to another. I really didn't want to be that guy."

And for the first time, I understand.

"What about you?" Dili prods, with a sly wink. "When did you realize I was the love of your life?"

"I've told you this many times, Okwudili," I answer. "From the moment I set my eyes on you at your fifth birthday party…"

"Bullshit, Ezi," he laughs. "What could you have known about love at the age of five? That was just childish infatuation. I want to know the moment you knew this was the real deal."

I pause to think about it and realize that there truly was a moment when I knew, without a shadow of doubt, that I was head over heels in love with him.

"Nnamdi and Azuka's Christmas Party in 2014, when you played that Stevie Wonder song on the piano," I say, a nostalgic smile on my face. "As you sang, I remember just looking at you, so captivated I could hardly breathe."

Our eyes lock, and in that instant, words are no longer necessary, as the love, the deep and beautiful love we feel for each other, does all the speaking for us. All the speaking we will ever have to do.

From that beautiful day of our reunion in May, we are inseparable, spending almost every waking hour together, save for when we have to go earn our daily bread. We spend as much time in Brooklyn as we do in Manhattan, enjoying the best of both worlds. Our families and friends are overjoyed that we are reunited, and we soon can't imagine a time we were ever apart.

On the Sunday before my birthday in July, a Priest we have befriended blesses our union in a small ceremony in the Sacristy of his Parish in Lower Manhattan. It isn't until October, after Dili processes travel documents for his mother and sisters, that we finally have the big ceremony not only we, but our friends and family, have looked forward to.

I finally get my wish of wearing a beautiful wedding gown and renewing our vows in a sunset ceremony on a rooftop with a panoramic view of the Manhattan skyline. As my brother Enyinna walks me down the candle-lit aisle, in my blush-coloured Monique Lhuillier dress, with Stevie Wonder's *Ribbon in the Sky* playing, I am so happy, it feels like I'm levitating, like I'm floating in the clouds.

I sight Dili at the end of the manufactured aisle, standing next to the Justice of Peace before whom we will be renewing our vows, and my heart bursts seeing the tears in his eyes. I beam at my husband, and this just makes more tears stream down his face.

Glancing around, I realize almost everyone is in tears. My tough cookie of a brother, Enyinna's eyes are glistening, and I can see Ebere and Dili's mother dabbing their eyes frequently. Many of our friends, Mia and Azuka especially, are also emotional, leaning on their partners for support, their eyes brimming. Even my dear Friday Harbor family, Dr. Chambers and Penny, look so happy they could burst.

But as for me, I am way too happy for tears. This is what I have dreamt of…for a lifetime.

As Enyinna hands me over to Dili, my husband kisses my hand, and we stand there as the *Stevie Wonder* song plays in its fullness.

As we listen to the lyrics of the song, my emotions finally find me. I can not believe that, after everything we have been through, we are here. We are finally here.

When the song plays out, we stand before each other, with the vows we have written for each other.

"Ezioma…I have to catch my breath to believe this is real, that I am marrying my true love, my heart's desire, and my best friend," Dili starts. "When you walked into my life, love walked in. It was a magical moment, one I will treasure forever. You are my light, my inspiration, and I am blessed to call you my wife. For as long as I live, I will shield you from the wind, cover you from the rain, and make a home for us inside my heart. Not just for this moment, not just for this hour, not just for this day, not just for this year…but forever. Ezioma, I will love you forever."

And despite everything I have done to keep them at bay, my tears gain their release and pour down my face, my heart completely overwhelmed by this declaration of love.

"Okwudili, I fell for you the moment we met as children, and I have been hopelessly in love with you ever since. As I make this vow to you today, I promise that my love for you will be an ever-flowing spring, never diminished, always sweet and life-giving. My commitment to you is one I give willingly, absolutely, and without hesitation. We were married before this day and I repeat the promise I made four years ago to love you unconditionally, with tenderness, and undying devotion. Not just for as long as we both shall live, but way beyond, because our love…" my voice breaks and I inhale deeply, determined to get the words out, "…because our love will outlive our physical form. Our love will last forever."

The rest of the evening is a beautiful blend of love, joy, happiness, good food and, of course, good music. Even though we are technically months away from our fifth wedding anniversary, the truth is that this is the day we have come together to *truly* become one. It is the most beautiful of all beginnings.

We honeymoon in the Maldives, and it is even better than the magical time we spent there in the Easter of 2016. Dili and I are two bodies with one soul, neither of us quite knowing where one ends and the other begins. If there is anything deeper than the word soulmates, that is exactly what we are.

We return to Friday Harbor for the last two weeks of our honeymoon. It is wonderful to enjoy the picturesque town in love and happy… not sick, dying, and insecure. But that is not the real reason we have returned to the town. We have been introduced to a Nigerian woman, Nene, who lives in Seattle, and who has agreed to be a gestational carrier for us. As my eggs are there in Friday Harbor, coming back to attempt to expand our family seems the most logical thing to do.

In December 2018, to our pure delight, Nene is confirmed pregnant with twins. We move her to New York, to a small apartment in Brooklyn, where we now spend most of our time, and it is the best Christmas I have had in a long, long time.

Even though it is still early days, as Nene isn't due until September 2019, I can't help but marvel over how far we have come. This time a year ago, I had just finished cancer treatment and was staring at a bleak and lonely life ahead. But here I am now, not only blissfully married to my heartbeat, but about to become a mother…of twins! If I'd been asked to go crazy and write what my desired outcome for my life would be, I never even would have been able to envision any of this.

As we, my husband and I, look forward to a beautiful life together, with our children, all I can be is grateful that God would take a love of convenience and transform it to something beautiful.

Something so very beautiful.

The End

# AUTHOR'S NOTE

I was pregnant with my youngest when I wrote this book, and I tossed aside all the rules in the book for this one. This was a love story I wrote just for me, and I threw everything I was in love with into it – music, Sex & the City, Ru Paul's Drag Race, and Grey's Anatomy (I wonder if you noticed the names of the doctors in Friday Harbor ☺). After writing it, I published it on my blog and went on to write other books, but it remained close to my heart.

Fast forward four years when the opportunity came to self-publish my books in paperback. After doing that for some of my newer titles, I decided to dig into my back catalogue. Choosing the first to run with was a no-brainer. Ezi and Dili have had my entire heart from when I set pen to paper (well, not literally, but you know what I mean ☺) in 2018, and I am so, so happy for the opportunity to share them with you.

At the time I wrote it, I didn't know anyone who'd suffered breast cancer. Everything I included in the story came from my research. But in the summer of 2019, one of my oldest friends got diagnosed and as she went through her treatment, it was a nightmare to see what I'd imagined in the hypothetical play out in reality before me. The good news is that, like Ezi, she beat it, and I am grateful for her life every day.

This wouldn't be complete without acknowledging my best friend and pseudo editor, Chichi Abiagam, who read this first and loved this first. I also want to thank Fehin Kusimo for helping to prepare it for this republish. You guys are amazing.

To all my readers from the days of my blog, to all those who have read this on the electronic platforms it has been published over the years, I say a big THANK YOU! Thank you for following me on this crazy journey. Thank you for supporting me. None of this would be possible without you.

And to my new readers meeting Ezi and Dili for the first time, I hope you love them like I do. Like we all do.

Much love!

A. N.

# AN ODE TO THE MUSIC

1. ***Handbags & Gladrags*** (1967) - written, composed, and produced by Mike D'abo, and performed by Mike D'abo (1967), Rod Stewart (1970), and Stereophonics (2001).

2. ***There She Goes*** (1988) – written by Lee Mavers, produced by Bob Andrews, and performed by the Las (1988) and Sixpence None the Richer (1997)

3. ***Once In a Blue Moon*** (1997) – written by Paul Tucker, produced by Mike Peden, and performed by Tunde Baiyewu

4. ***Russian Farmer's Song*** (2013) – written, produced, and performed by Keane

5. ***Moonlighting Theme*** (1987) – written by Lee Holdridge and Al Jarreau, produced by Nile Rodgers, and performed by Al Jarreau

6. ***Knocks Me off My Feet*** (1976) - written, produced, and performed by Stevie Wonder

7. ***Simple Kind of Life*** (2000) – written by Gwen Stefani, produced by Glenn Ballard, and performed by No Doubt

8. ***I Can't Help It*** (1979) – written by Stevie Wonder and Susaye Greene, produced by Quincy Jones, and performed by Michael Jackson

9. ***Edge of Desire*** (2009) – written by John Mayer, produced by John Mayer and Steve Jordan, and performed by John Mayer

10. ***The Fear*** (1999) – written, produced, and performed by Travis

11. ***Ordinary People*** (2004) – written by John Stephens and Will Adams, produced John Legend and will.i.am, and performed by John Legend

12. ***Me & Mrs. Jones*** (1972) – written by Kenny Gamble, Leon Huff and Carry Gilbert, and performed by Billy Paul (1972) and Michael Bublé (2007)

13. ***You Could Be Happy*** (2006) – written by Snow Patrol, produced by Jacknife Lee, and performed by Snow Patrol

14. ***Linger*** (1993) – written by Dolores O'Riordan and Noel Hogan, produced by Stephen Street, and performed by The Cranberries

15. ***Sunday Morning*** (2004) – written by Jesse Carmichael and Adam Levine, produced by Matt Wallace, and performed by Maroon 5

16. ***Drive*** (1984) – written by Ric Ocasek, produced by Robert John "Mutt" Lange and the Cars, performed by the Cars

17. ***Bohemian Rhapsody*** (1975) – written by Freddie Mercury, produced by Roy Thomas Baker and Queen, and performed by Queen

18. ***Sailing*** (1978) – written by Christopher Cross, produced by Michael Omartian, and performed by Christopher Cross

19. ***One Last Breath*** (2002) – written by Mark Tremonti and Scott Stapp, produced by John Kirzweg, Kirk Kelsey, and Creed, and performed by Creed

20. ***Love is Stronger Than Pride*** (1988) – written by Sade Adu, Andrew Hale, and Stewart Matthewman, produced and performed by Sade

21. ***Gravity*** (2006) – written by John Mayer, produced by John Mayer and Steve Jordan, and performed by John Mayer

22. ***In My Place*** (2002) – written by Guy Berriman, Jonny Buckland, Will Champion, and Chris Martin, produced by Ken Nelson and Coldplay, and performed by Coldplay

23. ***Live to Tell*** (1986) – written and produced by Madonna and Patrick Leonard, and performed by Madonna

24. ***How Can You Mend a Broken Heart*** (1972) – written by Al Green, produced by Willie Mitchel, and performed by Al Green

25. ***Ribbon in the Sky*** (1982) – written, produced and performed by Stevie Wonder

26. ***You Get What You Give*** (1998) – written by Gregg Alexander and Rick Nowels, produced by Gregg Alexander, and performed by New Radicals

27. ***Anniversary*** (1993) – written by Carl Wheeler and Raphael Wiggins, produced and performed by Tony! Toni! Toné!

28. ***Nothing Even Matters*** (1998) – written by Lauryn Hill, produced by Lauryn Hill, Che Pope, and Vada Nobles, and performed by Lauryn Hill and D'Angelo

29. ***Tonight (Best You Ever Had*** (2012*)* – written by Allen Arthur, Christopher Bridges, Keith Justice, John Stephens,

Miguel, and Clayton Reilly, produced by Phatboiz, and performed by John Legend

30. ***Me Myself and I*** (1989) – written by Paul Huston, David, Jude Jolicoeur, Vincent Mason, and Kelvin Mercer, produced by Prince Paul, performed by De La Soul

# BOOKS BY ADESUWA

**Standalones**

Accidentally Knocked Up
Faith's Pregnancy
You Used to Love Me
The Love Triangle
Golibe
Where Is the Love?
Iya Beji
You, Me…Them
A Love of Convenience
Jaiye Jaiye
Adanna
The Sisters
The One!
Call Me Legachi
The Marriage Class

**The Ginika's Bridesmaids Series**

Ginika's Bridesmaids 1: Ara
Ginika's Bridesmaids 2: Isioma
Ginika's Bridesmaids 3: Ife
Ginika's Bridesmaids 4: Ozioma
Ginika's Bridesmaids 5: Ginika
Whatever It Takes (a Ginika's Bridesmaids Sequel) (Summer 2023)
Any Love (a Ginika's Bridesmaids Sequel)
(Christmas 2023)
Love…Forever (a Ginika's Bridesmaids Sequel) (Christmas 2024)

**Malomo High Reunion Series**

# ADESUWA O'MAN NWOKEDI

An Unlikely Kind of Love
A Complicated Kind of Love
A Betrayed Kind of Love (December 2022)
A Broken Kind of Love (Fall 2023)
A Renewed Kind of Love (Summer 2024)
A Forever Kind of Love (Fall 2024)

# ABOUT THE AUTHOR

INVESTMENT BANKER BY DAY, romance writer by night, Adesuwa O'man Nwokedi began writing by accident and what started as a few scribbles for friends has led to 25 titles...and counting.

A self-described hopeless romantic, when she's not creating new characters, she's a loving wife and mom of three.